SOMETHING IS DOWN THERE . . .

He felt something around his feet, just barely touching his toes.

He tried to look down in the water.

The small, feathery touches around his legs had turned to something hard now, holding on to his legs, almost holding him like—

He brought his right hand down to feel what he was caught in, to push it away, to free himself.

What the hell?

It felt all sort of doughy, and soft, like, like—

Flesh. Gone puffy. Rotten.

"Oh, God," he said. And he screamed . . .

"A CONSUMMATE WRITER OF HORROR."

—Science Fiction Chronicle

Titles by Matthew J. Costello

MISSING MONDAY
UNIDENTIFIED
POLTERGEIST: THE LEGACY MAELSTROM
SEE HOW SHE RUNS
SEAQUEST DSV: FIRE BELOW
HOMECOMING
DARKBORN
CHILD'S PLAY 3
WURM
CHILD'S PLAY 2
MIDSUMMER
BENEATH STILL WATERS

BENEATH STILL WATERS

MATTHEW J. COSTELLO

BERKLEY BOOKS, NEW YORK

THE BERKLEY PUBLISHING GROUP
Published by the Penguin Group
Penguin Group (USA) Inc.
375 Hudson Street, New York, New York 10014, USA
Penguin Group (Canada), 90 Eglinton Avenue East, Suite 700, Toronto, Ontario M4P 2Y3, Canada (a division of Pearson Penguin Canada Inc.)
Penguin Books Ltd., 80 Strand, London WC2R 0RL, England
Penguin Group Ireland, 25 St. Stephen's Green, Dublin 2, Ireland (a division of Penguin Books Ltd.)
Penguin Group (Australia), 250 Camberwell Road, Camberwell, Victoria 3124, Australia (a division of Pearson Australia Group Pty. Ltd.)
Penguin Books India Pvt. Ltd., 11 Community Centre, Panchsheel Park, New Delhi—110 017, India
Penguin Group (NZ), 67 Apollo Drive, Mairangi Bay, Auckland 1311, New Zealand (a division of Pearson New Zealand Ltd.)
Penguin Books (South Africa) (Pty.) Ltd., 24 Sturdee Avenue, Rosebank, Johannesburg 2196, South Africa

Penguin Books Ltd., Registered Offices: 80 Strand, London WC2R 0RL, England

BENEATH STILL WATERS

A Berkley Book / published by arrangement with the author

PRINTING HISTORY
First Berkley mass-market edition / April 1989
Berkley movie tie-in edition / March 2007

Interior text design by Kristin del Rosario.

For information, address: The Berkley Publishing Group,
a division of Penguin Group (USA) Inc.,
375 Hudson Street, New York, New York 10014.

ISBN: 978-0-425-20108-4

BERKLEY®
Berkley Books are published by The Berkley Publishing Group,
a division of Penguin Group (USA) Inc.,
375 Hudson Street, New York, New York 10014.
BERKLEY is a registered trademark of Penguin Group (USA) Inc.
The "B" design is a trademark belonging to Penguin Group (USA) Inc.

PRINTED IN THE UNITED STATES OF AMERICA

10 9 8 7 6 5 4 3 2 1

PROLOGUE

GOULDENS FALLS, NEW YORK—1936

It was morning.

Cool, damp, with thin, wispy clouds ready to be burned off by breakfast.

Billy sat up quickly. He heard someone calling to him, a hushed voice from below his window, and for a moment he wondered whether the voice was part of a dream.

But he went to his window and saw Jackie Weeks standing below his window, looking right up at him, his wide-open eyes telling him to get a move on. Jackie was excited, but Billy just had that same uncomfortable feeling that he carried around all week, a feeling, he finally admitted, that was fear.

He waved at Jackie to let him know that he was on his way down, and then he jumped into yesterday's clothes, scattered on the floor of his room.

He pulled them on quickly, feeling their clammy coolness against his warm skin, and for a moment he wished he could just jump back into his bed and pull his covers over his head, shutting out the light, the morning, and Jackie Weeks.

But no, there was no way to do that.

After all, they had talked about this day, planned it for weeks, swearing each other to total secrecy. Swearing! Jackie had demanded.

Cross your heart and hope to—

Jackie called again, and Billy pulled on his worn sneakers, leaving the laces undone until he got outside. Then he moved as quietly as he could, just like the burglar from the Bulldog Drummond movie, stepping on his toes, wincing as the floorboards creaked out in alarm, hoping that his little sister wouldn't come stumbling out to pee or for a drink of water and blow the whistle on him.

Then he reached the front door and turned the doorknob slowly, silently, barely breathing, before pulling back on it, moving outside to where his best friend stood.

He saw Jackie roll his eyes in disgust before speaking to him.

"C'mon, Billy Boy, we're late already."

He nodded.

"My alarm clock didn't go off. It's old—"

"Yeah, well, we better get moving. The sun will be up in half an hour."

He crouched and tied his laces, pulling them real tight, until both his black sneakers were snug from his ankles to his toes. So they'd never come off no matter what—

"I've been thinking. You know, it's all fenced off, with signs and stuff. We could be in big trouble if we're caught in there."

Jackie rolled his eyes again. "Oh, brother. You're not punking out on me, are you? All your big talk of seeing the town one last time, seeing all the empty houses and stuff?"

"I'm just wondering." He stood up and looked at Jackie, a good five inches taller, seemingly years older. He never understood what Jackie saw in him. Here was Jackie, the best athlete in Gouldens Falls Elementary School, liked by all the kids, hanging around with someone who was the booby prize every time a team's captain lost out on the critical once-twice-three-shoot finger play that determined who got first pick.

"But you're smart," Jackie had told him one summer's day when they had gone fishing. "Real smart." And for some crazy reason this was important to Jackie.

"Well, are you ready, Billy Boy?"

Billy nodded.

Jackie turned, and Billy watched him dart into the woods that surrounded his house, heard his black Keds landing with an assured plop on the ground. Then he ran, not really able to keep up with him.

Jackie was the fastest kid in Gouldens Falls Elementary School. Nobody could catch him. They'd even put a plaque up, right in the school gym.

But that was all history now.

'Cause in a few hours the small redbrick school building will be at the bottom of the largest man-made lake in the whole state. Yeah, as if it were something to be proud of. As if he'd ever want to brag that his hometown was filled with fish and duckweed.

(And, for a moment, he remembered a bit of his dream from that night. He was in his bedroom, just walking around, when the water came in, a trickle at first, then slowly rising. He tried to get out, but the door just wouldn't open, and the water just . . . kept rising.)

"C'mon, Billy. Run, for Pete's sake!"

"No stamina," the coach had said. That was his problem. Just couldn't keep going, not the way Jackie could.

"I'm . . . coming," Billy gasped.

And Billy ran, head down, watching for branches and vines that might trip him up, barely noticing the dark woods growing lighter. Then he heard Jackie scream out.

"There it is!" And he stumbled beside his friend, and just ahead he could see the chain-link fence, topped with shiny strands of brand-new barbed wire. And behind it, the abandoned town of Gouldens Falls.

"Kinda spooky, isn't it?" Jackie said. Billy moved closer to him and they looked down at the town. "It's like a ghost town now."

Then he walked toward the fence.

And Billy followed Jackie. He came to the fence beside him and clawed the wire mesh, resting his face against the fence. And it was more than spooky. There was something bad about seeing a town so still.

"Look," Jackie said, laughing. "There's our church. I won't mind having that under fifty feet of water."

Billy nodded, even as he looked up and down the familiar streets that now seemed so strange, fenced in like some kind of—

"And Donnelly's Hardware Shop. My dad says his new place in Ellerton will carry a lot more stuff, lots more, maybe even hunting rifles and fishing gear."

"Yeah." But he wasn't really listening. Instead he looked at the streets, searching for some sign of life, knowing that there really couldn't be anything there.

'Cause they're all gone.

The old people and the kids. Donnelly and that nice waitress at Woolworth's who always gave free refills of Coke. All the cats and all the dogs.

And then he looked south, at the reason Gouldens Falls was surrounded by a ten-foot-high barbed-wire fence. He looked at the dam.

It wasn't big as far as dams went. No. He had checked out pictures of the Hoover Dam in the encyclopedia. Now, *that* was big. This one, the one they were calling the Kenicut Dam, was just small potatoes.

Still, seeing the massive wall at the south end of town, running all the way from one ridge to the other, sealing off the town, made him feel like he was seeing something important. Important and scary.

"They're all set up," Billy said quietly, looking at the roadway on top of the dam.

"Yeah. There's the special grandstand for the governor and the old-fart mayor, and a lot of other jerks."

"What time is it?" Billy asked. He wanted the trip over with, done, so he could get back home. Then he could join Jackie in bragging about their big adventure.

Jackie dug out a big pocket watch, its scratched gold cover catching the early-morning light. It was one of Jackie's treasures, he knew, from his grandfather. He knew Jackie just loved to be asked what time it was.

"Six A.M., Billy Boy. Time to pay our last respects."

And before he could say anything, to tell Jackie that he really didn't want to climb the fence, that all he wanted to do was get the hell out of there, Jackie started climbing. He felt trapped. By his friendship, by their plan, and by the fence.

And, no sweat, Jackie moved up the fence easily, clutching at the wire strands and digging his Keds into the mesh. He watched his friend climb, knowing that he'd have to go through with it next.

Then Jackie was at the top, gingerly stepping over the shiny strands of barbed wire, shifting his body around, crouching like he was going to take a dump or something.

And Billy kept his eyes on the twisted spokes of wire between Jackie's legs. He chewed his lips. "No problem, champ. This is just like Tim Tyler making his way over the snake pit."

That's another place that's going to disappear. The Glenwood was *his* movie theater, his favorite place in the whole town. He had seen *King Kong* there, and *Frankenstein*, and a ton of others, slumped down in his seat, feet up on the seat in front (until the usherette had come by and shined her flashlight in his face). There'd always be the greatest popcorn fights when some boring Western was on. He'd laugh so hard, it hurt.

The big old theater, his theater, would be under water in just a few hours. Did they leave the screen? he wondered.

Or the popcorn machine, half full with dried-out popcorn, soon to turn into a yellowish, soggy muck?

"Geronimo!" Jackie yelled with a scream that made Billy's hair stand on end. He saw Jackie leap off the fence, land, and roll into some bushes.

"You're next, sport."

Now there was this big new fence between them. Jackie's eyes were on him, burning. He could just turn and run away. So what if he lost his friend? So what if Jackie told the whole school he was a punk?

I'm not Tim Tyler. I don't need to cross rivers with alligators or quicksand pits.

But instead he reached up to the cold wire, grabbed it, and then started climbing, He moved slowly, making doubly sure of every foothold before climbing higher. He watched his hands grab the wire, saw the goose bumps on his arms.

"C'mon, Billy."

Then he saw the top, the strands of barbed wire ready to cut at him. It had been so easy for Jackie.

"Okay, Billy Boy. Nice and slow here. You don't want to lose the family jewels." Jackie laughed, but all Billy could think of was slipping, sliding down right onto the barbed wire.

He could jump off now. He could just leap off the fence, back where he came from, and run away. It would be all over. But he went up, feeling Jackie's eyes on him, wondering whether Jackie might be worried about him too. Then he reached for the top strand of barbed wire, clamping his hand around a bare section, and pulled himself up.

"Way to go! Take it easy now."

He heard himself breathing funny, like air whistling under a door in wintertime. There was no rhythm to it; he just sucked it in.

He straddled the wire and looked down at Jackie, knowing that the hard part was coming. He started to move one foot over the barbed wire.

"Nice and slow. Almost there. Almost—" Jackie's voice helped give him confidence.

Then he felt his balance go, and his body was just some heavy weight about to tumble down. His hands slid an inch, right over one of the barbs, and he screamed out.

But it stopped his fall, and he pulled his body into an awkward balance. He thought he might cry.

"Shit, you cut your hand."

Billy looked down. The blood coating the wire looked slimy and dark, not like when he scraped his knee. At least the wire wasn't rusty. *At least I won't get tetanus or whatever it is you get from rusty nails.*

"Bring your other leg over, Billy. You got to go over the barbed wire."

He nodded but didn't move. To move meant another chance to fall, maybe even more blood. It was better to just freeze. . . .

"You gotta move, Billy! Get your leg up!"

Then he let himself obey Jackie's voice, letting it take charge so he wouldn't have to think about the wire.

"That's it. Now bring it over. Easy. *Easy.* Okay, you're about there."

Amazingly his feet were on the other side of the fence.

"Now jump!" Jackie yelled.

No.

"Jump, Leeper, before I come up there and pull you down."

He would do it too. Jackie would really climb up and drag him down.

It was enough to get him to jump off.

"Aaaah!" He flew off awkwardly, his arms and legs reaching out in all directions. His shoulder hit the ground first, banging hard into the dirt. He thought for sure he'd broken some important bones.

"I thought you were stuck up there, chum. Sorry I had to get tough on you. How's the hand?"

He looked down at his hand, and the round hole in the center of his palm, surrounded by a small pool of blood.

"It's okay." He looked up at Jackie. "It's nothing."

"Great," Jackie said, gesturing at the town. "'Cause Gouldens Falls awaits."

It wasn't his town anymore.

Sure, the streets were the same, the houses, even the trees he used to pass as he made his way home.

All the same, yet now totally different. The people were gone, and the town seemed to be waiting for something.

"Isn't this great?" Jackie said. "Hey, watch this." And he turned to see Jackie reach down, pick up a stone, and fling it at a window. The glass shattered noisily.

"C'mon, Jackie."

"What's the matter? You think someone's going to complain? They're all gone, Billy Boy. For the next hour the town belongs to us."

He guessed Jackie was right. They were on Main Street, and it looked like a ghost town. The shops were all closed up tight, and down near the end of the block he saw the now blank marquee of the Glenwood Theater.

The owner was probably going to use the big black letters in his new theater in Ellerton.

He walked toward the theater, even as Jackie ran ahead, peering into each store.

"No loot, Billy. They've taken everything."

Jackie ran up the block, noisy and excited, and Billy just couldn't get himself to enjoy this. *I want to leave,* he thought.

It was quiet here until we came.

(His breath turned funny again. . . .)

We should leave now.

"C'mon, Jackie. Let's get back."

"Sure, I just want to take a look at—"

He watched Jackie freeze, his head tilted, as if straining to listen. "What is it?"

"Shh!" Jackie took a step, first north, toward the end of Main Street, and then to the east, moving near one of the small side streets. "I hear something," Jackie whispered. "Something like a kid, maybe a—"

"I don't hear anything."

(*No. I gotta go. I gotta—*)

"Just listen," Jackie hissed.

He tried, craning his neck left and right, trying to pick up the sound that had Jackie glued to the street.

Then he heard it, wishing that it had just been the wind or Jackie's imagination.

(*No. I gotta go. I gotta—*)

"Yeah. I hear something. It's . . . It's not a kid, though. It sounds like some lady. Yeah, some old lady calling out."

God, if it didn't sound like a voice. Somebody *was* left behind. Yeah, somebody's grandmother was left behind, that's all. Forgotten when everyone left a few days ago. Sure, that's what it was. . . .

"Hot damn," Jackie yelled out. "We're gonna be heroes, Billy Boy. We're gonna rescue someone."

Jackie walked down the side street.

"Where are you going?"

But Jackie kept walking.

"I'm gonna find who's calling out, Kiddo." Suddenly he was afraid for Jackie—Jackie, who knew no fear.

He ran up to him. "Look, I don't think it was anyone. Maybe it was just something blowing in the breeze. A creaking door or something. C'mon, we gotta get back."

(*Please.*)

But his friend just looked at him as if he were crazy. "What breeze, lamebrain?" And he looked at the trees, perfectly still, not even twitching.

So he walked beside Jackie, down Scott Street, not hearing the sound again, even though they both were quiet.

Not until they were opposite a big brown house with a wraparound porch that curved to the rear of the house.

And he heard the sound.

It was a cry.

He looked at Jackie thinking maybe he had imagined it. But then it came again, louder now, and oh, God, there was no question that it was coming from somewhere inside the house.

No question at all.

This big old brown house with all its shutters pulled down tight. Just like someone with their eyes closed. Like his dad on a Sunday afternoon, sitting in the dark green easy chair after dinner.

Then Jackie wasn't next to him; he was walking up the steps leading to the door.

"Hey, what are you doing?"

"I'm going in. If there's somebody inside, they need help. Coming?"

Jackie grabbed the doorknob and opened the door.

The sound was gone now.

And then, with a shake of his head, Jackie was gone.

Fine, 'cause he had no intention of following him.

He'd just stand here, at the curb, with the morning sun in his face, watching leaves barely rustling, listening to the occasional bird, waiting for Jackie.

Too long.

It had been too long.

He called out Jackie's name.

"Jackie! Find anything?" Then, louder, more urgent now. "Jackie!"

A grackle screamed overhead in answer, and he jumped.

He wanted to run now. Run all the way back to the fence and out of the dead town. He could watch it all get drowned while sipping pop and chewing on cotton candy up on the dam.

"Jackie, come on out!"

Where was he? In the basement, or somewhere where he couldn't hear? Or maybe in the attic? Maybe he was just playing a trick on him, trying to scare him like he always tried to do.

Sure. And the crying was maybe some old alley cat, hungry now that nobody was around to leave their garbage out.

"Jackie!"

He'd have to go in, inside this big old barn of a house with its windows covered. If Jackie was hurt, he'd have to help him. That's what friends did. Sometimes you just got to do things you don't want to do.

Just like in Spy Smasher comics. There's just times you gotta do things.

He moved dully, almost forcing his sluggish feet to inch up the walkway. Hoping that Jackie would pop out. He climbed the steps. He opened the door.

"Jackie? You can come out now. You spooked me out enough. Jackie?"

He was standing in the hallway, so dark that he could barely see anything. And he smelled the stuffy, stale air of the house. And something else. Another smell. Just like—

His breath went funny again.

Frozen. He was frozen here. Unable to move farther into the house. Unable to leave.

He heard steps and smiled.

"Where were—" he started to say.

But the steps were different. Slower, heavier. Not the steps of the fastest kid in Gouldens Falls Elementary School.

And he stepped back, just a bit.

Then someone was there. In the shadows.

He saw a face, with small eyes and a mouth.

Wet. The mouth was wet. Just like someone who gets up from the table to answer the door.

"Excuse me, mister. I was just looking for my friend. He heard something and came in the house. Did you see—"

But then his eyes picked up something else just barely

glistening in the hallway. A shiny, wet trail that led from the old man back to the rear of the house. Like someone had dragged something and left a smear.

And behind the man, he saw Jackie.

His golden hair lying on top of the wet smear.

(*No. I gotta go. I gotta—*)

And the man grinned, a wide-open smile that made Billy whimper.

"Please."

And the man's hands were on him, pulling him through the hall. And he screamed as loudly as he could. Moaning, twisting wildly in the hallway as the old man just dragged him along, and he tried to kick at him.

But then he was in a big room, filled with people, all of them dressed up like it was a party, sitting, talking, laughing, looking at him.

Then they stopped. And the old man let him go.

(The smell. Like when he and Jackie went fishing at the pond. When they cut the head off the catfish. Just to see what—)

Someone moved behind him. Someone big and slow-moving.

Someone who reached out for him.

Caressed him.

Held him gently by the neck and the legs.

(And he thought of his warm bed, all rumpled from sleep, and a bowl full of Wheaties, and playing catch with his dad.)

(*No. I gotta go. I gotta—*)

He pulled away, moaning and crying, slipping in all the stuff, all this—

(Blood.)

He turned and ran. *If they catch me, I'm gone.* Like the town. Gone forever.

The front door was still open, and his Keds twisted through the murky corners of the hallway until he burst out onto the porch. And he kept on running, pumping, gulping the air, asking God over and over to please, please let him live.

He never looked back. That would doom him. *They'd catch me for sure, if I did that.* Just had to keep going, had to reach the fence.

He got to the fence, and oh, how he climbed now, hand over hand, feet chewing into the mesh, fast, faster, until he reached the barbed wire and tossed himself into the air.

Toward the other side and safety. He didn't see the rock he was about to crash into, because at that moment he dared to look back. Safety and home so close, he turned around.

Then his head, flipping weirdly forward, banged into the rock. He yelled—a sound muffled by the thick woods—and a dark, almost calming blackness fell over him.

And Billy Leeper lay unconscious.

PART ONE

1986

ONE

Fuck her, Dan Elliot thought for the hundredth time today as he waited, sweltering inside his Land Rover, to reach the tollbooth for the George Washington Bridge.

I should have taken the Garden State Parkway, he realized with the keen navigational acuity so often provided by hindsight. He'd probably be in Ellerton by now, checked into the Motor Lodge . . .

God, how he hoped it had a pool!

And sucking on a Jack Daniel's on ice.

Fuck. Her. Just when things were starting to come together, a couple of choice articles assigned and some real interest in his novel. (At least his agent said it was real interest.) Yeah, finally it was beginning to look like he might just have a career going, and they wouldn't have to depend on her salary working as an accountant.

But then she told him (screamed, actually) that she'd had enough. Enough threatening notes from everyone from the Southern Pennsylvania Cable Company to Messrs. Sears and Roebuck. Enough rush projects that had him either locked away in his office–cum–laundry room for weeks on end, or disappearing into the Amazon River Basin.

And, she said pointedly, enough Jack Daniel's.

Fair. Okay. I can accept that, he thought, feeling like Tom Snyder interviewing an ex-girlfriend.

Like hell I can. And once again he let his pain recede, not to vanish but to be savored at various moments until he could have enough drinks to blot out the whole mess.

Like everyone else in the eight or nine crawling lanes waiting to cross the Hudson, he sat zombielike, holding on to the steering wheel, just inching ahead his Land Rover. Most of the people, hermetically sealed in their air-conditioned cars, looked up at him, sitting in the khaki-colored jeep in denim cutoffs, his T-shirt matted with sweat. Occasionally a woman driver would give him a slightly lingering glance. Despite his temporary dementia and need to shave, maybe he had not totally turned into some kind of toad.

Jane may be gone for good. (She did, after all, take every stitch of her clothes out of the cabin—*and* every photo.) But in time he might soon enough be able to crawl out from under his self-imposed rock and face the world again.

He reached over and picked up his Olympus mini-recorder. He pressed down the record button. "Get to the on-site engineer, Fred Massetrino, to set up a tour." He clicked the recorder off, thinking for a moment, and then: "Check for the nearest dive shop, maybe in White Plains." Click. Then again. "Get approval from the New York Water Commission, or whoever has authority." Once more. "Call Omni to see if the check has been sent."

He put the recorder down as he approached the toll plaza. It's amazing how slowly the people in the booths moved, as if this were the sleepiest damn day in the world, with just a few tired souls crossing the bridge.

He handed the toll taker his two bucks and finally got his Rover out of first gear as he crossed the Hudson.

There wasn't any way he could look around as he

crossed into New York, with the eight or nine lanes madly merging into three. It was like high-speed bumper cars.

And that was just fine with him.

Because he didn't like bridges. Not big ones. Not small ones. And the sooner he was off, the better it suited him.

Not that he ever told anyone of his secret fear. No, he didn't want anyone laughing about some odd phobia he had developed, like the nervous wrecks who yelled every time their DC-10s hit a bit of turbulence.

But it was different with him, different because he had a reason to be scared. Oh, yes. And as much as he didn't want to, he let himself remember.

He had been in Stamford majoring in journalism and beer blasts. It had been snowing, the first snowfall of the season. A wet, slushy fall that turned the roads into a shimmering skating pond. And as usual, he had had a beer or two more than he should have.

He was crossing the Housatonic River, on an old bridge with an ornate iron guardrail, circa 1930.

The railing was, unfortunately, long overdue for replacement. Maybe even the whole bridge was.

Suddenly a car to his left, a big black Caddy that he still saw in his dreams, cut in front of his Pinto. He turned sharply to the right. And then he straightened out. The only problem was, he couldn't straighten his little Ford firebomb out. It just developed a nice, smooth slide. All steering totally inoperative, moving at a solid sixty miles an hour, right toward the neat Art Deco guardrail of the bridge.

He didn't believe it when his car went flying off the bridge, ripping the metal post out and separating the gridwork like it was so much taffy.

Then he was airborne. A flying Pinto, he'd say, laughing, when he told the story countless times later, leaving out his screams and peeing in his pants.

And when the car hit the water, it snapped his head

forward, breaking the skin in a neat, curved line on his forehead, leaving a scar, as the car sank to the bottom.

Someone else would have panicked. No question about it. Here it was pitch dark, with icy water seeping in from the car's bottom at an incredible rate, and the air suddenly becoming stale and dank. But not Diver Dan. If there was one place he was comfortable, it was under the water. He had done his share of night dives, plunging into everything from the Caribbean to the frigid waters of Lake George. And even though this was not exactly an ideal diving situation, he knew if he kept his cool, he'd be just fine.

He let the water seep in for a bit and then lowered the passenger window a few inches, just as he knew he should. The water shot across, knocking his head against his door. But gradually the car filled, until there were only a few inches of air left and the pressure was nearly equalized. He took a big breath.

(And here he would demonstrate it for his impressionable dates or his fraternity brothers, comically puffing his cheeks out.)

And opened his window all the way.

The water was cold, but not as cold as he'd thought it would be. He crawled through the window and made his way up, wondering just how deep the Housatonic was and realizing it was a bad time to start thinking about that.

Not too deep, he discovered as he broke the surface and gasped for air. He was greeted by a crowd of onlookers, most registering a weird surprise at his sudden emergence. And he was glad that none of the idiots watching had decided to jump in and "save him" by opening his door. That just might have killed him, pinning him inside the car while the water rushed in.

Yeah, Dan thought, moving his Rover to the exit lane for the northbound Henry Hudson Parkway. Ever since then he'd had a tough time dealing with bridges.

Bridges and, for completely different reasons, women.

Bitchin'! Tom Fluhr popped open the door to his dad's creamy beige Lincoln Town Car. And, of course, it was goddamn spotless. Nothing inside except a magnetic coin caddy and the antenna jack for the cellular phone.

No phone, naturally.

But the car still had that sweet, sweet smell of newness and money.

Then he turned to look at Emily.

"I can't believe your dad let you borrow it," she said.

"Sure. I told him it was a special date, real special, and I'd be especially careful."

Right. Real special. 'Cause tonight's gotta be the night, honey.

Emily slid into the front seat, and her tanned legs stood out real nice against the plush material.

Real nice.

"Did you bring your suit?"

Emily hiked up her tank top, revealing her tanned, flat tummy and then dark purple bikini top.

"Great suit. And I've got the goodies." He pointed to the backseat. Emily turned around and looked over her seat. "Beer, Tony's Famous Combo Wedges, and munchies galore."

Oh, yeah. He looked at the sleek curve of her body bent over the seat, and her tight rear end pointing at the windshield.

Gotta be tonight.

He started the car and drove away.

"I just hope no one else has stumbled on our secret spot. You haven't told anyone, have you?"

"No, sir. I'd die first." She laughed. "Of course, there's got to be other spots around the lake where kids have broken through the fence to swim and hang out."

"But not as nice as our spot." He reached over and patted Emily's leg.

Emily smiled and leaned over to turn on the radio.

And he raised the electric windows while he cruised through Ellerton with Z-100 safely blasting away inside.

She was quiet during the short ride. Perhaps she was thinking what he was thinking. Yeah, enough damn waiting. Enough games, enough pulling his hand away, telling him she wasn't ready.

Yeah. It was going to be tonight.

He reached the reservoir just as the sun was dipping below the far ridge. Damn. It was later than he hoped it would be. He wanted some mellow afternoon sun. Yeah, and a bit of swimming and a few beers. And then, just as it got cooler, they'd cuddle on the blanket, getting warm, getting close . . .

He pulled into an impromptu pull-off that got his dad's twenty-thousand-dollar car off the road.

"Move out, girl."

He reached behind him and snatched up the bag of food and beer.

"It's cool," Emily said. She sounded disappointed.

"No sweat. We'll just take a quick dip and then warm up."

Then he followed the snakelike trail, his trail, that cut through the woods to the chain-link fence. The sun was already gone from here, and now he was pissed off at himself for not making the date earlier in the day.

"Ouch!" Emily yelled out, and he turned to see her rubbing her arm.

"A branch." She smiled. "Scratched my arm . . ."

He nodded and kept walking.

Then he was at the fence. He bent down and pried the twisted mesh apart. It was a neat bit of work, the way he cut the fence and then rehooked it. Undetectable even when you were sitting right on top of it. He held it open for Emily.

"This way, my lady."

"Why, thank you, kind sir."

He followed her to the small indentation on the western shore of the lake, shaded by a towering elm.

He didn't bother spreading the blanket. He just put the groceries down and peeled off his clothes, tossing his jeans and T-shirt to the side. He dived into the water, smoothly, sleekly, like the county diving champ he was.

It was cool, almost cold. Certainly colder than an ordinary lake. This baby was deep. Still, it felt good. Cooled him down.

He surfaced and watched Emily kicking out of her clothes. She dived in and surfaced next to him.

"Brrrr," she said.

"Cold, huh? We can always play arctic seal."

He started dipping under the water, swimming between Emily's legs, surfacing behind her, grabbing her tightly as he nuzzled her neck.

And he began to harden in his blue Speedo bathing suit.

"Tom," she scolded, laughing, "stop it!"

But that only sent him under again, making great arf-arf sounds, grabbing at her feet, pulling her under the clear water.

But then he surfaced, and the lake was bathed in shade. The sun was gone, and he felt it was time to move the show along.

He swam strongly back to shore and spread the terrycloth blanket. Emily followed him, snatching the towel from him to dry herself off.

Tom spread the food on the blanket.

He watched her feast on the wedge, dripping oily bits of onion and provolone onto the blanket, munching down whole handfuls of Charles Chips.

"The best," he announced.

They were drinking Heineken, courtesy of Leo's lenient deli. Yeah, where IDs are never a problem.

He was in heaven.

"I've got a room reserved; my name is Dan Elliot."

The Ellerton Motor Inn was another one of those generic motels touting that they had a pool, color TV, and (in big letters) free HBO. With the parking lot more than half empty, business seemed to be none too swift.

"Let . . . me . . . see." The plump manager was leafing through his book. "Yes, here we are."

The manager looked up; his eyes narrowed. "And how will you pay for this?"

"Visa." He prayed that he wasn't so late with his payment that his card had been cut off.

The manager, a Mr. Feely from the name in black-and-white letters on the back wall, took the card and searched a book filled with twelve-digit numbers of thousands of terminated credit-card desperadoes roaming the country.

He placed the card into the roller. "We'll write it up when you check out." He smiled as he handed the card back. "How long you here for?"

"A week. Maybe a bit more."

"Here for the big celebration, huh? Should be some party."

He smiled. Ellerton was making a big deal out of the fiftieth anniversary of the dam, with fireworks and concerts planned. But it wasn't the dam that he was interested in.

Not at all.

"Yeah," he said, letting his impatience show.

"Room twenty-eight, right near the pool, Mr. Elliot," Feely said, catching his drift.

He picked up the key and drove his Rover over to the room. He opened it and ran back to pick up his bags and camera cases first, plopping them on one of the twin beds. Then he went back for his Panasonic portable typewriter and his diving gear, leaving the heavy tank and wet suit near the door. He saw Feely watching him from the office.

Nosy old bastard. Probably has peepholes in some of the rooms.

When everything was finally out of the Rover, he opened his floppy leather bag and dug out a small blue book. *Hagstrom's Guide to Westchester and Putnam.* He flipped it open to a dog-eared page.

It was four-thirty. If he hurried, he might be in time to catch Mr. Fred Massetrino before he left for the day.

And see just how much he knew about the quaint little burg of Gouldens Falls.

TWO

He threaded his way through the tree-lined roads of suburbia, his Hagstrom's open on the seat beside him.

This is the end of the rainbow, all right. The pot of gold for all those hard working eager beavers who trot into New York City and spend their day juggling other people's money from one low-risk, tax-sheltered investment to another.

To judge by a quick look at Ellerton, nobody in the world could ever be in need of a hot meal or a tennis racket. *Control* was the key word here.

The grass was tamed into submission with nary a single timid dandelion rearing its puffy head. No litter marred the streets, and no noisy kids cluttered the corner. Sure, the brats were all away, upstate, at Camp No-See-Um.

Yes, everything in its place.

He glanced down at the map, checking for the name of the road he was looking for.

Kenicut Drive.

Then, as if by magic, the road suddenly appeared on the left, a narrow, two-lane highway that angled sharply upward.

He shifted gears and took the turn. And the scenery changed as he left behind the split-level ranches.

First there were sand-colored buildings, all with heavy green doors shut tight. Then, to his left, a big open field and, at its center, a massive poollike area, filled with brown pipes.

These were the aerators. An enormous metal grid just rusting away now that Kenicut Lake was no longer in use as a reservoir.

Like some kind of big spiderweb, like something you'd get in your basement.

The road grew steep, and he curved around to pass THE OVERLOOK INN—SERVING ITALIAN AND AMERICAN CUISINE. A few cars were parked outside the strategically located restaurant. Perhaps he might even risk eating there later. Hunger can do that to you.

Then he saw the lake.

And it didn't look like an ordinary lake.

(But you didn't expect it to, did you?)

He entered the roadway that crossed the dam, and he saw the water, saw how choppy it was, its small waves jumping back and forth as if confused as to where to go.

Of course, that was to be expected. All that water just sitting there, flat against a stone wall. It makes for a strange and powerful wave action. Without the gradual slope of a shoreline to stop the actual waves, to break the little fuckers, it could get incredibly choppy. In a storm it probably sprayed right onto the roadway.

(And wouldn't that be fun to drive over, Danny Boy?)

He slowed and looked around for a place to park his Land Rover. But outside the Overlook, there didn't seem to be anyplace to stop and walk around. He wanted to look at the lake, and also look over the wall, on the other side, to the plaza at the bottom of the dam.

Well, that could wait for later.

Now he'd better find the site engineer's office and start

things rolling. With a two-week deadline—which he went and stupidly guaranteed, saying he'd give up his precious kill fee—he needed to move things along fast.

Just as he reached the eastern end of the roadway and the dark lake was behind him, he saw a small building with a car in front of it, and a sign: FRED MASSETRINO—SITE ENGINEER.

He checked his rearview mirror and turned in. He hopped out of his Rover.

The door to the car next to him suddenly opened, startling him.

"Mr. Massetrino?" the woman asked.

He smiled at her. She was pretty, with long dark hair. Nice and long, just like—

"We had an appointment?" she said, taking a step toward him.

"Sorry. I'm not the engineer. I was kinda hoping that he'd be here myself."

She looked away. He hadn't exactly made her day.

"Damn. This is the second time I've tried to see him. I'm just going to have to call the county supervisor's office and report him."

He walked to the door of the small office, noting the heavy Yale lock bolting it shut. "Says here he's on duty till five. I guess it was a slow day at the dam."

"Very funny. And he wasn't here yesterday. This really screws me up."

Now he took in other particulars, the bland cut of her suit, her bright eyes, the absolutely luscious-looking lips.

It had been a long time.

He stepped over to her and stuck out his hand. "Dan Elliot," he said, taking her hand and giving it a gentle squeeze.

"Susan Sloan," she said.

She didn't exactly seem interested.

"Why are you looking for the elusive Mr. Massetrino?" he asked.

"I'm a reporter for the *Ellerton Register,* and I'm doing a piece on the golden anniversary of the dam."

She rubbed her fingers through her hair.

Just like—

"I was told that he was the one to talk with about the dam's history."

"Perhaps." He wished he had taken time to shower, maybe shave. He just had to stop looking like a slob. No way any respectable woman would give him the time of day. Not as long as he kept on looking like Jungle Jim on a bender.

"What do you mean?" she asked, seeming to look at him for the first time.

"Oh, just that he may know how the dam operates, where the water comes from, where it all goes, and all that crap. But its history? I don't think so. . . ."

Got her now. Just have to pull back a bit on the line. Just a bit.

"Then who should I talk to?"

Dan smiled. "Well, for starters, you could talk to me."

She laughed. "You? Why you?"

"Take a look at the lake." She glanced at it, but he walked over to her and turned her around. "No, look at it. Under that lake there used to be a town."

"Gouldens Falls."

"Right. And Gouldens Falls was my parents' hometown."

Her eyes widened. "Really?"

"Yes, really. But if you want, as Paul Harvey says, the rest of the story, you'll have to adjourn with me to the Overlook Inn. The cocktail hour is upon us."

She seemed to hesitate a moment, as if weighing his offer. Then, finally, she smiled and said, "Sure. After all, I was ready to interview somebody today. And you're available."

"Exactly." Now he grinned, thrilled to have someone to talk with. Maybe his long period of emotional wound-licking was about to end. He sure as hell hoped so.

He got into his Land Rover. "I'll follow you." Then he let her ease her blue Escort out before backing up to trail her to the roadside tavern.

"They were kids, I guess ten or eleven years old or so, when it happened." He ran his fingers over the tabletop, following the dead-end trails made by the carved initials of countless visitors.

"They moved the houses, right?"

"Wrong," he said. A waitress sporting a blue gingham apron set down his Jack Daniel's and Susan's white wine. He took a good-sized sip of it before continuing. Got to watch it. Got too much of a taste for this stuff lately. "Some of the houses were moved. But for nearly everyone it was cheaper to take the federal money and just move. So everything was pretty much left there."

"Everything? Just left there?"

"Sure. The bank, the churches, the homes. Apparently some scientists had told the state that the submerged buildings and trees would have minimal impact on the water quality. And the plant was set up to filter the water, anyway."

"So your parents saw the town flooded?"

He shook his head. "No. They didn't. You see"—and he leaned forward—"something else happened that year, something that scared the shit out of some of the good folks of Gouldens Falls." He took a big gulp of his drink, finishing it. "Months before the flooding, there had been strange stories about the town, that something was . . . wrong with it."

"Wrong? What do you mean?" Susan took out her steno notebook.

"I'm not too sure. My parents didn't like talking about it. They just said it was a good thing that the town was under a couple hundred feet of water. Real good. Later, though, I did some checking in the old papers saved on microfilm.

And I find out that on the very day of the opening of the dam a kid disappeared."

"Disappeared? I don't understand."

"Neither did anyone else. But one of the stories in the paper said that some of the boy's friends said that he had planned on sneaking into the town on the last day."

"You mean, he was drowned, trapped in the town?"

He caught the waitress's eye and held up his empty tumbler, tilting it back and forth, indicating his need for a refill. "No one knows." He smiled.

Susan now took the first sip of her chilled white wine, the tiny beads of sweat slipping downs its side.

"So why are you here?"

"Because despite my disheveled appearance, I'm a writer too."

"Oh, really? What kind?"

"Everything and anything that pays more than five cents a word. But mostly stuff for magazines like *Outside, National Geographic, Natural History,* all the outdoor publications. I do my own photographs of faraway places and animals."

But I've been known to do press releases for the local McBurger. "Hey, kiddies, come see the all-beef clown!"

No need, though, to tell her about that.

"Sounds exciting. So what brings you to Ellerton?"

The waitress arrived and put down his second drink. He took another sip.

Easy this time. Take it slow.

" 'The Town That Drowned'," he said. "The true story behind what really happened in 1936. If . . ." Another sip. "If I can find it."

"Oh." Susan looked at her watch. "Hey, I've got to go. My daughter's getting home from day camp. She gets real upset if I don't get home on schedule." Susan stood up.

"You're married?" He tried not to let his disappointment show.

"No." She smiled gently, maybe even encouragingly. "Divorced."

He grinned.

My lucky day. Already the next week was looking a lot better.

"Well, then, how 'bout we meet here in the A.M. and see if we can rouse Mr. Fred Massetrino. Say nine o'clock? We can interview him together, while I scout out the dam."

"Agreed." She smiled and extended her hand. "And thanks for the wine."

"My pleasure."

He watched her leave, enjoying feeling almost human again.

Then he sat down. He'd be plotzed soon if he didn't eat something. He picked up a grease-speckled menu.

He scanned the gourmet entrées. Ah, there it is. The classic hamburger deluxe complete with fries, lettuce, and tomato.

A true American delicacy, he thought, and he signaled the waitress to come and take his order.

Fred Massetrino sat alone at the White Horse Bar, staring into his sixth or seventh beer of the day; he stopped counting a long time ago. Some smiley-faced reporter on the tube was talking about another baby that crawled through an open window, plummeting to its death on the hot sidewalk.

Nice story. Real newsy.

This was followed by an ad for the beer-drinker's beer.

But any beer is the beer-drinker's beer. Oh, yeah. He downed his glass and let it come down hard on the bar to catch the bartender's attention.

'Cause I'm having more than one.

He dug out another five-dollar bill to lay on the bar to

keep his somber party going. The bartender, a dopey-looking string bean whose pants seemed to just about stay up, tapped the bar, signaling that this one was on the house.

And Fred nodded. *Thanks, man. Big deal. I only had to drink five beers to get a fuckin' freebie.*

Dammit, tomorrow he had to get it together. He was gonna get screwed royally if he didn't stay in his office. Someone, sooner or later, was going to blow the whistle on him.

And he had missed his appointment with that lady reporter.

Hell, he was risking his job, his pension, all the goddamn time he put in for the County Water Commission as site engineer. All going down the tube.

Yes, he thought with a smile. Site engineer. Nice title, even if he really was the site caretaker, custodian, garbageman, picking up the crap left by the kids, checking the fence, putting up new signs that read: NO ENTRANCE FOR ANY PURPOSE WHATSOEVER.

But that wasn't it, that wasn't what was really bothering him.

No. It was something else.

Something that made his fat stomach go loose when he walked beside the lake in the morning. Something that made him think he heard someone calling him when he sat alone in his office. And he'd think he'd heard someone whispering, giggling, calling—

"Fred . . ."

And every time he'd leave his office and go looking outside, there'd be nobody the fuck there. Nobody. Just the damn lake, all choppy and churning like it was alive or something.

And that's the weird part.

Oh, Jeez, I'm losing it.

It seemed alive. Like the damn lake was watching him,

watching him as he checked the fence (until he stopped and ran, really ran like hell back to his office). And he thought he saw things in the water, sometimes the water turning so clear on blue-sky days that he thought he saw the tops of houses, or the dead, waterlogged branches of a tree, and then—oh, Jesus, no—some puffy, water-bloated head floating right up, looking at him.

Oh, God, he was losing it. No doubt about it.

Too many years hanging around that weird lake.

But he had to be there, had to be in his shit-can office, or he'd lose his job, his dream of retiring to Florida, the whole sweet deal. Tomorrow. He'd get a grip on himself tomorrow.

And now he just kept chugging down his brewskies, glad to have the White Horse to keep him sane.

That is, if he still was sane.

Tom reclined on the blanket close to Emily, ignoring his goose bumps.

"I'll have you come up to Cornell for the first big weekend." Truth? Why? He didn't know. "It's homecoming, and they always book some big comic or a rock act."

"Great," Emily said. He could hear that she wasn't convinced. Sure, she was no fool. She probably had more than a vague idea of what could happen to their relationship once it went long-distance. He moved right along. "I'll be rushing the frat houses by then, checking them out. Maybe we'll have some hot parties to go to."

There was a pause. And he braced himself.

"Where will I stay?"

He reached over and placed his hand on her stomach. "You could," he said slowly, "stay with me."

"Tom, we talked about that. I'm not ready yet. I mean—"

Shit. More fun and games, huh?

He withdrew his hand. "I know, I know. Soon you'll be ready to let me sleep with you. Soon. Only thing is, you can't tell me when." He stood up and let his pent-up frustration spill out. "God, you know how many guys would have dumped you a long time ago with that kind of attitude?"

Cock teaser. He almost said it. But he held back, not wanting to get too low.

"Well, so could you. I'm not about to be bullied into—"

"Fine. Then why don't you go screw yourself. I think I've had enough crap, waiting for you to be ready to fuck." He looked at her. "You know, I'm getting a little tired of playing with myself after our dates."

Emily stood up. "I want to go home."

There it was. He'd pushed all her buttons, all the wrong ones.

He looked away, out to the lake, almost dark now. He could hear her putting on her clothes, stuffing her towel into her bag.

"Oh, you do? Well, I want another swim. So you can just wait."

Prissy little bitch. Always in charge, always calling the shots.

He moved to the water.

"I'll wait in the car," she announced as he turned. She walked away, following the trail to the fence and the car.

Screw it. Let her cool her heels.

He walked a few steps into the water.

Chilly.

Almost too chilly.

But before he could decide to chuck the whole thing, he dived into the water, surfacing to slice through the water with powerful, practiced strokes.

Not so cold once you were in it. Kinda nice, actually.

But what a bitch. How many goddamn months had they

been going out? And he never pushed her. Never. But there's a limit to how long a guy can wait, for christsake. This is 1986, after all, not the freakin' fifties. Then, as he treaded water, he felt himself begin to simmer down. Emily was a serious girl. And when she finally slept with a guy, that would be it. Forever. Maybe she was old-fashioned, completely out of sync with the rest of the world. But she was special. Real special. Maybe even worth waiting for. He decided to swim back, catch her, and apologize (once more!).

He was good at that. He put his head down and brought his legs up to swim back. He kicked and pulled through the water, glancing up to see how close he was to shore.

The shore didn't look any closer. He seemed to be in the same damn place. He swam some more, feeling the choppy water spitting and gurgling around him. He looked up.

What? There was the shore, and their blanket, and the brown food bag. But he just didn't seem to get any closer, no matter how hard he kicked. He tried some more kicks, some more strokes—

Some more fear.

What the hell is going on here? He looked up out of the water. He should call for help. No, he'd feel too stupid with the way he'd acted. He swam harder. But the shore was still far away. His stomach grew tight. What the hell was going on?

"Emily! Something's wrong. I need help."

He waited. Could she hear him through all the trees? "Emily!" He heard the leaves rustle with the sudden breeze.

Great. Well, he knew he could tread water a long time if he had to.

If he couldn't get to shore, for whatever screwy reason, he'd tread water till Emily came back looking for him, until—

What was that?

He felt something around his feet, just barely touching his toes.

Probably a small pumpkin seed swimming around. The lake was filled with the tiny fish. But then he felt it again, around both legs—tiny, feathery touches all around him.

He tried to look down into the water.

But he couldn't see through the now dark, totally opaque surface.

Shit. I'm getting out of here. And he started swimming, real hard now, as hard as he could toward shore.

But his legs didn't move. The small, feathery touches around his legs, those "little pumpkin seeds," had turned to something hard now, holding on to his legs, almost holding him like—

He brought his right hand down to feel what he was caught in, to push it away, to free himself. His head kept bobbing slightly under the water.

His hand traced a path down past his hip, past his thigh, trying to feel what in the world held him tight.

What the hell?

It felt all sort of doughy, and soft, like, like—

Flesh. Gone puffy. Rotten.

"Oh, God," he said. And he screamed, his voice echoing over the lake. "Emily! Help me! Emily!"

And then he couldn't bring his hand up. It just wouldn't move.

Oh, Jeez. No. This can't be happening. This can't be—

His free hand was paddling the water crazily. He was barely keeping his head above the surface, and he gulped down whole mouthfuls of water.

And then he splashed his free hand down. And he felt something close around it. And then, almost gently, begin to pull him down.

No, please.

He screamed.

But it was cut off by the water filling his wide-open mouth.

And then there was only the churning sound of the lake water slapping against the dam, and the occasional throaty hum of a car quickly passing by.

THREE

He looked down at her face.

Like some slinky strumpet from a black-and-white fifties thriller, her face caught the glow of the motel sign through the narrow slits of the blinds. Her eyes were closed, and the tip of her tongue pressed against her upper lip.

She's got all engines firing, Max Wiley thought. *But is she thinking about me?*

Was she running some catalog of bronze beefcake through her mind? Yeah, so that other thrust was another hot picture. A lifeguard. Click. The pizza boy. Click. A slide show of studs.

She opened her eyes, her face grim, determined, hell-bent to nail down the big *O*.

I'm trying, baby. I'm trying.

He leaned forward (oh so glad that the three sessions a week at the Ellerton Sports and Racquet Club kept the beginnings of a paunch in check).

She was so young. Short blond hair and a lean dancer's body. He deserved this. Sure, he'd set up his own consulting engineering firm (billing a couple of million a year), and he was mayor of one of the sleekest towns in suburbia.

(And a devoted father too. Sure, always taking the kids to a ball game or a movie, whenever there was time, whenever he wasn't—)

She gasped, and Max Wiley let himself go, falling onto her thin frame, their sweaty bodies sticking together. He lay on top of her, coming down, and he caught a look at his Rolex.

"Jesus," he said, rolling off her, grabbing at his watch. "I gotta go. It's already past midnight."

He stood up, immune to the lure of any postcoital languor. His wife knew he screwed around—no evidence, but she was no fool—and it was best not to push it. He had a good thing going. He had his cake. And he ate it.

As often as possible. He picked up his clothes, neatly draped on a chair.

Jamie Collins lit a cigarette, letting the sheet slide off her breasts.

"Couldn't you wait until I was out?" The power she had over him was gone . . . for the moment.

"I like a smoke . . . no, I *love* a smoke after sex."

He shook his head. For six months they'd been meeting, at all sorts of odd hours, hitting every fleabag motel within a forty-mile radius. Always careful, he never let his pecker get in the way of his judgment.

Usually. But after he met Jamie, being interviewed for her community college law class, he quickly offered her some part-time work at his company. Some filing, some letter writing (what a god-awful speller), and fun and games in the land of suburban sex.

Yes, he was simply joining a long line of politicians, from FDR to JFK to poor Gary "Monkey Business" Hart. Nothing went better with politics than backdoor bimbos.

But young . . . these days they had to be young.

Inexperienced and germ-free. These days he didn't look at anyone over twenty-two or twenty-three.

Jamie was slipping into her skirt, a blousy plaid number in the new short style that Max was decidedly in favor of. He loved watching her dress and undress. Slowly.

And she knew that too.

"Hey, I've gotta go, sweetheart. I'll probably catch hell, anyway."

"Sure, Max. Go ahead before you turn into a pumpkin or whatever."

He hesitated. "Need any cash? If—"

"No," she answered quickly, sharply. "I'm fine."

A touchy moment navigated. "Right. Okay, I'll run, then." He walked over to her and kissed her cheek, suddenly feeling almost paternal.

Or maybe this one was running out of steam.

He opened the door and walked out to the parking lot, looking back and forth, checking to see if anyone was lurking about who might spot him.

But then again, who'd be coming or going at a motel at this hour? It would have to be another pillar of the community like he was. Still, this was a moment when his stomach tightened. He had to walk to his Porsche (parked discreetly around the back, near the overfilled dumpster), and calmly, casually get in (Don't run, man!) without some local yokel spotting him and screaming out—

"Jesus H. Christ! There's our ever-lovin' mayor! Now what in the hell do you think he's doing here? You don't suppose . . ."

Step, step. A hot-rod Camaro took the nearby corner too fast, tires squealing and screaming in protest, before the driver straightened out and gunned the car. Step. Step. The low, throaty hum of a truck echoed out of the distance and grew in intensity. Step. Step. He turned the corner of the motel just as the truck passed.

Now all the driver could see was the back of his head.

And there was his cream-colored Porsche, waiting for him, mottled by the dark shadow made by the fat old maple tree standing right next to it.

Made it. Safe and sound. Yeah, folks, once again Max Wiley risked his fame, fortune, and an upcoming shot at a congressional seat for his number-one passion in life.

He unlocked his car, opened up the door, and saw the car phone flashing.

A dozen creepy thoughts went through his head. His house was burned down, maybe, and his family trapped. Sure, happens all the time. (Wouldn't that make for some wopping guilt? Oh, yeah. Wouldn't that be fun to live with?)

He quickly slid into the black Leatherette seat and pressed the button. The phone buzzed briefly and he picked it up.

"Hello." His throat felt tight and dry.

"Max, it's Paddy Rogers. I'm at the Kenicut Dam, and I thought I should let you know what happened. Besides, I think I'll have to call the New York police for some help."

It was rare for Ellerton's police captain—six months away from retiring, thank God—to call him. Only one call in the past four years, just once when that crazy Henderson kid locked himself in the high school and began destroying it room by room.

"What happened, Paddy?" The captain was one of the few people he respected. No, respect was not quite the right word. He was nothing less than a local version of J. Edgar Hoover, with the meaty head of an Irish cop on the beat. Rogers knew, it was rumored, everything about everyone in town.

Which meant he probably knew how the mayor spent his free time.

"Tommy Fluhr went for a swim . . . at the reservoir. Emily Powers was there."

"Yeah." Max knew Tommy Fluhr's dad. They both were good for two martinis. No more, no less—at the Embassy Club.

"Something happened to him. Our best guess is he got a cramp and went under. Emily Powers was with him, but she didn't see anything."

Wiley started the car. No point sitting at the motel waiting for someone to come cruising by and spot him. He lodged the phone in his shoulder, backed the car to the left, and pulled it out of the lot. Gravel sprayed backward as he eased onto the road.

"What do we have to do, Paddy?"

"What we have to do, Max, is get a N.Y.P.D. diving team up here. We can use two Westport cops I know, but they don't have any electronic equipment. If he drowned, we need a body."

"What do you mean, 'if'?"

He heard the cop pause.

"Nobody saw him drown, Max. Nobody knows what happened to Tommy. He wasn't drunk. They hadn't eaten yet. And he was a champion swimmer."

Then Wiley thought of the celebration. The biggest event in Ellerton. The fiftieth-anniversary celebration of the dam and the reservoir. Speakers, parades, all ending in a grand celebration on Saturday night with fireworks, picnics, and—

The perfect way to launch his congressional bid.

This, though, was bad news. Nasty news. A mysterious drowning in a local lake. He didn't want his name connected with the drowning.

Dammit. Something had to be done. It had to be . . . contained.

"Paddy, let's hold off a bit. I'll be right there and we'll see what's what. Maybe the body's floated to the top, somewhere off to the side. Do you have some boats coming?"

Paddy grunted affirmatively.

"Yeah, we'll just sit tight a bit until we can look things over." A disturbing thought crossed his mind. "Any reporters there?"

"No. It's a bit late for them to be listening to the police radio. By tomorrow morning, though, we should have a crowd of them."

"Right. Well, by tomorrow everything might be all explained. I'll be there in a few minutes, Paddy."

He hung up and quickly dialed his home number.

After three rings the answering machine clicked on, and Wiley left a message, glad that no one was waiting up for him.

With no one waiting, there was so much less guilt.

By the time he pulled off Kenicut Drive to the small parking lot near the dam wall, he saw that Paddy Rogers had two enormous klieglike lights scanning the surface of the dark reservoir. He stopped his car, pulling right next to the captain's personal patrol car (a jet-black Chrysler with a blue bubble light spinning around). There were two boats in the water, each with small lights swinging this way and that. A faint fog seemed to be slowly rolling off the nearby hills, and Wiley felt cool, with just the thin sport coat to keep the damp chill off.

He looked around for the captain and saw him standing near the open gate leading down to the water, talking to two of Ellerton's finest.

"Captain," he called. Rogers finished his instructions and walked, not too quickly, over to Wiley.

"Find anything yet?"

Rogers shook his head. "No, Max, I've got two boats out there, going back and forth looking for the body. And there's teams of cops circling the reservoir, checking the shore." He looked right at Wiley. "So far, Max, they've found nothing."

Wiley nodded. Got to contain this. Keep our cool. Just an unfortunate drowning. A tragedy. Nothing, though, to get bent out of shape over. Happens at the Jersey Shore every summer. Right, it's just a freak accident.

"It . . . I mean, the body, will pop up eventually, right, Paddy?"

Rogers rubbed his cheek and looked to his left. One of the klieg lights seemed to pause a moment, as if its trolling of the surface had picked up something.

"Got something?" Rogers called out to the guy operating the light.

"No, Captain, just a funny wave. Water's a bit choppy."

Wiley looked at the reservoir. It looked positively sinister. He never liked it. Big, black, now with a whispery fog starting to creep over the surface. The boats, with their small lights, seemed alien, probing. And the water was unbelievably choppy, the wind whipping over the surface, causing tiny whitecaps to appear.

He pulled his jacket tighter.

"Sure, the body will probably surface tomorrow," he repeated.

Rogers looked at him, and Max could feel the captain's withering glance. And he wondered, *What does this red-nosed bastard know about me?*

"Bodies tend to pop up pretty quickly, Max. You see," he said, turning away and walking down toward the shore, "they're buoyant. They float. Unless something else happens. If they're punctured, then water can get in and weigh them down. They get soggy . . . like a piece of bread. Or sometimes, like in a plane crash, they get snagged on some metal. Or they just stay strapped to their chairs." He laughed. "Especially if the FASTEN SEAT BELTS sign is on."

"Then sometimes they pop up later, all filled with gas, a puffy human raft. I saw one once when I was a rookie in New York." Rogers looked right at him, apparently enjoying telling the story. "Yeah, somebody reported a body in the East River, and we went there with these long poles with hooks at the end for pulling it in. They reached out, Max, and punctured it, and pulled the fucking thing in. It popped like a balloon."

"Nice."

"One of the young cops said, joking, 'Look what I caught.' But nobody laughed. Not when the damp body balloon rolled over, eyes wide open, Max, and some green shit was lodged in its mouth—"

Wiley felt the evening's steak au poivre begin to rumble around, eager to begin a return journey up his gullet.

"And I had to get my ass down near the water and haul the thing up, actually grab an arm and lift the bloated thing onto the dock."

Rogers paused, rubbed his lips back and forth (as if getting rid of an unwanted taste or flavor, Wiley thought), and looked out at the reservoir and his boats.

"If Tommy Fluhr had a cramp and drowned, we should see his body soon. But—"

The captain started walking away from Wiley, along the shore, and Wiley followed. "I don't think that's going to happen here." He followed Rogers around the reservoir's edge until they came to the remnants of a cozy little shore-side picnic. A checkered tablecloth. A six-pack of Heinekens (minus one). A crumpled bag of chips.

Tommy Fluhr's clothes were scattered around, probably growing damp now just sitting on the ground. A heavy-duty lantern was stuck in the crotch of a tree, aimed down at the scene.

"So what do we do?" Wiley knew his voice sounded distant, hollow.

"With your permission I'm going to request a diving team, Ed Koch's best, complete with sonar and dredge equipment, though what good it will do, I don't know."

"What do you mean . . . 'what good it will do'?"

The captain's walkie-talkie crackled, and he picked it up. One of the boat teams reported finishing its crisscrossing search of the reservoir.

"Then do it again," Rogers ordered. He looked back at Max. "There's not much of a muddy bottom for us to dredge,

Max," he explained. "There's no way to do much digging for Tommy's body. There's a fuckin' town down there, under the water, Max. A town . . . with streets, buildings, . . ."

Wiley looked out at the water, the other shore almost invisible now as the fog became even more dense. Rogers put a hand on Wiley's shoulder—not a friendly gesture, Wiley thought. "And if that's where his body is, the divers will have to go down there to find it."

Wiley looked at his watch. One A.M.

And he hoped the body popped to the surface. Before sunrise. Before the reporters came.

Before the divers had to go down to look for it.

Already Dan was behind schedule.

Thanks to sleeping too late at the fabulous Ellerton Motor Inn (due, no doubt, to his last and totally superfluous Jack Daniel's double), he barely had enough time to crawl into yesterday's clammy clothes and rub a toothbrush across his teeth.

Breakfast was a lost cause (with tantalizing images of pancakes, syrup, and melting pats of butter, of course, very clear), and he was still going to be late to meet Susan Sloan.

He didn't need a map to get back to the reservoir. Years of shooting photographs in dense forests and honest-to-God jungles where a wrong turn could mean more than a missed deadline had taught him to pay real close attention to signs, directions, and broken twigs.

Still, when he arrived at the site engineer's office, he thought he might have made a mistake.

The gravel pull-off—that's all it really was—was filled end to end with police cars, both state and local. Braces of dogs were barking hungrily, eager to give chase to something. And he saw boats in the reservoir, long, squat things almost like the lobster boats that he spent a week shooting in Stonington, Connecticut.

Something, quite obviously, was up.

He slowed, then noticed a narrow space just wide enough for his Land Rover. He pulled in and hopped out, looking around for Susan.

He saw her, down near the open gate to the reservoir, steno pad dutifully out, talking to some middle-aged cop. He waved to her and she smiled. (Just a small smile but a smile nonetheless.) He walked over to her, brushing his mustache with his fingers, trying to arrange it into some kind of orderly configuration.

"By this afternoon, maybe even at the latest. We're still not too sure—" The police captain (or maybe general, for all Dan knew, judging from all the decorations on his coat pocket) stopped talking.

"Oh," Susan said, smiling. "Captain Rogers, this is Dan Elliot. He's writing a magazine article about the dam and the town of Kenicut."

The captain looked at him, not exactly a friendly stare.

"What happened?" Dan asked.

Susan quickly filled him in on the details of Tom Fluhr's disappearance.

The only thought he had then was a guilty one. Was this going to screw up his story somehow? Already he saw police barriers going up, and it probably wouldn't be too long before the whole areas was closed down tight.

No story. No sale. No money.

"That's terrible." He looked at Susan. "We were hoping to tour the dam today, as background to my story. I even wanted to dive in the res—"

"That's out of the question. For now, anyway. Not until we find the body."

A young cop came up and said something quietly to Rogers. "I have to go. If we find out anything more, Susan, I'll be sure to let you know." He gave a small nod to Dan, turned, and started to walk away.

"Captain . . . sorry, but do you have any objection to our

going on with the tour?" Dan gave his most cooperative grin. The future of his story lay in the captain's hands.

"No . . . that's okay. Just keep away from the shore . . . for now, at any rate." He walked away.

"Great timing," Dan said.

Susan brushed some stray hairs off her forehead. Unlike himself, she looked fresh and professional. "Don't tell me," he said. "I look like shit."

"You don't look great. Did you have some trouble getting back to your motel last night?"

"Sort of. Look, I know you've probably got to file something on this, but can you still help me with this Fred Massetrino? He might prove a bit more cooperative with a real live local reporter along."

"No problem. There's nothing much to report on the story, anyway. Some divers will be coming this afternoon, but that's about all the news. I'm still doing background on the celebration."

"Divers. From where?"

"New York. A special police team. The crew that normally gets the plum East River jobs. You know, floating body parts and gangsters in concrete shoes."

Dan turned away, looking at the swarm of cops. "I've got to go down with the divers. It might be my only shot at some photos of the sunken town."

"I doubt—"

Dan came close to her. A shower and a clean pair of khakis would sure hit the spot. "Don't you worry about that. I'll get to go with them. But first let's dig up Massetrino before he disappears on us again."

"Rogers said he was in his shed, and he looked like he had already had his first drink of the day. So we'd best get him while he's still coherent."

"Good idea."

Dan grabbed her hand and walked past the crowd of cops on the left, and some snarling, impatient dogs on the right. He made his way right to Massetrino's door (with its washed-out nameplate: F. MASSETRINO—SITE ENGINEER).

"Mr. Massetrino," Dan called, knocking loudly.

He looked at Susan. She was, if anything, more beautiful in daylight. Her jet-black hair glistened (it would look great on a pillow), and her classy business suit showed off her lean but not uninviting body. He still hadn't a clue whether she had any interest in him.

"Mr. Massetrino." Dan knocked again, looking at Susan. "Sure is one hell of an elusive—"

The door creaked open. And for a moment Dan was actually shocked by what he saw. The old guy looked like he hadn't showered in a couple of weeks. He was sporting an unkempt, grizzly gray beard that made him look like a wild man.

Dan felt almost dapper standing next to him. This guy was one step from cleaning windows in the Bowery.

But it was more than that. His eyes were a road map of red lines, covered with a mucous film, sunken into the hollows of his face.

Fred Massetrino was either mad or scared shitless.

"Mr. Massetrino," Dan went on, quietly now (as if addressing a bank president), "Ms. Sloan and I were hoping you could give us a tour of the dam, as arranged by the County Water Commissioner's office."

Dan dug out his letter of permission and stuck it out in the direction of Massetrino.

The eyes blinked, but there was no acknowledgment.

Massetrino opened his mouth. Gummy. With strings of . . . something holding his two lips together.

"No. Not today. Someone"—Dan saw his pupils dilate a moment—"drowned. A kid. A stupid kid." Massetrino seemed almost to snarl. "I'm always telling them kids to get the hell away. Always picking up their garbage, their beer cans . . ." He looked at Susan and tried to lick his lips.

"And other stuff. Now this happens. No tours today, mister." Massetrino started to close the door.

Dan jammed his foot in the door, something he'd seen done in a Bogart-Cagney movie. How come they never winced in pain when the door dug into their big toes? he wondered.

"You don't seem to understand," Dan said calmly. "I've got to take pictures, see?" He held his camera up. "And write a story. It's my job."

"Captain Rogers said it would be okay," Susan added.

"Right. The captain said everything is fine, Mr. Massetrino. So why don't you open the door, let us in, and we can start our tour of this historic structure."

Massetrino was erect. The DTs had to be just around the corner. Dan felt guilty about bearing down so hard.

Almost. But not quite.

Massetrino licked his lips. Not much real moisture there.

(*And I bet I know just what you're thinking about, pal. I've been close to that particular hell myself. When Sharon left, all I had left was the solace of Miller time and grabbing all the gusto I could. Somehow, though, the brink was seen, duly noted, and stepped back from. Just a step. At least for a while.*)

"Please, Mr. Massetrino. Mr. Elliot and I have important assignments. It's a big week for Ellerton."

Massetrino looked up at Susan, and slowly Dan saw him accept the inevitable. "Yes, a big week," he repeated dully. He let the door open, straightened up—almost to human proportions, Dan thought—and cleared his throat.

"Damned inconvenient. *Damned* inconvenient. But if the upstate guys say it's okay, who am I to complain? I'm no complainer. I do my job. I'm just looking at my retirement, friends. That's all Fred Massetrino worries about."

He stepped out into the light, like a debauched groundhog

checking out his shadow in February. He rubbed his grizzly beard.

"We're ready when you are, Mr. Massetrino. Right, Susan? Just lead on."

Susan nodded, and Dan thought she might be a bit uneasy about the tour guide.

"Okay," Massetrino said dully. "Then you might as well start at the top"—he grinned—"and work your way to the bottom." Massetrino walked away.

Dan watched him thread his way through the police and the growing crowd of semiofficial busybodies. He saw beefy guys wearing volunteer fireman jackets and ambulance caps. Nearly every car had a police light on the roof, whether it was an official car or not.

"Where is he taking us?" Susan asked.

Dan shrugged. "I don't know. But I'd hazard a guess there's an entrance to the inside of the dam somewhere here. There's bound to be a ladder down."

Massetrino climbed up stone steps that led to a walkway that ran parallel to the road on top of the dam. Cars whizzed past him as Massetrino hurried ahead.

He took the steps two at a time. "C'mon, Susan, old Fred seems ready to give us a quick tour."

He waited for Susan, and together they hurried to catch up with him.

Then Dan noticed it.

Massetrino wasn't looking at the water. Not a glance. There were cops out there in boats, and dogs circling the shore of the man-made lake, and lots of interesting activity. But old Fred just plowed on—spitting now and then, hawking great gobs of who knows what onto the ground—but he didn't look once at the water.

Just like—

Just like he was scared to look

(Scared? What could he be scared of?)

Massetrino reached the end of the roadway and quickly

went down another cracked and curved staircase to the left. He vanished.

Dan paused and looked at the lake, heard it lapping at the side of the dam not more than five feet from him.

One way or the other, he knew, he was going to see the town under that lake.

And more, he promised himself. *I'm going to find out why the hell it was buried under a square mile of water.*

"Are you coming?" Massetrino barked.

Dan smiled at Susan, then hurried along.

FOUR

Even here!

Even here he heard the voices. Much fainter, of course, because of the thick stone. But still, as Fred made his way down the spiral metal stairs, he could hear the voices chattering just beyond the walls, laughing, calling—

Fred . . . come with us. Out here. In the water.

He held the railway even tighter, to keep his balance.

(To keep his sanity.)

Curving around the metal staircase, trying to remember (*Please let me remember*) where the bottle was hidden. Was it behind the maze of pipes just below, lodged safe and sound in a moldy corner? Or was it farther down, hidden in one of the countless other dark nooks and crannies inside the dam?

He licked his lips.

Fred . . .

He thought he heard another laugh then, lower, deeper. A new sound almost like the sleepy growl of an animal.

The damned reporters following him were talking too. (Laughing. Sure, they didn't know. They weren't here every day to hear the voices.)

And wouldn't this be a wonderful place to watch the Earth's last moments?

"This happen often?" he said, turning to Massetrino.

The site engineer just stood there, licking his gummy lips some more. "No," Massetrino answered dully. "Every few years there's a quake. Something small."

"That wasn't all that small, friend."

"There's a fault line just about five miles from here," Susan said. "Right near the nuclear power plant on the Hudson, if you can believe that."

"Of course. That's where I'd build a nuclear plant, wouldn't you? Why not put it on a beautiful river just outside one of the world's largest population centers? Makes perfect sense to me."

Susan continued. "It's called the Ramapo Fault, and it runs right through Bear Mountain Park. Apparently three separate mountain ranges meet there."

Massetrino started to shuffle away. "Our guide is moving on. We'd best catch up to him before he leaves us trapped in this mausoleum."

It was just a joke, but when Massetrino seemed to disappear into a corner, the image seemed a bit too real.

It would be a nasty place to spend the night.

Then old Fred was back, the familiar aroma of a fresh belt emanating from his mouth.

Needed a constitutional, eh, old boy? Something to put the starch back into your shirt. A song on your lips and a smile on your face. Only Fred looked to be about as unhappy and confused as ever.

"Yeah, it was a strong quake," Massetrino said. "Never felt one like that, not here." He looked up and around at the pipes. "These pipes here . . . could be real bad if they broke. They carry water from the top of the wall. Some of them," he said, reaching up and running a hand along one large, sweaty pipe, "go directly to nearby towns for their water supply. Some used to go right to the Croton Aqueduct . . . for New York City's water."

He looked at Susan. "But not anymore."

"Why not?" she asked.

"There's no need. The Ashokan system upstate has more than enough dam water. Now, this reservoir is nothing more than a local convenience."

"But it was needed when it was built, right?" she asked.

Dan was listening, but he was also taking pictures, of the stairs, looking up to the open metal door and down to the even larger maze of pipes and the jumble of machinery.

Massetrino hesitated.

"Well," Dan asked, turning to him, "it was needed, then, wasn't it?"

Massetrino looked around, almost as if he were checking to see if someone was eavesdropping on him "I . . . don't know. I mean, there must have been some reason to build this thing, had to be." He stepped closer, looking in Susan's direction (who gave Dan her best don't-leave-me-alone-with-this-guy look). "I just don't know if they ever really needed this reservoir." He looked at Dan. "Ever."

Massetrino coughed, a phlegmy sound that echoed oddly in the dark passageway. He spit over the side of the railing. "I'll show you the pumps now. More stairs, though," he said. "Careful. They get damp lately somehow."

He shuffled along the metal walkway.

Dan wanted to put his arm around Susan. It seemed like a natural thing to do, to pull her close and keep her warm. But there still hadn't been anything from her except a professional interest. At this point in his life he couldn't handle anything resembling rejection.

Massetrino was climbing down again, the steady slide and plop of his feet a rhythmic spore to be followed. It got colder, and the air was thick and damp stuff, difficult to breathe.

"How big is this thing, anyway?" Dan called ahead.

Massetrino again cleared his throat. "What you can see, outside, is only about one third of the dam. There's twice as much buried underground. Most of the pumps are at ground level. You'll be able to see them . . . then leave from the bottom."

"Get the feeling he wants to get rid of us?" Susan whispered.

(And she came real close to him that time, she did. Real close.)

"Hey, I'm sort of eager to get out of here myself. You wouldn't have any lunch plans, would you?"

"Not at the moment."

"Then shall we hit the local greasy spoon? A cup of java and a stale cruller would hit the spot after the dungeon tour."

"Sure." She smiled.

Massetrino had stopped and was delivering another of his bits of trivia about the dam.

"Each pump here can handle up to fifty thousand gallons a minute. In case of a flood, there are special overflow gates to direct the water to the Bronx River."

Dan stepped close to the railway. The pumps overlapped and crisscrossed each other in a chaotic way that made it impossible for him to see what pipes connected where. They were covered with a black, crusty coating that made them look alive, organic.

(Like the fossilized entrails of some prehistoric creature.)

He took a half dozen quick photos, finishing the roll. "Hold on. Need a new roll of film," he said, slipping his camera off and opening it up.

"Where's that water come from?" he heard Susan ask, leaning over the railway beside him and looking down at the ground.

"What water?" Massetrino grumbled.

"There. On the ground. All over the ground. Near the pipes."

Dan was still fiddling with his film, threading it into the sprocket, closing the back of the camera.

"What the . . . what the hell?"

Dan looked over at Massetrino, scanning the floor, and he looked up.

(Just as if he had suddenly noticed someone standing there in the shadows watching him.)

He saw a crack.

"From there," Dan said quietly. He took a photo.

The crack ran from the ground, up eight or ten feet, a dark gash, moist with the slight trickle of water running to the floor.

"Oh, shit," Massetrino mumbled.

"Your dam's broken," Dan said. He took a photo of the narrow gash.

"Is that new?" Susan asked. "Did it just happen today?"

"No . . . I mean, I—"

"Of course it didn't just happen," Dan said, clicking away. "Look at the trail the water's made traveling over the stone. See, there, a thin line of algae. It's been here for months . . . maybe longer."

He turned to Massetrino. "When's the last time you were down here to check the inside of the dam, eh, Fred?"

He took a photo of Massetrino, the gibbering idiot in his domain.

(And wouldn't that be a nice item to put in a frame over the mantelpiece. Uncle Fred in shock, watching his dam leak.)

"I don't know. A little while ago. Just last . . ."

He trailed off into some incoherent muttering.

"That water's coming from the reservoir?" Susan asked.

Massetrino nodded.

"You better call some people," Dan said. "The Water Department. Whoever the hell's in charge of your dam."

"Yes, I . . . I should go now."

The trickle was small but steady. A thin, shining ribbon running along the inner stone wall.

And on the other side, thought Dan. Enough water to wash Ellerton away in minutes.

"Dan, I've got to get out . . . tell the paper."

"Right, reporter lady. We'll head back now."

Massetrino didn't move.

"You staying here?" Dan asked.

Massetrino shook his head. "No. I don't want to. I got to tell—"

But Dan was already leading Susan back to the main staircase, up and out of the wounded dam.

Max Wiley sat in his office, achy and tired, wanting nothing more than to lock his office door, curl up, and go to sleep on his couch.

But too much was happening for such a luxury.

Rogers had called him twice. First to tell him the divers were coming that night, then to report that he was calling off his search teams at the reservoir. There was, quite simply, no sign of Tommy Fluhr.

And as expected, the local rag called for a quote. The *Ellerton Register* offered more typos for your twenty-five cents than any other paper. The fact that it had not supported his run for mayor still stuck in his craw. Certainly it wouldn't back him when he declared for Congress.

If he ever got to declare for Congress.

But PR was power. If the fabulous Ellerton celebration of the Kenicut Dam got screwed up, it would reflect directly on him.

(Already he was calling it the damn dam, grinning at his feeble joke. He liked saying it out loud, under his breath . . . "The goddamn dam.")

Then, surprise, boys and girls, an earthquake. Not a small

one, either. No buildings or trees down—the Hudson Valley was too geologically old for such a catastrophe. That was for the Californians to worry about.

But big enough to give the houses a good rattle, send a few plates and pictures crashing to the floor, make a few little kids cry and run for their mommies. Hell, it was enough to wake him when he was trying to sleep in, and he had been dead to the world.

The boiler, he had thought, blinking awake. *It's going to blow, taking me and the house with it.* His kids were away at camp, and his wife had already gone to the real-estate office where she nailed down an extra few hundred dollars a week. It would have just been poor Max going kaboom.

But it ended, and it was only a few moments before he realized that it was an honest-to-God earthquake.

If that didn't beat it all. A drowning (a *champion* swimmer drowning!) and a freakin' earthquake.

He picked up the schedule for Saturday's celebration. A full day's worth of activities. Tours of the dam. Historical Society lectures. Naturalists running field trips around the reservoir. (Here's where the frogs like to fuck, ladies and gentlemen.) And bands and barrels of beer and soda. Followed by all the neighboring fire departments parading their heavy trucks over the dam's roadway while the massive fireworks display (contracted, you bet your life, by the ever-present Carlino Brothers, who seem to win every fireworks bid in the county—a nice bunch of boys if you didn't get them mad) lit up the summer sky.

Plenty of opportunities for his photo in the paper, interviews, and even a Sunday magazine feature. Yeah, lots of golden opportunities to get his name in black and white in the paper. Lots of good publicity, the ever-lovin' lifeblood of the politician on the make.

The phone buzzed, insistent and annoying.

He pushed a button and picked the receiver up. "Yes," he said distractedly. Damn. It was the town supervisor, Jack

O'Keefe—another old-time employee of the town who remembered when Ellerton still supported a working dairy farm and a cup of coffee was a nickel. "Jack, how are you doing? What can I do for you?"

Wiley listened (all the time trying to think of a quick fix for the headache O'Keefe was dumping on him).

"A crack? In the dam?" Max said lightheartedly. "Gee, nothing too severe, I hope."

But the supervisor didn't seem interested in allaying Max's fear.

(Just fix it, you stupid bastard, Max wanted to scream. Get some goddamn cement and patch the friggin' crack!)

"That bad, huh? I hope we can get everything in good shape for Saturday. We have tours planned, you know, and—"

But the supervisor refused to be lured into making everything okay for Max. He took the biggest, grimmest brush and painted Max a nice dismal picture.

The dam interior had to be closed. The State Water Commission had to be notified. Emergency evacuation plans had to be developed. No alarms were to be sent out, but the local authorities needed plans. Notification had to be given to the cops, firemen, and volunteer ambulance people, not to mention the mayors of nearby towns stretching from Harley-on-the-Hudson to Rye, on the Connecticut border.

And best of all, the papers already knew about it. In fact, it was a reporter who first saw it. Lots of publicity about this story.

"Jesus," Max said. "Jack, do what has to be done, but please, let's not go to pieces over it. Don't go overboard with all this alarmist junk. This is an important week for Ellerton."

(But Max could sense that O'Keefe saw through that little lie. No problem. Max felt as transparent as glass. Some people wouldn't buy a load of bullshit no matter how you dressed it up.)

Then the supervisor was gone, off to set a bunch of nasty wheels in motion, and Max Wiley felt like he was tied to something beyond his control.

He pushed the burton of his intercom.

"No more calls," he told his secretary. "From anyone. Until I tell you otherwise."

He leaned back in his comfortably padded chair, put his feet on his desk, and stared out the office's picture window, looking out over Ellerton and beyond, to the great wall of the Kenicut Dam. A wall that, unfortunately, happened to have a crack in it.

FIVE

Claire Sloan hated camp. This camp or any dumb camp. While the rest of the girls laughed and ran around together acting like total jerks, the whole dumb thing just made her want to throw up.

First there was swimming, every day, twice a day, no matter what, like the kids were frogs or something. And loads of dumb little arts-and-crafts projects (with the fatty "art" counselor telling her she *had* to make a coaster, 'cause everyone was making a coaster—*everyone*). But the games were the absolute worst. Field hockey, volleyball, kickball, one stupid game worse than the other.

(It didn't help that she was so klutzy. Here she had an absolutely beautiful mom who probably used to be *great* at everything, while she was totally uncoordinated.)

Rainy days were better. Then, at least, she could spend just about the whole day reading. Jean Auel's book about growing up smart in the good old Neanderthal days. Ursula Le Guin's SF fantasies—so real, she could picture absolutely everything. And her new favorite, the best book of all time,

Anne of Green Gables. They took her places. They took her away from camp.

The other kids didn't bug her, though. In fact, they liked sitting with her at lunch, swapping desserts, and listening to Claire goof on the entire camp staff one by one, ripping them to pieces. *That* was fun. And sometimes, like now, she could sneak to the side, plop down next to a tree, and read without some gung-ho counselor bopping over and ordering her to play the game or jump into the water, or whatever.

But at least this wasn't sleepaway camp. That would be the end. The absolute bottom. She couldn't imagine a whole summer (imagine, a *whole* summer) at the mercy of the dopey counselors and camp food, with the nearest bookstore miles and miles away.

(And something else—though she'd never tell anyone, not a soul. How could she explain her dreams? How would she explain waking up and screaming in the middle of the night, begging for it to end before she slowly realized that's all it was . . . just a dream. Just a spooky little dream.)

The same dream.

Every time.

The same ugly little nightmare.

Of course, her mother would have loved for her to go away to camp.

"Everyone loves it," she argued. "All your friends—"

"But all my friends don't wake up screaming at night," she said.

And her mother finally agreed, telling her, though, that everyone has nightmares.

(Even if Claire did hear her call the doctor and ask about something strange, called "night terrors.")

The books helped. Sometimes she dreamed about other things . . . about beautiful Alpine meadows, and crenelated castles, and horses galloping along a bench.

Books took her away.

She heard someone yell from the field, and she looked over.

The kickball game seemed to be running along just fine without her. The two counselors, tall and gawky Mary Stanger and Pam Marsh, the snot, were so busy blabbing to each other that she could stay away.

She started reading again.

Anne. Now that was a beautiful name. Not like Claire—why, it almost sounded like *chair.* Such an old, dull name, it just didn't sound like the name other kids had. Like Tammy, or Terry, or Sandy. Claire just didn't fit. Mary Stanger looked over at her as if she had just discovered her missing camper.

Just go on with your talking, jerk.

Stanger signaled to her to come over to the field, but she quickly stuck her face back in the book. Then the counselor shrugged and went back to talking.

Claire. She'd been named for her grandmother. And for that reason she almost didn't mind. Almost. She and her grandmother had something special between them. Ever since Claire's father left when she was four, Grandma was there. Working in their small garden, pulling up weeds and talking, really talking to her, about school, her friends, and books.

It was Grandma who gave her *Anne.*

"There's more when you finish that one," she'd said, touching Claire's head ever so gently. ('Cause she knew she was no huggable kid. Only special people got close to her. And she liked it that way.)

Mom was great, really super. But Mom worked a lot at the paper, even at night. And Mom maybe forgot what it was like to be a kid. The only way she got Claire to agree to go to camp was if she could also go spend a week at Grandma's house. It wasn't far away, but it was a whole different world. There was an actual farm—with cows, sheep, and everything—right next to the house. And big fields with tall grass that she could wander into until she found the perfect spot to lie down and read.

One more week at camp and she was free.

And tomorrow afternoon she'd even get out early to baby-sit for Mrs. Benny's two kids. Mrs. Benny was nice, even if the kids were total brats, and she paid well.

"Sloan, you're supposed to be playing kickball with the rest of your group," Mary Stanger yelled at her.

"C'mon, Mary, let me just—" she called back.

"Up and at 'em, Sloan," Stanger barked back.

Claire made her most disgusted face.

Probably neither of them would know a book if it fell on their heads. *I'm trapped in a world controlled by illiterate counselors.*

She closed her book with a loud snap.

"As if kickball was really important," she muttered to herself.

And she strolled over to the hot field.

"No dice, Dan. Sorry, but they say there's too many problems with insurance and they don't want anyone mucking about until the body is found."

Dan put down his coffee cup. "Damn!" He looked up at Susan. "Who'd you talk to?"

Susan slid into the booth and picked up the second half of her tuna on rye. "A couple of people. The County Water Commission, the town supervisor, and even the police chief. I left word at the mayor's office, but he flies whichever way the wind blows." She took a bite.

Great. Just how was he going to do a story on the town with the place off-limits? He considered bagging the whole project, packing up, and heading back to Pennsylvania. (And watching all the bills accumulate. Wouldn't that be fun?)

Then he looked at Susan. She seemed to feel bad for him, unless he was misreading the look in her eye.

"Hey," she said, "you've got time to make your deadline. Stick around, do some research . . . we can go down to the reservoir tonight, when the divers come. Meanwhile I'll try to see what I can do."

There, he thought. The first sign of—dare he hope it?—an interest.

"Hit the local library, get all your background stuff, and wait and see what happens."

He smiled. Right, he could do that. He could even make a dive without permission, maybe at night, if it came to that. Could make some ghostly, if highly illegal, photos. But it wouldn't be the first time he'd broken the law to get a picture. Not by a long shot.

"So where do you suggest I start, Susan?"

"The library. It's small, but the Ellerton Historical Society keeps their files there. I'll hit the newspaper's morgue. All the back issues of the *Kenicut Chronicle* are on microfilm there. I'll try to keep you posted on how things look for a dive."

He asked for directions to the library, which Susan supplied by making a little sketch on the puzzle placemat. "Great. Sounds like my whole day is planned."

"But not your evening. Any interest in a home-cooked meal?" she said.

"Absolutely." He grinned, then pulled back. Not wanting to appear to be too eager. Best be suave, aloof, and laid back rather than appear in his true state—as one of the walking wounded. "What time?"

"Say five, five-thirty. My daughter gets dropped off from camp around then." Susan slid off the bench. "Nothing fancy—just spaghetti and meatballs."

"Love it. I'll bring the Chianti."

"We could swap notes on the reservoir—" She looked at her watch. "Oh, I've got to run."

He dug out his wallet and uncomfortably, if cavalierly, put down a ten-dollar bill for their lunch. "You go ahead.

I'll see you tonight." Susan smiled and walked out of the Old Taconic Diner.

Dan reached over and picked up her leftover morsel of a sandwich and wrapped it in a napkin.

People are starving in Chile, he told himself. Or then again, maybe they weren't. But you never knew when you'd get hungry doing research.

He left the Pullman-shaped diner, walking out of the frigid air (the sign read, IT'S COOL INSIDE, and it didn't lie), and into the growing heat of the afternoon.

The library was down a dead-end street at the end of Ellerton's main business section. It looked like an old church, or maybe some kind of strange meeting hall. It had a bunch of oddly shaped gables and a tiny widow's walk that could just about accommodate one standing person. The whole building was painted a brilliant, glaring white, with garish red trim. It looked like a little old witch's cottage more than a library.

The inside was even more disappointing, with only two rooms filled with books, a small, freestanding card catalog, and a tiny librarian's desk. This was the domain, he read, of Miss Sarah Rider, a gray-haired matron who didn't look a day over seventy-five.

"Hello," he said, breaking the sepulchral silence and drawing glances from the only two other customers browsing in nearby stacks. "I was wondering if you'd be able to help me."

"Why, I'll certainly try. You've never used our library before?"

He smiled at her. "No, miss, I'm actually doing some research . . . for an article."

"Why, how exciting. Tell me, what kind of article are you writing?"

"It's about Gouldens Falls. You know, the town—"

"How marvelous! Why, that should be a wonderful story. So tell me, how can I help you?"

"Well," Dan said, pressing home with what he thought should be an obvious point, "I'm looking for information about the town and the dam. You know, photos and articles from when it was built—1939."

Miss Rider's face clouded over, a befuddled expression, like he had just asked for something completely off-the-wall.

"I don't know that we have too much. . . . I mean, there are the official town records down here, for Kenicut and Ellerton. But I don't know what else."

"I thought that the Historical Society kept its archives here."

"Oh, they do, sure they do. I just don't recall there being too much. No, I don't . . . but you go on upstairs and look. Everything will be in the big file cabinet with a *G*, a *G* for—"

"Gouldens."

"Exactly. Then, if you want, you can check the town record books down here. The room is upstairs, just a bit to your right."

"Thanks," he said, and he went up, and wondered . . .

Could that be all the information there is? A dam is built, a big project, a town buried. And there are only a few files on it?

The archives room seemed to be an old bedroom, now filled with heavy, olive-green file cabinets. A swirling Persian-style carpet, well frayed at the ends, sat incongruously in the center of the floor. There were no chairs and no tables.

It obviously was not a place devoted to heavy research.

He opened up the *G* file, expecting to see it jammed full of file folders. But it contained only a few inches of folders, with only one skinny folder labeled "Kenicut/Dam."

He pulled it out.

(Outside, through the closed windows, he heard some birds screeching—some jays, he guessed. It was stuffy, hot in the room, and he walked over to the window and tried to open it. He pulled up, but it was painted shut. His sweat dripped onto the carpet.)

He went back and opened up the file.

And for the first time he saw Gouldens Falls.

It looked more modern than he had imagined. For some reason he had expected horses and old wooden houses. Maybe an old country store. But this was a town, circa 1936, a rather normal-looking town, its wide blocks lined with houses with Georgian-style porches. And small buildings, like the Woolworth's, with its flaming red sign merely a dull gray in the black-and-white photo. And the picture of a movie theater. Its marquee proclaimed a DOUBLE FEATURE—DRACULA AND FRANKENSTEIN.

A town like hundreds of other small towns, Nice, safe, and secure.

Then there were pictures of the dam being constructed.

He saw the heavy stone blocks made out of poured concrete stacked neatly by the incomplete, sloping wall of the dam. In one photo workmen were at the top, leaning for a moment on their shovels, posing for posterity. There was a shot (taken from the town, he figured) looking up at the just completed dam.

And finally there was another picture (maybe the last one) of the town, now completely surrounded by a chain-link fence. Some of the houses were gone—removed, taken to new locations. It was a photo taken from the top of the dam, looking down at the town.

How long? How long was it before the water came and made it disappear forever? The next week, the next day . . . the next hour?

He knew then, standing there, that he'd get to see it. That one way or another he'd dive down and—

"Excuse me."

He jumped (and some of the pictures slid out of the file onto the floor).

"Oh, I didn't mean to startle you. I see you found the file."

Dan smiled. The woman's croaking voice seemed to have come out of the wall. Her orthopedic shoes, God bless her, made her as soft on her feet as a cat burglar.

"It's just that I thought of something else that might help you."

"Oh, what's that?"

"Well, not something but someone." She squinted up at him. "The Methodist minister, Reverend Winston, is a bit of a history bug. Yes, and he's probably learned a lot of interesting facts about our little dam here."

"Oh, really? That sounds promising."

Anything would be better than this pithy package of information. He had written articles before on nothing more than a wing and a prayer, but this was getting ridiculous. "Do you have his phone number?" he asked.

"No, but I certainly can help you find it. There's a local directory downstairs."

She led the way down to her desk.

The librarian quickly found the rectory number, then stood back and watched as Dan dialed.

After two rings Reverend Winston answered—a mellow, lulling voice that was probably not much in the fire-and-brimstone department.

When Dan mentioned what he wanted, he thought he heard Winston's voice falter.

"Yes, I have been collecting . . . information."

Dan waited for the minister to offer to show his goodies, but when he didn't, he pressed on.

"Will you be willing to talk with me for my article?"

(Another pause. And now Dan recognized the sound of the voice. It was the same sound he'd heard as a boy, when his parents talked about the town of Gouldens Falls. The same hesitation.)

"Why, yes, I suppose so. If it could help you. Mind, there's lots I don't know. Lots. Still, I could tell you as much of the history as I've been able to find out."

"Super. Then how about tonight? Say, seven o'clock . . . seven-thirty?"

"That'll be fine. I retire early. My parish is small but old. There are many people who need to be visited. I'm out much of the day."

"Thank you, Reverend. I'll see you then."

He replaced the receiver and gave Miss Rider a wink.

"And thank you. I'll be sure to mention in my article the wonderful service provided by you and your library."

The librarian blushed.

"Now, if you wouldn't mind, I'd like to see the town records."

The librarian bustled over to the small pair of shelves devoted to reference books.

The door to the small wooden office, his cruddy shack, was locked, bolted tight from the inside. He sat in the corner, in the dark, streams of sweat running off him and dropping onto the dusty floor.

(I've got to clean up this pigsty. Before anyone comes and looks at it.)

The bottle in his hand was half gone; shit, maybe more—it was always hard to tell when it started slipping down to empty. Every nip he took, burning on his tongue, burning its way down, was going to be his last sip for a while. But then he'd raise it up and take another hit and—uh-oh—the old booze-level mark slipped down a few more notches.

He was safe here. The voices were still all around. Playful, teasing, but he knew what they wanted. They wanted him to leave the shack, to come out in the air where they could get at him. Sure, the police were gone now, leaving only a few barriers up and one cop to walk around the reservoir. They could get him if he left his little office.

But there was no need to do that, was there? He could

stay here with his trusty bottle and ignore the crazy voices. Let the fuckers shout and scream, he didn't care. Not at all.

He was safe.

Some more sweat plopped off him, and Fred brought his arm up to wipe his brow. He smelled himself in the room, like some boxed animal, an overpowering stench that almost made him gag.

Later he would try to leave.

Later when the voices stopped.

Besides, this bottle was almost a dead Indian.

And the nearest one was hidden all the way inside the dam.

He took another gulp.

SIX

Claire was ignoring her mom's guest, this guy who looked like some moron from a Camel ad. Yeah, he looked like a regular Captain Adventure with a camera. And boy, was he ever trying hard to win her over. Smiling at her, asking about camp—

("Puh-lease," she told him. "Ask me anything but that.")

But she had *his* number. He just wanted to get close to her because of her mom, just like other guys who drifted in and drifted out of their lives. Mom was the big attraction. Even her father, who'd vanished when she was a little squirt. Twice a year he came by, dropped some gifts on her, and left.

(Even her mother didn't know about her crying into her pillow later, feeling a strange kind of pain that just wouldn't go away.)

"Can I help you set the table?" he asked.

"I do it every night by myself, Mr. Elliot, so I don't think I need any help."

"Claire!" her mother barked from the kitchen. "You

could try being a tad more polite to our guest. Just because you had a bad day at camp—"

"Mom, every day is a bad day at camp. It's like a prison. Thank God there are only three more days."

"Well, tomorrow is a half day, Claire. Mrs. Benny will pick you up after lunch to go sit for her. So enough rudeness here, girl."

She shook her head. "Sorry, Mr. Elliot."

"The name's Dan. And don't apologize. I hated camp too."

She was corraling the knives and forks. "You did? You look like just the kind of person who'd love camp." She paused a beat. "No offense."

Dan came close to her. There was something about this one that caught Claire's interest. Most people bored her crazy. There was just nothing to them, like the cotton candy she bought at the Catholic school carnival each year that just melted away. They were cardboard people, not like the people in books, characters who lived exciting lives—

This guy seemed to be more like them, to have secrets . . . layers.

"You know what asthma is?" he asked.

"Yeah, it's some kind of breathing thing, right?"

"All your tubes get clogged with mucus and it can be very hard to breathe. It also made it very hard for me to play with the other kids. I never knew when an attack would come. I used to carry an aspirator, a little spray thing that helped me through an attack." He reached over to her and took away some of the fistful of knives and forks she held.

"One time—I think I was ten or eleven—I was at camp, having a pretty miserable time of it. There were these relay races, which I hated."

"Me too."

"I slipped away with some friends, out into the woods. We called ourselves the Avengers, after a TV show."

She looked at him now, listening to his story, wanting more.

"Anyway, we climbed a tree, a big old elm tree that had to be just about the tallest tree around, with loads of real heavy branches. It was a perfect climbing tree." Dan smiled. "It was perfect, so we climbed it."

Listening to him was like a story, like something from one of her books. She saw him, in her mind, change into a small boy—still with curly hair and blue eyes, of course—and she saw the woods. But most clearly of all she saw the wonderful elm tree.

"So what happened?"

"We nearly got to the top. I was always trying to prove that I was the same as everyone else . . . you know, just as strong as they were, just as good." He laughed. "It's called denial. You know, when you try to deny something about yourself."

"I know," she said, meaning it.

"So I was ahead of them all, getting to where the branches started getting thin and weak. Some sunlight was hitting me, and the air was clean and fresh. I felt like the King of the Mountain."

Dan scooped up some napkins from a plain wooden holder and started placing them under the utensils.

"Then I stepped on a branch—only a few feet from the top—and it snapped. All of a sudden it just gave way. I tried to hold on to the tree, but it was impossible." Dan laughed. "It was like a Looney Tunes cartoon. One minute I was there, and the next minute I was flying through space. If I hadn't stopped falling, I think I would have died."

Claire was chewing her lower lip. "God, what did you do?"

"I hit a branch—about halfway down—and it broke my fall. Then I was hanging there, like some kind of monkey, trying to scramble up the branch." His eyes seemed to cloud over and she thought, he's back there too, he's reliving it right now.

"Then the attack came. My asthma. Couldn't have been a worse time. I couldn't breathe, my lungs started to clog up, and I was hanging there gasping. I think I started to cry."

"And you couldn't get at you aspirator?"

"Right." He smiled.

(And now she knew he wasn't like the others her mom brought home. He was real, with secrets to be shared.)

"I was ready to let go. I couldn't hold on anymore. That's when my best friend, a kid named Simon, started screaming at me. 'Get up, you jerk,' he yelled. 'Get your butt up.' And all I did was listen to my friend's voice, yelling over and over, telling me to climb onto the branch. I listened, and for one of the few times in my life I did what I was told."

"You got up?" She smiled.

"Slowly, barely able to breathe, but I got up. Then, shaking like I'd seen my own ghost, I reached into my jeans pocket, popped out my trusty aspirator, and sucked on it. It was ten minutes before I was breathing normally again."

"What a great story!"

"Only," he said, grinning, "it's not a story. When I think of camp, I think of that day and just about nothing else."

"Claire . . . would you come and help me carry out the food?"

"I'll be back," she said, suddenly afraid that her new discovery would disappear.

Her mother was at the sink, gently tossing the spaghetti in the air one more time to get the water off.

"I like him," Claire said quietly. "He's a real person."

Susan Sloan handed her daughter the spaghetti and pushed a strand of Claire's hair off her forehead.

"And so do I," she whispered to her.

The knock on the door was a slight, tentative thing. Wiley knew his secretary was gone for the day, no eager beaver she, and he quickly deduced who it might be.

"Come in," he said.

Jamie Collins walked in, a playful smile on her face. So young. So loaded with energy. She closed the door behind her. "I thought you might like some company."

"Oh, God, I don't know. Things are really getting crazy around here."

She stepped closer to him, and he picked up the rich, musky aroma of her perfume, a scent that carried with it memories of their tryst. The motels and beds might change, but that smell stayed the same.

She smiled. "Problem with the company?" And she rested her hand on his shoulder.

"No," he said, letting his hand travel up her leg, slowly tracing the exquisite shape of her firm, sleek legs. "There's divers coming to look for that boy's body—at night, no less. I figure I should be there."

She slowly knelt down beside him.

(And now he felt himself start to harden. More than most girls he dallied with, Jamie knew how to tease. She moved slowly, almost catlike, and it drove him crazy.)

"So you won't be going home for a while, then," she said, licking her lips.

He leaned back, pushing his chair away from his oversize (and underutilized) desk. He saw her eyes fall to his crotch.

"Oh," she said, reaching out to him, letting her hand gently grasp the now obvious bump in his pants. "Then we have time to play."

His answer was a grunt, and he reached down and pressed a button under his desk that locked his door.

And for a little while, with her dark eyes looking up at

him, enjoying his pleasure, wriggling in his seat, Wiley forgot all the problems that seemed to have come out of nowhere.

"I'll clear," Claire said, popping up from the table and grabbing a few dishes.

She was a serious kid, Dan thought. Not your average bubble-headed eleven-year-old. He had been on trial the moment he walked in the door, and somehow letting his guard down, exposing himself to her, had won her over.

She was also in pain.

From the divorce, perhaps. But also something else, something else she was hiding, very deep.

"Thanks, sweetheart," Susan said. She looked at Dan. "Some coffee? Maybe a bit of ice cream?"

"Sure. If there's time. I have to go in a bit to meet the local historian. I was wondering if we could swap notes before I leave."

"Sure, though I didn't get to run through all the papers and microfilm. But I can tell you the strangest thing I found out."

"What was that?"

"The dam was approved in a matter of weeks and then built in thirteen months."

"That's odd?"

"Very. Most of the big WPA projects took a year or more for all the state, local, and federal paperwork to be filed. But this project just breezed through, and the rate of construction was incredible. Similar reservoirs in other parts of the state took up to five years to build."

"So what's it all mean?" Dan glanced out at the kitchen. Claire was digging out great spoonfuls of green ice cream and dumping them into bowls.

"Someone wanted the project done quickly, and they had enough clout or money to make it happen."

“Was there any clue to who that might be?”

“None. At least not in the papers. What did you find out in the library?”

He smiled, remembering the thin file on Kenicut. “Not much, I’m afraid.” Claire arrived with the ice cream. “Mint chocolate chip?” he asked.

“Absolutely,” Claire said. “It’s Mom’s and my favorite.” She went out to the kitchen for her own bowl.

“Anyway, the town records give the date when the project was first proposed, when construction began, and not much else. There’s only one thing that seemed peculiar.”

“And that was?”

“It was only after the project was approved—actually approved—that I found a published reason for its construction. It’s like it was some kind of Mafia kickback deal, where they set the whole thing up and then think of a reason. But I can’t imagine how so many people, at the state level and all, could have gone along with it.”

“Well, I have another year’s worth of papers to go through tomorrow.”

“And maybe kindly Reverend Winston will be able to help me out.”

“Hey, everybody, your ice cream’s melting,” Claire shouted, scooping up a great greenish gob of the desert.

“Say no more, sprout, I’m digging in,” Dan said, obeying. And he looked at Susan, letting a dangerous thought linger for a moment before giving himself over to his mint chocolate chip ice cream.

Damn, he had to leave.

The divers would be coming soon, along with a whole crowd of busybodies, cops, firemen, anyone and everyone who wanted to watch the dive into the reservoir.

He could tell them what was wrong. Sure. But nobody asked him. The damn bottle was empty, and he had been so good about trying to save it, to ration it, taking small slugs. No, sips! Trying to make it last. Now, dammit, it was all gone. There was no way around it. He'd have to go get the other bottle.

The other bottle, he thought. The one that's tucked away inside the dam itself.

Sure, he could try to get to his car instead and get away, just drive away to the White Horse and meet all his old pals . . . Johnny Walker, Jim Beam, and the old fart himself, Old Granddad.

But the voices wouldn't allow that, now would they? He knew too much. He had figured out too much. They wanted him to stay right here, nice and close, where he could hear them, talking to him from under the water.

(*Gone,* he thought. *I'm completely gone. Crazy. This is what it's like. To be nuts. To hear things that aren't there. To imagine strange, bad things, things that just aren't real. Couldn't be real. But somehow*—he laughed to himself—are *real.* He laughed out loud. *As real as this dumb-ass office and the dam itself. As real as sin.*)

But he had to leave now. In a while there'd be too many people around, walking and nosing about, for him to go into the dam. The dam was supposed to be locked up tight, and he had a key. Oh, yes, he still was, after all, the site supervisor.

He stood up.

He unbolted the door and opened it. He smelled the fresh air.

Just have to be quick, that's all. Get over to the dam, climb down, get the bottle—

(It's still in there, isn't it?)

And then back, safe and sound. Snug as a bug in a rug.

He looked around for the cop left on guard duty. For a moment he couldn't see him. Then he noticed a blue shirt ducking in and out of the trees over at the north end of the lake. Perfect. He was well away from Fred's little jaunt.

Then he saw his own beat-up car, and again he wondered whether he should try to get to it. It was just a walk of fifty feet or so. And then, hopping in (quickly!) and driving away. Maybe he could do it . . .

But maybe, just maybe, they wouldn't let him.

No, they wanted him here now. He knew that. He *accepted* that.

He let his office door swing shut and then started to walk over to the stone stairs leading up to the wall, then across the walkway. (Making double sure not to look at the water. No, sir.) And he was amazed at how steady on his feet he was. What had he downed—about a fifth of bourbon—and look at him! One foot in front of the other, just like a regular person. He grinned, pleased with himself.

This is nothing, he thought. A piece of cake.

The roadway curved to the left, leaving the dam, and he came to the matching stone staircase at the eastern end leading to the metal door. *(To which I've got the key, yes, indeed.)*

He stepped down—a little wobbly here on the steps. Damn things must be a bit tilted. He had the key out and ready . . . best not to waste a moment, not a second, in his task.

The key didn't fit at first, until he turned the thing around and he heard the heavy bolt slide away. He pulled open the metal door and went in.

Tomorrow the state engineers would snoop in there, bright and early, to see the crack. *That's when I lose my job,* he thought. *That's when they find out that I haven't been staying on top of things.*

No, I've been a bit preoccupied.

He went down the staircase, the rattle echoing in the narrow cavern. Across the walkway, past some pipes, to another stairway. Then down again—halfway—to where he knew the bottle was hidden. He stopped and felt in the wedge-shaped pocket made by the pipe in the wall. He felt nothing.

"Shit. Now where the hell," he said, spluttering, his hand flopping around in the wedge, trying to feel for the bottle. Then he began to panic, because if it wasn't there, he'd have to try to leave.

He heard something.

A voice.

(But not in his head. No, this was a regular voice. An out-loud voice. Coming from just above him.)

"Who the—" he shouted. "Who the hell—"

Again he heard it. Like someone whispering, talking about him.

He looked at the walkway above him. A big rat was staring down at him, big oval eyes, its pointy canines just protruding from its thin rubbery lips. The ugly sucker squeaked. Watching him.

"You goddamn—" he yelled, and he reached up and banged at the metal flooring, sending the chattering rat darting away.

He saw the bottle. Somehow, maybe in the earthquake, it had slipped a few feet. Now it was barely balanced on the pipe where it curved away from the wall. The engineers would have been sure to spot it the next day.

He reached over and grabbed it. (Thinking What the hell as he unscrewed the top and took a healthy hit from the bottle. Then another. Just enough to help him back to his shack, back to safety.)

He stuck the bottle under his belt, close to his belly, and after checking that it was secure, he stood up, hustling now, rushing. He reached the door and shut it gently. (Didn't want the cop to turn and see him now.) He got his key out and locked the bolt. Then back across the roadway, ignoring the late commuters coming from the Ellerton station driving past him. Again pleased with how well he was moving. He was damn proud of himself. Just as long as he didn't look at the water. Just as long—

But somehow, just out of the very corner of his eye—he wasn't looking, not really—he noticed something floating near the surface. Something whitish and big.

And he looked.

His pace slowed as he started trying to make out what the damn thing could be. Yeah, it was something white, just below the surface.

"What the hell?"

There were no voices. The voices were somehow gone. There was no sound in his ears at all. Nothing except the occasional hum of a passing car.

It felt safe.

He went to the stone guardrail and looked down at the thing. It was floating, bobbing up and down, getting closer to him.

Soon he'd be able to see it.

He kept staring down at the thing, trying to see what the hell it was, just under the water. It came closer, almost to the edge where the reservoir's water slapped against the dam's wall.

It bobbed up.

It was a face. Under the water. Its eyes wide open. (Not regular eyes. Eyes like he'd never seen before.) And the mouth was open too. (Like when he went crabbing with his kids and they'd pick up the fish head with notches cutting into it that was tied to the string. And for a while nobody could say anything, then they'd see the head, all chewed up, one eye left, then a crab just about to scuttle off, if he was lucky.)

Then the voices came back, like a surprise party erupting from a closet. He started to back away.

But it was too late. The face was coming up out of the water, leaping up at him, while its hands (so cleverly hidden before) reached out and grabbed Fred's sweat-stained shirt and pulled him in.

He thought he screamed. He thought he yelled loud enough that the cop heard him. He *had* to have heard him.

But he just didn't realize that his scream, his full-throated, whiskey-coated yell, just didn't carry too well under the dark, cool water of the Kenicut Dam.

SEVEN

She took the airplane demo seat belt—now worn almost threadbare by years of lifeless safety demonstrations—and replaced it in its small compartment.

The man in front of her was watching her mannequin routine with unusual attention, even for a horny businessman. She was more than used to being scrutinized by planeloads of men, all of whom fantasized that they actually had a chance to score with her, a real live stewardess. Of course, none of them had a shot at it, and any imagined extra-friendliness that they perceived was just standard company policy.

But, thought Karen McCammon, there were always exceptions. And this fellow—with his jet-black hair, blue eyes, and rugged, tanned features—might have a real opportunity.

He turned her switches.

She smiled at him, hoping he wouldn't read it as mere flight-attendant formality. When she leaned over to pull out the life vest, she was aware of his eyes traveling the extended arch of her body.

"Since we'll be traveling over water," her friend Sally Jo

announced over the PA, "life vests are available directly under your seat." Karen wrapped her sample life vest around her neck.

"I'll get you another drink just as soon as this is done," she said quietly, leaning down to him.

"No problem. I always like to know as much about safety precautions as possible."

He had reserved two seats—not that he needed them. She could see that underneath his elegant, cream-colored suit (perhaps a Giorgio Armani) he was lean and muscular. His hands looked powerful, with long, tapered fingers and well-defined veins. No, he was simply someone who wanted privacy and had the means to pay for it.

"We hope you enjoy flying with American. The flight attendants will begin serving complimentary beverages just after takeoff."

She put away the vest and sat by the main door for takeoff. Once the plane was in the air, she walked past him, to the back and the DC-10's mini-kitchen. Sally Jo was there, with Jack and Allison, preparing the rolling "booze-mobile," as she called the drink cart.

She grabbed the ship's manifest from its slot and flipped through the pages.

"I wanted to find out who's the guy in 2-A. He's just my type."

"That's a rarity. I thought you didn't date customers," Sally Jo said.

Karen grinned. "I don't. But for every rule there's an exception. This guy's gorgeous, and if he's buying two seats across the Atlantic, he's not exactly impoverished."

"Gold digger."

"Ah, here it is. Martin Parks." She looked up at Sally Jo. "Now to think of some clever conversation for later, during the movie—"

"When the lights get low, why not invite him up to see your etchings?"

"Coming through, ladies . . ." Jack's petulant voice startled Karen.

"Sorry," she said. He was so damned serious about the job, Karen couldn't believe it, as if he actually swallowed all the propaganda about being part of the in-flight team. *We're glorified waitresses,* she thought. *We're paid to hand out tiny steaks and moist towelettes. That, and keep smiles plastered on our faces when the plane starts bobbing like a cork.*

(*See? We're not scared, ladies and gentlemen. No, sir. And we fly* all *the time.*)

"C'mon," Sally Jo said to her. "The sooner we have everyone served, the sooner you can strike up a friendship."

The flight proceeded smoothly, outside of a few bumps when they hit their northernmost point. She was too busy to say much to Martin Parks, but she was glad to see that he had not put on his headphones for the movie.

After dinner the cabin lights were lowered, and everyone seemed to be watching the movie or dozing. Karen pulled the curtain that separated first class from the car section and looked down at her well-tailored passenger.

"Get you something?"

He looked up at her casually, almost too casually. Perhaps he wasn't interested. There was no wedding ring, but maybe he had someone waiting for him. Or, God forbid, maybe he was gay. All the good-looking ones were.

"No," he answered. "Not at all. You must be tired," he said slowly. "Standing up . . . on such a long flight. Why not have a seat?"

He seemed courtly, almost old-fashioned. He couldn't have been more than thirty-eight or so. Yet he seemed refined in a way that most of today's hotshot, mile-a-minute executives couldn't even dream of.

"It's against company regulations. But, heck, for a minute or two it won't matter." She slid down into the seat next to him.

He smiled at her (and for a moment it seemed as though he knew what she was going to say).

"Do you travel often?" she said, immediately embarrassed by her dumb pleasantry.

He laughed, making it worse. "Oh, my, yes. I've traveled an awful lot." He looked right at her. "Too much, I think"—and here he laughed out loud—"I think I'm already to settle down. Find a nice quiet town someplace."

Now Karen started to question her pursuit of this man. Things weren't proceeding as they should. No, he should appear flattered, or maybe a bit flustered. They both should be acting very coy.

But Martin Parks seemed to have expected her advance, and now it was—what?—merely amusing him. He seemed to be toying with her.

"I better check the other—"

His left hand, which she had previously admired, reached out and closed around hers gently. "They're all asleep or at the movies. Why not keep me company a bit longer? I find you attractive." He smiled.

She nodded, thinking, *This is ridiculous. What am I worried about? I'm with a planeload of people.* "I . . . I am enjoying being with you."

"Sure you are. Perhaps—and correct me if I'm wrong—you assumed I was wealthy?"

"No . . ."

He squeezed her hand. She tried to wriggle away, but he ever so lightly held her in place.

"Come, tell me the truth. I'll *know* when you are telling the truth."

She looked around, worried about passengers seeing them.

"Mr. Parks, please let go of my hand." She allowed her voice to rise, and an elderly couple across the aisle looked over. Strange as it seemed, she was on the verge of getting angry at Parks. He might be wealthy, but he was obviously strange, almost sinister.

"Yes," he went on, "you were thinking about dinner maybe, after the flight, and perhaps even something more."

"Please," she said. "I'm sorry. Just—"

He came close to her, his face—so calm and intelligent before—now touched with an odd glee, enjoying playing with her. "So what about it, my sweet Karen, shall we get together after the plane lands?"

She looked back to the old couple, now talking with each other, oblivious to her problem.

(I should stand up, just pull away from him. That's what I should—)

"Well. . . ?" he asked, squeezing harder, no longer gentle.

"Please, Mr. Parks, I—"

His face went stony and the blood seemed to drain out of it, and Karen, without realizing it, moaned.

The plane dropped.

One minute it was flying smoothly, halfway through its downward arc over the North Atlantic, and then it became the world's worst roller coaster, plummeting through the air. It lasted maybe a second or two, but it was enough to send meals flying into the air, bits of overdone filet mignon slapping people in the face. Hot coffee and cold drinks flew above the seats, scalding passengers who were startled awake, adding to the screams.

The screaming was louder than the incessant whine of the engines, a crazy mixture of wails and yells and high-pitched shrieks.

Nobody heard the *ping* of the seat-belt light coming on.

"Well . . . ?" Parks said, still holding on to her, his smile an ugly thing now.

She was crying, her mascara going all smeary. "My . . . my . . . p-assengers. I have to—"

She didn't wonder why she could hear his voice over all the screams.

Then, just as the pilot came on the PA to calm everyone, saying, "It's okay, folks, we just ran into a little—" the plane started weaving, left and right, wildly. The wings dipped, like a dinghy in the middle of an ocean gale. Those people with their seat belts unfastened, tumbled over the people next to them, into the gap of the center aisle, trapped in weird, unhealthy-looking angles. Karen fell onto Parks, real close to him—

(Just like she wanted to be.)

He stared at her, sneering, and then—as if it were just a passing thought—it changed, his smile returning.

The plane leveled out.

"No?" he said. (Still audible above the terrible howls that filled the cabin.) "You're not my type, anyway." He laughed, a small titter at first, then growing into a full-out belly laugh.

He let go of her hand.

And she pulled back, standing, crying.

He looked at her, all business now.

"I would like another martini, though." He glanced over his shoulder and waved his hand backward. "When things settle down back there."

She staggered away, through the curtain, back into the mayhem of tourist class where the hurt and burned passengers were still screaming. She went back there slowly, shakily, away from Martin Parks.

"Herbal tea is about all I can manage at night. I do have a nice selection, though. Rose hips, Apple, and Sleepy Time—don't you just love the picture on the box?"

Dan politely picked up the box of tea and spent a moment glancing at a bear dressed in a striped nightie and nightcap. Reverend Winston's living room was tiny, just about enough space for two people to sit, surrounded by walls and a floor filled with stacks of books. This, the rectory of his parish,

St. Mark's, was on the second floor of a small two-family house. Dan could hear a TV blaring from the room below them.

"Very cute," Dan said, smiling, putting the box down on the small coffee table (on top of a worn copy of Hazlitt's *History of Medieval Europe*).

"Yes," the reverend said. His eyes looked bulbous, almost froglike, under just about the thickest pair of lenses Dan had ever seen. The good vicar was an old man, with thin white hair sparsely covering his head and a wrinkled face that seemed to carry a line for each year of the man's life. When he got up, he shuffled from place to place, and if his parish was made up of people in old-age homes, it wouldn't be long before the reverend would be joining them there.

Dan took the teacup, now filled with its poultice of caffeine-free spices floating on the top. He poked a finger in the cup and submerged it.

"Let it steep for a moment."

Dan nodded. "You seem to be a fan of history."

Reverend Winston looked around at the books that encircled him. "Decidedly. History offers a . . . solace. Something like religion. It says that mistakes can happen but humanity somehow corrects itself. And no matter what darkness mankind itself may enter, somehow there always seems to be a way out. A salvation, if you will." He looked at Dan. "Somehow there's always hope. And that is the business I'm in."

"Speaking of hope, I was hoping that you might help me with my story. The local library was really devoid—"

The minister's hands fluttered in front of his face. "Oh, that's not a library. It's just a few rooms with books. You'll have to go to White Plains. . . . They have a real library."

"But I was told that you have researched the story of Gouldens Falls."

Winston put down his teacup. "Yes, I've done some

reading about it. Some. I'm not sure how relevant to your story it might be."

In such close quarters, Dan quickly sensed the reverend's discomfort.

He leaned forward. "My story, Reverend, is 'The Town That Disappeared.' I've yet to find a good reason for their putting a dam here. It was done so quickly. It should have taken—"

"Years. Yes, and it was approved"—Winston smiled at Dan—"almost overnight. I wondered about that too."

"And it was built so quickly."

"Some people couldn't even get their homes moved," Winston said wistfully. "Not enough time, they were told. Can you imagine that?"

"No."

"Others just took the money and ran. Some to Ellerton." He paused. "Others went much farther away."

"My parents came from the town."

"And what did they tell you?" Winston's eyes blinked.

"Nothing, really. But they seemed to think it was a good thing the town was drowned."

Winston shook his head and took another sip of his tea. He licked his lips. "They weren't alone, Dan. Not at all. There was a kind of . . . superstition about the town, a feeling—"

"A fear."

"Yeah, I guess you could say that. People had a bad feeling about the town."

"Why?"

Winston pulled himself to a standing position, struggled to get out of the all-too-easy chair bolted to his behind. Dan stuck out a hand to help pull him up, but Winston ignored it.

"Got to stay independent," he said, smiling. "For as long as possible, anyway."

Dan watched the vicar walk over to a large bookcase.

His gnarled fingers traveled along the spines of oversize books and albums before stopping at a brown leather volume, at least a couple of inches thick. Winston pulled it down and cradled the heavy bulk under his arm. He lowered himself back into his chair—going down was obviously as tricky as getting up—and flipped open the album.

Pay dirt, he thought. If he was lucky, this old book could save the article. Now, if he could just get his camera down there.

"I'll let you take this, of course, if you'll promise to take good care of it. It's taken me, why, I guess, almost ten years to collect everything here." He was flipping through the plastic-covered pages. "But I'd like to show you something . . . before you leave. Then I do have to get to bed." He flipped some more. "Something that I think is important." He stopped. "Here." He turned the book around, rested it on his knees. Dan came off his chair and crouched next to the man. Winston's hand shook as he pointed at a yellowed, almost brownish newspaper article.

"Jackie Weeks, that's his picture."

Dan looked. The boy wore a toothy grin and close-cropped hair. Freckles covered his face. He wore a striped shirt.

"He was never found?"

"Never. The story soon got out that he went over the fence and slipped into the town the day the water came. It took, you know, nearly three weeks for the entire reservoir to fill. But by the end of the first day, a foot of water covered the entire town, like some great flood brought by torrential rains. They looked for him then. Before the water got too deep. Even while speeches were going on. Policemen and firemen in hip boots sloshing up and down Scott Street, past the post office, the movie theater. But Jackie Weeks was gone."

"Strange story."

The reverend paused. And Dan thought that his pasty skin seemed to look even whiter. The bony fingers shook.

"But I'm afraid that's not the story."

"What do you mean?"

The reverend pointed again at the picture of Jackie Weeks. "This boy went in, all right, and . . . something happened to him. But he wasn't alone. Two boys explored Kenicut that day—two. Poor Jackie, rest his soul, ended up staying there forever."

The way Winston said *forever* made Dan's skin feel cold, like a stray breeze blowing through the window and chilling his sweaty skin.

The reverend spoke quietly. "The other boy got out."

Winston flipped the pages of the album.

It was a photo. A placard read, GOULDENS FALLS ELEMENTARY SCHOOL—EIGHTH GRADE, 1939. A teacher stood at attention beside thirty or more of her charges, all looking uncomfortable, the girls in spanking clean dresses and the boys in their Sunday white shirts.

One boy's face was circled.

A short fellow with bright eyes that looked right at the camera.

"Billy Leeper," Winston said, almost gently. "He was there that day. With Jackie. He saw what happened."

Winston touched the boy's picture, as if reaching across the decades. "He was there and he got out." Winston looked at Dan. "If anyone knows what happened to Jackie Weeks and the town of Gouldens Falls, it's Billy Leeper."

EIGHT

"Not a minute too soon," Dan said, sliding up next to Susan.

"Oh. I thought you were going to miss the show."

He looked around at this circus, this carnival of thrill seekers gathered around the lake. "The old reverend was a tad more interesting than you might imagine."

"Step back, folks . . . behind that barrier."

Some well-padded fellow, wearing an Ellerton Volunteer Firemen windbreaker and clutching a heavy-duty walkie-talkie, was gesturing at them to step back.

"Back a bit more," he barked, eyeballing Dan.

"We can't stay all the way back there," he said quietly, leaning close to Susan. "Let's see if we can get closer."

The southeast corner of the dam was flooded with spotlights, giant klieg lights that gave every slack-jawed busybody standing within their glare that illusion that they were part of the action.

Everyone loves a crisis, Dan thought.

"I don't think we can—" Susan started to say.

But he grabbed Susan's arm and guided her past the

barrier. "Just walk like you know what we are doing and direct me toward the police chief."

Susan shook her head. "You're crazy, Dan. But he's over there. His name's Paddy Rogers. A tough Irishman. Over—"

"I see him."

The chief was standing near the edge of the water. There was a beached boat beside him, filled—almost dangerously, it seemed—with electronic equipment.

Damn, this could be perfect. If he could just go with them now.

"Introduce me," he said. "Build me up."

He dug into his pocket for his business card and found one, which turned out to be a bit too dog-eared to use to make an impression. He steered Susan right next to the burly chief.

Rogers turned around and stared at both of them.

"Susan? What are you doing here? I told my boys to—"

Dan could sense the bum's rush coming, and leaped into the fray. "Chief Rogers, I'm Dan Elliot." He grabbed Rogers's hand and gave it an unwanted shake.

"He's a writer for—"

"Lots of places. The *L.A. Examiner, Time, Playboy* . . . you name it."

"Well, I'm sorry, Mr. Elliot, you'll have to move back over three with everyone else," he said, gesturing. "Behind—"

One of the divers came up to the boat, threw his flippers in, and turned to the chief and said, "We're all set to go."

"Fine," Rogers said, turning away from Dan. "Just give—"

Dan quickly checked the diving team's equipment. This was no Sunday diver gear here, no AMF flippers and toy snorkels. The wet suits were German-made—the best available—with an extra thermal layer. Real toasty. And the regulators, like the oversize tanks, were state of the art.

But the sonar gear could put a small sub to shame. It filled about half of what was a flat-bottom New York police boat. A large chunk of the floor space was taken up by a two-way radio.

They'd be able to talk with the divers between gulps of oxygen.

He had to be there. By tomorrow the whole reservoir might be out of bounds.

"I'd like to go," Dan said, touching Rogers on his shoulder. "I'm a diver, registered and all. I could help—"

"Out of the question, sir," Rogers snapped. "Susan, would you please escort your friend back—"

One of the divers, not more than twenty years old, came up to Dan. "Where have you dived?"

"Name it," he said. "Everywhere from Cancun to a nasty frozen lake outside of Yellow Knife, Canada. I also did a piece on skin diving in the Amazon River."

The cop grinned. "Oh, yeah . . . I read that. Great stuff. Made me glad that all I had to deal with was the East River."

"I hyped it a bit for the reader, you know, about the piranha and all. But—"

"C'mon," Rogers said, taking him by the arm. "That's enough. These fellows have work to do—"

The city cop interrupted. "Chief, if you don't mind, we might be able to use him—topside, that is. It could help to have another diver there . . . in case there's a problem. It would free Jack up to check the sonar."

Dan grinned, but Rogers still held his arm.

So close, he thought.

"I don't know . . ."

The other diver, somewhat older, called for his partner from the front of the boat. "All set. Let's get moving." He started the throaty inboard engine.

The crowd's chattering faded, and the boat's engine sputtered to life in the shallow water. The radioman climbed in, and a puff of smoke was suspended over the crowd's heads.

C'mon, man, Dan thought.

Rogers looked right at Dan. "Okay." He looked at the divers. "This is your show. But no pictures, Mr. Elliot. Not tonight. Not until we know what happened here."

"I'll leave my camera right here," Dan said, smiling, unslinging it and handing it to Susan.

He again pumped the chief's unenthusiastic hand.

"Thanks." He jumped into the boat, eager for them to pull away from the shore, before the stubby police chief changed his mind.

The plane touched down rockily, rudely slapping the runway at JFK. People clapped. Others began to cry, tears of relieved happiness. Most sat in numb silence.

Karen listened to the head attendant calmly tell the passengers to please wait until the plane had taxied up to the tentaclelike exit ramp. But they ignored her, popping off their seat belts, scrambling to pull down their too bulky carry-on luggage.

Standing. Waiting.

Oh so eager to get off the plane.

Each and every one standing behind Martin Parks (who, she saw, carried only the slimmest of attachés).

The plane rolled to the ramp, taking, it seemed, so much time, crawling up the ramp. Outside, the air was filled with the sound of planes roaring into the sky like clockwork.

And still their plane rolled, creeping up to the American Airlines terminal. Then it stopped. The captain (and she wondered what kind of shape he was in) flipped off the seat-belt light.

The main exit door opened.

And Parks looked back at her.

Smiled at her.

And held it for just a moment. A horrible moment.

Then she slowly slid into a vacant seat. Her skin was cold. She brushed feathery wisps of hair away from her face, her cheek, wisps that weren't there.

Her stomach spasmed and she began coughing, then vomited. Over and over, as if trying to scrape some horrible poison out of her insides.

The passengers ignored her.

They just wanted out.

But all Karen could think about (again and again, like some terrible, nagging dread that just wouldn't go away) was . . .

Who was Martin Parks?

And, God help them, where was he going?

The New York cops made Dan feel totally welcome.

The two divers, he learned, were Tom Flaherty and Ed Raskin, veterans of four and eight years respectively. The dour sonar man was Jack Russo.

"Nice of you to invite me," he said.

"I liked your article," Tom said, smiling. "Besides, Jack, here, can get a bit fussy watching all his dials. Tends to forget about us bobbing around down below."

"I do not."

"Easy, just kidding, Jacko."

The other cop—who didn't seem as lighthearted—was beginning to put on his tank and weights. "Let's get started, Tommyrot. It's body-bag time."

"Ed's been having a bit of a time eating after work." Tom grinned. "Too many gooey bodies have put him off his . . . what's your favorite dish, Ed?"

"Linguine with clam sauce. And dry Chianti."

After cruising out into the lake for a few minutes, Russo put the boat in neutral. He then hit a button and an anchor slid noisily into the water. Tom turned on the radio. "Dan, it's as simple as pie. Just press here to talk, otherwise leave the line open. Jack, here, tends to chatter a bit much, so it'll be a pleasure to—"

"Be careful right under us," Russo said. He was scanning the sonar screen. "There's something pretty large about thirty feet down. A building, most likely. There's a good-sized drop-off about twenty feet to each side."

All this easy banter . . . graveyard chatter, Dan thought. Helps to keep the willies away, probably. "Why start here?" he asked.

"In river work you go back and forth," Tom explained. "Assuming, of course, that what you're looking for hasn't been carried out to the ocean. But a lake's different."

"We'll work in semicircles," Ed said. "In the center of that circle is—"

Dan could figure that one out. The spot where Tom Fluhr vanished.

"Right," Tom said.

He watched them finish suiting up. All in black except for the shiny tubes leading to their tanks.

Oh, the pictures he could have gotten! But being here was better than being on shore (with every beered-up geek from miles around). And if the body turned up, and if it was a simple case of drowning, he'd be home free.

They'd probably love the publicity. Love for him to take pictures of the Town that Drowned.

Sure they would.

If they find the body.

Yeah, and if it turned out that Tom Fluhr had, indeed, just drowned.

Claire always knew it was a dream.

That wasn't the scary part. There was no way she'd be tricked into thinking it was like real or something. It was just a dream.

She knew that.

A dream.

The same dream all the time.

But that didn't help her. It almost didn't matter. It was like being forced to sit through the same yucky movie, night after night, knowing when all the bad scenes were going to come.

And it always started with her swimming.

It was some kind of beach, she guessed, though she never recognized it. Or any of the dumb-looking people standing knee-deep in the water (so cold!) with their brats flopping around, screaming, "Look at me, Mom, look at me, Dad!"

She'd walk past them. Past the happy families, feeling the icy water climb up her legs, covering her tummy, daring her to take the plunge.

Which, after one long look at the blue sky and the puffy little lamb clouds, she did.

She loved it under water. Kicking seallike, harder and harder, as if it were the most important thing in the world, to just keep moving, farther and farther, until she surfaced.

And then she saw that the sky had changed into a dark, dull gray. ("Lightning weather," her mother always said. "Better come out now, honey.")

She turned. (Knowing it was a dream. Just a dream.) And everybody was gone. No moms, no dads, no brats, no beach towels, nothing.

Just little Claire going for a swim. All by herself.

So she'd leave the water. Staying on the surface now (the better to see the lightning come, she'd think, kicking and stroking while her eyes kept searching the clouds for the first nasty yellow streak).

Then she'd see them. Coming onto the beach. The people.

Who weren't people. People don't walk that way, she told herself. (In this just-a-dream.) No, people don't stumble around like wounded animals, growling, looking as if they'd like to bite someone.

She always felt that there was a place that she could stop the dream. Some magical point at which she could say, "Okay, that's enough, let's wake up now. Maybe pee. Get a slug of apple juice."

It was too late. Now. Maybe always.

Suddenly she knew she'd have to get away from them, and she turned around.

(Horrible moment. It was the one picture that could make her go all cold and sick the next day, even when she was reading in bright sunshine surrounded by hundreds of kids.)

Dozens more of them—these grayish "not-people"—were behind her, coming from the lake, right toward her. Led by—

(And, of course, she knew this was coming. *Knew* it. It always came.)

Her mother. Reaching out for her, her gray and slimy face still just recognizable. She opens her mouth.

("Don't talk," Claire wants to beg this mom-thing. "Don't—")

Something slithers out of her mouth, lizardlike, leaping from between the brown, rotted teeth, plopping down to the water.

And if she's lucky, really lucky, her real mother hears her screaming out loud, hears her cries, and comes in and shakes her harder and harder to end the dream for this night.

But the real mom doesn't come. Not tonight. Only this dream thing, which comes closer, resting an oily hand on her.

And pulls her down, into the water, down with all the other not-people. Down where lizards crawl into open mouths (and no one minds!). Down.

But she never gets there. She awakens. Crying, moaning into her pillow, her fist tight, bunching up the sheet, trying to pull away.

Awake. Screaming. But awake. In minutes she stops.

A regulator clock ticks off seconds in the hallway. A car passes. In a few moments, when her breathing slows, she hears the loud hum of the refrigerator.

Her bed is wet again. An accident. At eleven years old! But she doesn't cry.

She just wonders when she'll stop having this same dream.

Over and over and over. She gets up and wedges her chair against the door.

He stared at them. With envy, with a crazy kind of itchiness that only another diver would understand.

"Can you hear okay . . . through the headphones, I mean?" Tom asked.

"Clear as a bell. If they work that well under water, then—"

"They do," Russo said, turning to Dan. "Just don't blast their eardrums by getting too close to that microphone."

Their masks nearly covered their whole head. Their mouths were completely free to talk, and the regulator—which automatically kept a supply of fresh air pumping in—was just below the chin.

It was great stuff—the ultimate diving technology.

He had used a radio once. Just once. In Lake George. In the middle of the winter.

To use it, the diver had to talk like Cloris Leachman in Mel Brooks's movie *High Anxiety.* She managed to speak through the whole movie with clenched teeth (telling a feverish Harvey Korman, "I'll let you wear my underwear.") Took practice, that's all. It was a freakin' night dive too. Night, ice, and a goddamn body hunt.

Only that time the body was about six years old.

Jesus. He remembered downing a few shots of Jack Daniel's before going out. Had to keep the old blood circulating. Wet suit or no, he knew the icy water would soon be keeping him perky enough.

And he remembered the look of the parents. Lost. Sick. Yuppies up for a week of skiing. It was their only kid, a little boy.

"Boys do like to explore," the local sheriff had told them. (All heart, the fat bastard.)

Only this kid had wandered down to the December lake ice (funny, it sure looked solid) and even got pretty far out, slipping and sliding, enjoying the fun, the ice, even the too warm glow of the sun on his face.

Bunches of people saw him vanish. A few even tried to get out there to pick him up. But with the cracking ice, it was clearly too late before things were properly organized.

They wanted to pay him to dive for the body. (Schneiderman, who had a dive shop down near Saratoga, would have taken the money. A job's a job.) But Dan said sure, actually sneered at the sheriff who had mentioned cash.

So he had a few toots, and with everyone on shore watching—and not one of them envying him—he dived in. The radio had been Dan's idea. Part of a test, but also, ice could be funny. Guidelines get snagged. Divers trapped. He didn't want to take any chances.

Over the side—resisting the temptation to make the normal *Sea Hunt* banter (the parents were standing right there beside the radio, for chrissake). Over the side, right through the hole that gobbled the little boy.

I'm coming.

Just a tad late, son.

The lights made the icy roof above glisten with a dull bluish glow. And it's there that the body would be, most likely pressed flush against the ice, waiting for spring.

He saw it almost immediately. And he cried.

So small, my God, so damn small, all snug in its sleeveless parka and L. L. Bean mini-boots.

"I . . . I've got him," he had said.

Then, knowing they were listening, "I've got your boy."

He reached up, thankful that this wasn't to be any long night of searching, and thankful that he wore gloves.

He grabbed him gently—the body floated downward so easily—and cradled him lifesaver-style under his arm as he followed his guide rope back to the hole.

"I'm heading back," he said.

He came out of the hole first, grabbing the support plank that crisscrossed the surrounding ice like enormous wooden snowshoes, distributing his weight. Then he pulled out the boy, lifting him, heavy now in the air.

He carried him back to his parents.

A week later he left the Lake George area.

He knew he'd never dive there again.

"We're all set, Dan. . . . You okay?"

He smiled. What did that little mental trip take? he thought. A second? Two . . . three? More than enough time to bring it all on home.

"All set," he said into the condenser mike.

"Move north once you're down," Russo said. "Away from the damn building, or whatever it is."

"Right, Chief," Ed said. "Let's get going."

The divers flipped backward, like funny targets at a carnival being knocked down.

And for now Dan was glad he was just sitting on the boat.

NINE

"Jeez, it's cold," Tom said, letting his body just float for a minute, getting his bearing.

"A mountain-fed lake, Tommyrot," his partner said, the voice amazingly clear in Tom's ear.

"It's a long way from Battery Park."

"Head due north about ten yards." Dan's voice sounded more distant. But it was certainly better having him directing them than Russo, who tended to bark in their ears.

Ed was already kicking away, and Tom followed, his light trailing downward.

At first all he could see was a murky blackness. It seemed to gobble up all the glow of the waterproof tungsten lamp. Then, peering through the snow of tiny bits of suspended algae, he made out something solid.

It was dark and flat.

"A roof," he said aloud.

Just about the strangest thing he'd ever seen on a dive.

But Ed was already past it.

"Jack says you can head down now, guys," Dan told them.

"Right."

Down. Street level coming up. It looked like Noah's flood, take two. Only this time nobody gets out alive.

He kicked back, guiding his body right over the edge and then straight down. His light picked up the front of the building.

It was a movie theater. Unfuckin' real. He made out the letters. The Glenwood.

There were even some letters on the marquee. An *F,* a *D,* and a few vowels hanging off cockeyed. Did someone forget to take them down?

(And he imagined an audience inside, some waterlogged collection of stiffs munching on buckets of buttered algae watching—what? *20,000 Leagues Under the Sea? Jaws?* And were the seats left behind in the theater, the red velvety cushions worn almost white by years of squirming fannies, now all bloated with water?)

He nearly crashed into the street.

"Watch it!" Ed yelled at him. "What the hell is wrong with you?"

He kicked around, curling, prawnlike, and faced Ed.

"Sorry. I was checking out what was playing. I've got a heavy date later—"

"Cut the chatter—" It was Russo, obviously taking the microphone away from Dan. "You're on Main Street. Try going south, down the block . . . see if the body could have gotten . . . caught up on something. Then I'll guide you down one of the open side streets."

"Jack, you see something on the sonar screen?" Ed asked.

"Nothing free and moving . . . just the outline of the buildings."

Ed leveled out, splaying his light in front of him, waving it back and forth.

Tom followed his example. But the last thing he was

looking for was a body. No, it was too strange down here to look for anything as mundane as a body.

The Gill-Man maybe. But not just a corpse.

Most of the shops were still there. Many of the large glass windows were intact, while fish swam in and out of the broken ones . . . little schools of pumpkin seeds checking out Donnelly's Hardware, zipping into the Rexall Pharmacy for an egg cream.

"Too weird," he said. "Too freakin' weird."

He wasn't looking where he was going. He hit something, crashing headfirst, and he brought his hand quickly up to check that his faceplate was okay.

"You okay, Flaherty?" Russo called down.

"Sure." His gloved fingers checked the seal of his mask, while he strained to look down into the bottom, inside the mask, checking for the telltale sign of leakage. "Just hit a street sign."

"Asshole," Ed commented.

"We're live, guys," Dan reminded them.

Tom looked up to the sign. Main Street. And he thought of the guy who must have put the sign up. Little did he know that what he was putting up would become some kind of underwater signpost.

He hoped the body showed up soon.

Real soon.

He passed a foundation, an open basement filled with years of debris, dead leaves, bits of wood, decades of flotsam and jetsam from hurricanes and garbage chucked out of cars.

Whoever owned this particular building obviously took it with them. It looked just like some giant extraction. Yeah, the buildings were all teeth—squat molars and pointy canines, and this one had been yanked away.

He was glad when Ed swam over to check out the garbage at the bottom. *Better him than me. . . .*

"Nothing here. Just a lot of—"

Ed paused. Tom waited a minute for him to finish his sentence. And when it didn't happen, he knew he'd have to swim over and take a look too—

(And maybe even get down and dig through all the decaying shit.)

Ed was there, his hand gingerly picking through the layers.

"What is it?" Tom asked, sounding almost annoyed.

"Dunno. Saw something. Like . . . yeah, there it is."

He reached over and pulled something out of the muck.

For one horrible moment Tom didn't know what it was. It could have been anything. Anything.

But then the water-bloated shape came into view. It was pretty well chewed through to the bone, but amazingly enough, the head was pretty intact. Intact, that is, except for the eyes.

"A delicacy for some fish, no doubt."

"Some mother rat, eh?" Ed said, suspending the carcass in the water, looking like a dumb-ass big-game fisherman.

"Got anything, fellows?" Dan's voice crackled in his ear, picking up a bit of static now.

"No. Just an old rat."

Sure. Just an old—

"I've got a block for you to head down." It was Russo again.

"We're all ears, Jack."

"About fifty feet ahead of you, on the left, there's a small street . . . Scott Street, if you bump into another sign. It will bring you close to the shore, and you can work your way out from there scanning the tops of the houses, backyards—"

"Great, and maybe, if we're really lucky, we'll get to go into some of the buildings. Won't that be fun."

"I see it," Ed said.

Tom lost track of his partner and quickly kicked ahead,

swimming hard, his light just barely picking up Ed, already kicking his way down the small side street.

"Wait up, Cisco," Tom said.

And sure enough, there was a sign, cantilevered at a sick-looking forty-five-degree angle.

Scott Street.

Nice kind of block, Tom thought. Right out of *Our Town.* Just the perfect, small-town kind of block. One he wouldn't mind moving to, if it wasn't under water. He turned the corner, kicking past Smiler's newsstand and down the street.

"Who's that?" Wiley asked Paddy Rogers.

The police chief shrugged. "Some writer. Barged in here with Susan Sloan and talked his way on. The divers said they could use another hand."

Wiley could see him crouched by the radio. The boat looked stranded in the dark lake, surrounded by the hills and water. It might be the middle of summer, but Wiley was feeling chilly.

"No luck yet?"

"Nothing. They're starting to come closer to shore now, near the spot where Tommy Fluhr went down."

Wiley put an arm on the chief's shoulder. And while the old bastard didn't recoil, Wiley felt him tense under his blue jacket. Small-town cop, he thought. Just a local redneck who doesn't realize that things are different now. There are no communities anymore—not in the 'burbs. People sleep and fuck there, that's all. And send their kids to yuppie camps in Vermont. And if all the paid officials do their bit to keep things nice and quiet and friendly, then everything will be fine.

"You know, Paddy, they're setting up for the celebration tomorrow. Putting together a platform for speakers, banners, you name it."

He looked right at Rogers, who kept his eyes on the boat. "I hope this is all taken care of real soon."

"Soon as possible, Mr. Mayor," Rogers said. He cleared his throat and then hawked a great gob to his left.

The old fart.

He turned away from Wiley. "Just as soon as we come up with the body."

Claire got up. Not that she wanted to. She would have liked to stay in bed . . . let the dream fade and maybe fall back to sleep, listening, listening for the sound of her mother's car. But she had to pee, and it was nagging at her, forcing her to get out of the bed. And her mouth felt dry, like she couldn't get her tongue wet no matter how much she tried to swirl around the inside of her mouth.

So she got up, crawled out of her bed, pushing aside her purple poppet that didn't seem to have the friendly, smiley expression it wore in the daytime.

It looked scared, worried.

She walked.

Fighting back the fear. Kid stuff, she thought. *Baby* stuff. Nightmares and being scared of the dark. It was all *so* stupid.

The more she tried to tell herself that, though, the more difficult it became to pad into the bathroom, past dark, empty rooms, down a bleak hallway—the light switch at the other end.

"Hello," she said, passing first the living room, then her mother's bedroom. Monsters have to be polite . . . it's a rule. Before they jump out and eat you, they've got to say hi back.

Then they rip you to tiny pieces.

But she kept moving, feeling better when the too bright light of the bathroom was finally on. And, of course, there was someone else there, looking right back at her.

In the mirror. A young girl. Just like her. Same eyes, same hair, even the same nightgown.

Something was different, though, as she studied her image in the water-spotted glass of the mirror.

For a minute she didn't know what it was.

Then it was clear.

The girl in the mirror looked alone, lost, and so, so scared.

She needed help, that girl did.

Someone who believed in dreams.

Claire touched the glass, hand to hand, wishing that it was already next week and that she was already away at her grandmother's.

Away from this place—and her nightmares.

Dan looked out at Susan. She was standing in a small group by the edge of the water, near the police chief and some other people who all stood with their arms folded, studying the small boat.

Damn peculiar. Like some kind of strange wake, only everyone has to wait for the body to show up. And just as soon as the corpus delicti appears, everyone can go home, crawl into bed, and go to sleep with the damp chill of the lake in their bones.

Susan looked cold, standing stock-still, arms folded, watching the boat just bob around.

They had a radio receiver on the shore so they would get the same blow-by-blow of the dive. But so far it had been pretty much like watching radio. Not a lot to be seen or heard.

And he wondered whether he should have told her. About his meeting with Reverend Winston. About Billy Leeper.

(Didn't want to scare her off? Now did he? She was being pretty tolerant of him as it was. Damn tolerant. If he told her what he really suspected, really thought—)

No, there'd be time for that later.

He gave her a wave, a dopey gesture spurred by his guilt, no doubt. She waved back.

Unaware that there might be more going on here than a drowning and a dam built for no good reason.

The radio crackled, and Tom's voice came out of the small speaker: "Where to now. Dan? I'm afraid we haven't a clue where we are."

He picked up the microphone.

It looked like a backyard.

Sure, that's what it was. Somebody's backyard. There were even the remains of a tree stump. Maybe it had been an old maple or something, chopped down for firewood before the water came.

Only Tom could see that the stump looked all strange, puffy, like some kind of a great underwater fungus, bloated, about to release millions of spores.

He looked left. The back door of the house was still there, complete with a battered screen. Might have been banged shut a thousand times in the summer. Now it was closed up tight. No robbers coming down this way.

"Dan . . ." Tom said into his microphone. "Can you get Jack to tell us which way to go? We can barely see ten feet down here."

Tom swung his light around to catch his partner, suspended in the gloom. And for a moment Tom wished he could swim back to the door, yeah, open it and go inside the house.

It was like the feeling he got when he walked across a bridge and looked down into the water, wondering . . .

What would it be like if he jumped in?

Just for a minute.

And feeling that strange tingling sensation, as though your body could act on its own, leap over the side as if to say—

(You thought of it, baby, so here it is.)

What's a house like after fifty years under water? Did they leave anything behind? A fake Persian rug in the living room? A red-and-blue ball in the baby's room?

"Jack says to keep moving south," Dan announced. "You should come to another block soon that will—wait a minute."

Tom swam hard to catch up with his partner. He heard Dan talking to Jack, the microphone button left on, but it wasn't carrying clearly enough.

"Wait a minute," Dan said, now speaking into the microphone. "Jack thinks that he may have . . ."

Another pause, and more talking back and forth.

May have what, dammit? He was abreast of Ed now. Ed tapped his arm, a sudden gesture that startled Tom.

"Watch the fence," Ed said, pointing to the remains of a stockade fence, weaving around crazily, seemingly on the verge of collapse. "What's the story, Dan?" he said, letting his voice rise.

"Jack thinks he's picked up something, guys, near where you are."

Instinctively Tom made his light do a slow 360-degree turn around him, but there was nothing there but the ever-present suspended particles of algae and sand.

"Don't see anything," Tom said. "How about you, Ed?"

"Nothing."

"It's just ahead," Jack said now, taking the microphone again. "Not more than twenty, thirty feet—"

"Is it large enough, I mean—" Ed started to ask.

"It could be a body," Russo said. "Are you sure you don't see it?"

"I don't see any—" Tom started to say, but then he noticed that Ed wasn't beside him . . . like he just suddenly vanished into the gloom.

"Hey, Ed, where the hell are you?"

"Over here!"

Tom barely saw his partner's light dimly wave back and forth. "I still don't see anything."

Shit. This was too creepy. Too creepy. Whatever it was, he hoped that Ed—good old rock-solid, brass-balls Ed—would find it. And soon too.

"You've got to see it!" Russo was yelling excitedly, forgetting as usual about the eardrums. "You've got to see . . . them."

"Them?" Tom said. "Now, what the hell do you mean, 'them,' Russo?"

"He's got a couple of blips." It was Dan's voice. "He's trying to get an exact fix. But there's two, maybe three things moving around down there."

"Great."

And Tom decided then and there that he was going to swim over to his partner and stay right by him. Hold on to the bastard, even. Maybe he had enough balls for both of them.

Maybe.

He followed Ed's light, moving back and forth, searching for the source of the blips.

"Hey, friend, here I—"

He swam into it.

Big and dark, it thudded into him, and he yelled. Quickly—oh, real quickly—he kicked back like a fish trying to pull away from a hook. And he brought his light up to see what he had just swum into.

It was a leg.

Most of one anyway. All torn and jagged at the thigh (with a good-sized chunk of whitish bone sticking out of the top). The pant leg and shoe were still on, though, ready for a nice underwater stroll.

"Jesus," he said, "I think—" He back pedaled some more. "I think I found the boy. Part of him, anyway."

He turned to search for Ed.

And then the matching head was right there at his shoulder, looking right at him.

He screamed.

On board the boat, Russo quickly hit the squelch button, preventing the sound from getting back to the shore party.

Ed swam over to him.

It was just a head, suspended in the water, eyes open, the mouth puckered as if it were about to speak.

Say, have you seen my leg? I know it's around here somewhere. . . .

"You okay?" Ed asked, his gloved hand tapping on his faceplate.

"Sure. Just wish it had been you that found it, instead of me."

Ed was removing a large plastic bag from a small pouch strapped to his side.

"I'll put it in, if it's okay with you."

"Be my guest," Tom said.

He watched almost with amazement as Ed matter-of-factly took the head and guided it into the bag. Then he grabbed the leg, seemingly strolling in the other direction, and put that in.

"Let's call it a night," Ed said, sealing the bag with an industrial-strength twist tie.

"No argument here," Tom said, and he started kicking his way upward, checking his depth gauge, taking the necessary time to decompress.

And not a second more.

When he finally reached the surface, he thought he might throw up. He pulled off his face mask and gulped the cool night air.

Russo brought the boat alongside, and then Ed popped up, the heavy brown plastic bag in his hand.

Tom wasted no time scrambling onto the boat. He saw

Russo pull the bag on board, filled with the two body parts and water. Ed clambered in after it.

"I just have to get rid of some of the water," Russo announced to everyone as he undid the tie and started tipping the bag.

They all watched Russo tilt the water out, taking care to keep the two body parts in the bag.

"Just a bit more. The morgue doesn't want a bagful of—"

The boat rocked.

A wave—a damn wave!—from somewhere hit the small boat. Ed was standing and nearly tumbled forward onto the bag. Dan grabbed the side of the boat to get his balance.

Tom slid against the side of the boat.

But Russo let the bag slip out of his hand. The open end was tilted down, facing the trough of the queer, tilted wave that had just rocked the boat.

The head rolled out. Three, four turns, around and around until it came to stop right at Tom's feet, looking up now at the night sky. That's when he saw it.

This wasn't a kid. It was a man, some grizzled old man with a beat-up face and thin, grayish hair.

"Who the hell is this?" Tom said. "It's not that boy, dammit. Who the fuckin' hell is this?"

The boat was still. Dan stood up and walked over to Tom. He looked down.

"Fred Massetrino," Dan said flatly. His nostrils flared, picking up a strange smell. "He's site supervisor at the dam."

"And the boy?" Ed asked.

Dan looked at him, then at Tom.

"Still down there, I guess. Still down there . . ."

They sat there for a full minute before Ed went over and replaced what was left of Fred Massetrino into the bag.

Russo started the engine and slowly took the boat toward shore.

PART TWO

TEN

They were walking slowly, Susan noticed. Though dead tired and lusting for the rumpled sheets of her queen-size bed (alone), she wanted Dan to stay . . . at least for a few more minutes.

A few minutes to talk some more, about the boat, the dam, and Fred's body. Hoping all the time that talking about it would make it seem somehow less strange, less bizarre.

I spoke to him that morning, she kept telling herself, remembering their tour with Fred Massetrino. *That very day.* And how many hours later would he find his way to the bottom of the reservoir, down to the remnants of Gouldens Falls?

It was a picture she just couldn't chase from her mind.

And she would like to reach out, take Dan's hand, and just hold it—like a schoolgirl. Something warm and living to keep Fred's grizzled face out of her mind.

But he might misinterpret it, walking her to her door, holding her hand. . . . She was too tired for a long explanation of why, tonight, she didn't want anyone coming inside.

(And always the same excuses to put men off: "Claire might wake up . . . I've got an early day tomorrow"—anything but an honest "No, buster, I don't want to screw you.")

Not that she found Dan unattractive. Just the opposite, actually. He was a far cry from the usual single (and married) businessmen who hit on her. He was exciting, unpredictable, and maybe even a bit dangerous.

Before anything would happen, though, she would have to know him better. She'd been burned too many damned times, humiliated by good-looking hunks with all the sensitivity of rattlesnakes.

Still, she wouldn't discourage him.

"So," she said, turning around on her small front porch, "what are you doing tomorrow?"

"Kindly Reverend Winston, dear fellow, gave me Billy Leeper's address, if you can believe it. He lives out on Montauk, sort of retired, and I thought I'd go talk with him."

She laughed. "Montauk? Not exactly around the corner—what is it, three, four hours away? Why don't you call?"

Dan smiled (and Susan was glad to see that he didn't take offense at her rude chuckling). "Turns out he has no phone. He's been invited to the celebrations countless times, but he's ignored all their letters."

"Maybe he's dead."

Dan leaned against the door. "Winston didn't think so. He heard from him a few years ago, when he was first researching Gouldens Falls. He said Leeper described himself as pretty much of a hermit since his wife died."

"So you're going to drive there, just hoping he'll talk to you?"

"Hell, Billy Leeper was in the town on its last day. Actually in the town. And he was with that other boy, Jackie . . ."

"Weeks."

"Right. The boy who didn't get out. I'd like to talk with him about the town . . . and that day."

She nodded, dug around in her bag for her keys. "More power to you. It will use up a whole day, though."

"I can't dive tomorrow, anyhow. They'll still be looking for the other body—"

"And meanwhile trying to figure out what happened to Fred."

Dan came closer, and she stiffened, expecting the first step in his bid for a shot at her.

But he spoke slowly, deliberately.

(Scaring her.)

"Susan, I don't know what happened to Fred. Maybe they'll find out, maybe they won't. Until they do, I'd like you to be careful . . . maybe even stay away from the reservoir."

She stuck her key in (perhaps a bit disappointed that Dan's expected move didn't come). "Well, tomorrow I'm busy writing up festive ideas for the big weekend. Cool summer recipes and all that. So I won't go near there—not that I'm worried."

"Good girl. Hey," he said, looking down at his watch, "I've got to go. I plan on being on the road at six at the latest. That's mighty early for me."

She took a step inside her door.

"Need a free dinner tomorrow?"

"Sure. If I'm lucky, I'll be back by four—five, maybe. And there's a bonus. You'll get the true story of Billy Leeper, assuming I get to see him."

"See you then," she said, and stepped inside the front door. She slowly shut it behind her, letting it click into place, then turning the bolt.

Then she heard Claire.

Whimpering softly, almost inaudibly.

"Claire, honey!" she called, even as she hurried toward her daughter's room, knowing—

It's another one of those nightmares.

"Claire." She saw her all curled up on her bed, her light on, her blanket wrapped tightly around her.

She went to the bed, sat, and pulled her close.

"Claire . . . you've been dreaming again. It's okay, honey, I'm home now."

Her daughter heaved against her, sobbing now, arms wrapped around her tightly.

"Oh, Mommy, Mommy, I hate that dream. Why does it keep on happening?" Claire cried, sounding so young and defenseless.

Susan ran her hand through her daughter's hair. It rolled in waves, just like her father's, catching every bit of light. Not a day went by when she didn't look at Claire and have to think of her father.

"I don't know, baby, but it's all over. Try to go back to sleep now. Shut the light out and—"

Claire reached and closed a hand around her mother's. "Stay with me . . . for a few minutes."

Susan smiled (not letting herself worry, really worry, about her daughter . . . not now). "Sure, honey. I'll stay here awhile."

And she sat in the semidarkness, with just the glow of the hall light.

Please, God, she prayed. *Please.*

Make the nightmare stop.

Please.

"I'm comin', dammit. Hold your damn horses."

What the hell hour was it, anyway? John Feely wondered, his head all fuzzy and banging from the five beers he'd downed before turning in.

He and his wife took turns coming out to the motel office after midnight, and he hated it . . . padding across the cold linoleum floor, wondering whether it would be some punk with a handgun looking for crack money.

"I'm comin'. Jesus!"

The buzzer kept ringing. Louder as he came to the front desk (with its plastic card displaying all the credit cards "gladly accepted").

And it was not the typical graveyard-shift customer.

No, In fact, Feely felt almost embarrassed by cursing out this . . . this . . . gentleman.

A nice suit; a nice, real respectable-looking attaché case; and every hair in place.

Feely thought he must look like the biggest piece of shit in the universe.

"Sorry, mister"—Feely smiled—"I get a bit grouchy being waked up and all, after going to sleep. You know—"

"Perfectly. I understand. You do have a room?"

"Oh, sure . . . sure. By the weekend we'll be filled. The celebration and all."

"Yes," the man said. "I know all about that."

No, sir, Feely thought, not the usual post-midnight sort at all. They usually ran to hyped-up truckers looking to catch an hour of sleep or a break from white-line fever. Or a young couple stumbling around, no luggage and out for a quickie.

This guy looked like some kind of bank president.

"What card will you use?"

The man smiled. "Is cash acceptable?"

Feely rubbed his chin. "Sure. How long you planning on staying?"

"Just till Saturday."

Feely passed the man a registration card and an official Ellerton Motor Inn pen ("Reasonable Rates, Clean Rooms"). He watched the man fill it out.

"Fine, Mr. . . . Parks." Then he checked out the rest of the card. "There's no . . . address here or—"

Parks put two hundred dollars on the counter. "No," he said. "There isn't." He smiled right at Feely.

(And damn if Feely didn't know he'd better think twice about mentioning the registration card again.)

"Sure . . . thanks, Mr. Parks." He grabbed a key from off the back wall. "Here . . . it's number eleven, nice and quiet, around the back." He saw the man's eyes narrow. "Unless, that is, if you'd rather—"

Parks's hand closed around the key. "No, that'll be fine. Just tell the maid not to come and clean up. I prefer . . . not being disturbed."

"Sure, just—"

But Parks had already turned, pushing open the glass door, and gone out to a big black car parked in front.

And suddenly Feely wasn't all that sleepy. No, all he wanted was another beer, maybe a quick check to see if *The Honeymooners* was on. Watch Ralphie boy for a while.

He picked up the registration card.

Martin Parks was all it said.

"Damn peculiar," Feely said. "*Damn* peculiar." And he flipped the card into his desk and padded back to the refrigerator and TV.

The house couldn't have been more unapproachable.

Sure, there was a road of sorts leading up to it, but a normal car would probably break an axle on the holes and rubble.

Even Dan's Land Rover would have a tough climb.

He shifted into first gear, alternating between front and rear traction, gently climbing the steep, curving path leading to what the local gas jockey had told him was Billy Leeper's house.

What a bitch, he thought. Most of Montauk was flat—another part of the terminal moraine called Long Island, which had been formed by one hell of a bulldozer glacier a hundred thousand years or so ago. Except somehow this one spot was built up to a pointy, almost jagged hill.

As the Land Rover climbed, more and more of the Montauk beach below came into view—too early to play host to the swimming crowd but dotted with surf casters trolling the waters for striped bass and blues.

The house had to have been a real monster to build. Half of it was on stilts, thick chunks of telephone poles that held it level. The front half was surrounded by chunks of grayish rock, seemingly tumbled around at random.

No one would try to build a house here . . . not normally. Not unless they were looking for something really difficult to get to—with a good view all around.

The Rover lurched forward, then slipped back, digging into a massive hole. The rear wheels whined, spraying sand and chunks of rock into the air.

"C'mon, get moving," he said, quickly shifting traction to the front wheels, and the Rover pulled forward again.

As he got closer, Dan could see the house more clearly. Small, a dark little house with a black tile roof, painted a deep brown. The curtains were shut, and a small battered jeep—army-surplus, maybe—was parked to the side.

If cheery Captain Ahab had a summer cottage, this might have been it.

He stopped the Rover.

No sign of anyone stirring inside.

Well, Billy Leeper, if you're dead, this is where we find out.

He made sure that his Rover was in gear, and the parking brake as tight as possible. Then he opened the door and strolled, almost casually, up to Leeper's house.

Nine A.M. A respectable time for a surprise visit.

Sort of. There was no bell—nor any electricity, from the looks of things. He knocked again. Then again.

"Mr. Leeper!" he called. He strained, trying to hear if anyone was coming to the door.

"Mr. Leeper. Mr—"

The door opened. It was dark inside, gloomy, and then there was someone there, halfway between the shadowy interior and the early-morning sunlight.

"Mr. Leeper, my name is—"

"Just go away, son. I'm still asleep. I haven't been . . . well lately."

He started to shut the door.

"I've come about the town, Mr. Leeper. About Gouldens Falls . . . about the dam."

The door stopped.

A reprieve, Dan thought. For a moment, at least.

"What about the town?"

It was a harsh voice, filled with the scratchy, rumbling sound caused by age and work.

Dan didn't know what to say. Tell him he's a writer, or maybe talk about the celebration, or . . . or . . .

(I'm a gambler, he thought. *A fuckin' risk taker. So gamble—)*

"A boy has died in the reservoir, Billy . . . drowned. They can't find the body. And someone else, the engineer . . ."

The door opened a crack more.

Dan felt the man scrutinize him, checking him carefully.

"You can come in . . . but only for a few minutes."

Then Leeper opened the door and let Dan enter.

They sat at a small wooden table filled with the countless crisscrossing marks of countless meals. Leeper had pushed away an assortment of dirty plates and glasses to make room for a pair of just rinsed cups.

"The tea water will be ready in a minute."

Dan had quickly told him about his article as Leeper had pushed away the curtain covering the small kitchen window, letting some light into the room. Dan could see him clearly now. His face was rough, weather-beaten, and he had big, gnarled hands. They were strong hands. Powerful. Leeper grabbed the edge of the sink.

"What's really on your mind, Mr. Elliot? Why'd you drive all the way out here to see me?"

He looked at Leeper, trying to decide how best to win his confidence. If Leeper had secrets—and there was no way to tell if he did or not—how could he get at them? When in doubt, he finally decided, jump in feetfirst.

"I'd like to know about that day, the last day, before the town disappeared. About you . . . and Jackie Weeks."

Billy Leeper turned toward the teakettle and moved it, as if trying to hurry it along. And Dan tried to see the young boy, from fifty years ago, hidden now in this old man.

"You know, Mr. Elliot, I've got a pile of letters over there . . . some of them inviting me to the celebration. After a while I didn't even open them. You see," he said, turning back to Dan, "I've no intention of going to that town, or seeing that reservoir, or getting anywhere near that damned—"

His voice rose with each word, his eyes gleaming even in the shadows, spittle spraying from his mouth, landing on the table, hitting Dan.

"—town!" he yelled. "I came here . . . to this rock . . . to get away."

The kettle started whistling, faint, tentative, then insistent, high-pitched.

Leeper let it shriek. "So you see . . . I'm not the person you want to talk to. Not at all."

He turned away slowly, took the kettle off.

"Still want your tea?"

"Sure do. It's been a long time since breakfast for me."

Leeper grinned and poured. "Sorry for the noise level, Dan, but . . ."

He looked up at him. "I think I understand. My parents came from that town . . . they were just kids, too, a bit younger than you."

Leeper paused. "Elliot? Elliot . . . from Gouldens Falls? Oh, wait a minute. There was an Elliot family that lived on Lakeview Drive."

"That's them."

Leeper seemed to study Dan for a moment, then sat down. "So you want to know about that last day . . . what I remember of it, anyway?"

"I think I need to know about it. There's just too much I don't understand."

Leeper laughed, a loud, almost manic sound, and it startled Dan. It was the kind of laugh you'd make looking at a fool, an idiot.

"Some things you don't understand, huh? That, my friend, is putting it mildly."

Leeper took a sip of his tea. "Well, then, I'll start at the beginning, Dan Elliot, the beginning. Which should have been the end. Yes. But it wasn't."

Dan gingerly took a sip of his scalding tea. It burned his tongue. And he listened.

Leeper laughed. "Not by a long shot."

ELEVEN

"Joshua, Joshua!" Claire barked, trying to copy the not to be denied sound of an adult order. "Come away from there!"

Joshua, though, was five years old and took a gleeful joy in doing just the opposite of what he was asked. He kept walking into the woods, his small sneakers padding off the closely cropped grass onto the thick underbrush.

"Oh, brother." Claire moaned to herself. Not five minutes in charge and already she was totally losing control of the situation. The girl, Samantha, was peacefully playing on the Benny family's massive swing set, waiting for the promised time when just she and Claire could play Barbie.

Except that now Joshua—horrible creature—was already making this baby-sitting job an even bigger headache than camp.

And if there was one thing Mrs. Benny had said—at least a half dozen times—it was to keep the kids out of the woods. No matter what.

Because the woods led to the fence. And on the other side of the fence was a reservoir.

And she's so worried about the children.

("Especially little Joshua," Claire could mimic. "Little Joshua, the monster.")

Though, come to think of it, drowning would suit the little beast perfectly.

"Joshua, you stop right now, you hear me?"

"He won't stop," Samantha said, and Claire turned to look at her. She didn't seem to care what happened to her brother. "He does what he wants to do. Even Daddy—"

But Claire darted off, giving up on orders and ready to rely on her two hands.

It took her only a few seconds to catch up with him and grab his shoulders. (Not too tightly, she knew. Couldn't have him moaning and groaning to his mom about the "mean baby-sitter.")

"Hold it right there, Josh."

"Leggo," he said, pulling ahead like some goofy puppy on a leash. "I want to see the water. There was a boat—"

"And you can see it just fine from your living room. You get a real nice view."

"But I want to be close to the boat. C'mon, Claire," he said, turning to her, beginning to plead. "Just a look, okay?"

"No way, Jay. Your mom said you stay on your property, and that's what you're going to do." She was trying to make her voice sound like that crazy lady on *Mr. Rogers' Neighborhood,* the young woman always talking so nice and understanding to all the dumb puppets.

And to believe she actually thought she'd get some reading done today. "So back we go, it's almost lunchtime."

Lunch would give her a break. The two kids would be inside, and Mrs. Benny told her that they could watch some TV after lunch. Which meant they could watch as much as they wanted, until twenty minutes before old Mom was due back.

After preparing them some quickly made peanut butter and jelly sandwiches (during which Samantha told her that she's seven, and she *doesn't* like the crust cut off anymore), Claire guided them down to the family room and turned on the tube.

There, she thought. Finally she could curl up somewhere and read.

At first she plopped on the ratty downstairs sofa. But the crazy sounds of screeching feet putting on their cartoon brakes, and heads vibrating like bells after being bonked by enormous mallets, made it impossible to concentrate.

So she left them to Tom and Jerry, and crept away upstairs to the modern living room, where an enormous overstuffed couch awaited her.

Besides, she thought, *I can hear them downstairs.* And she started reading.

Max Wiley reluctantly had taken the morning off to make one of his infrequent visits to the mayor's office, a tiny, depressing cubicle in Town Hall.

If he spent more than fifteen minutes a week there, it bugged him. But that morning he was going to be a busy little public official, with three people already booked to meet him.

Damn, this wasn't what he'd bargained for. The job was supposed to be no real headache—that's how Tom Farrell, his predecessor, had described it to him. "No real headache, Max. And it can be a nice little stepping-stone."

Except this week he seemed to have stepped onto something other than a stone. Paddy Rogers had popped in to give him the bad news bright and early.

"Best to think about canceling the celebration, Max," the old fart had said.

Max stood up, the two of them already making the small office seemed cramped.

"What the hell for?" he asked.

And Rogers told him. "You've got a missing body . . . and a possible—make that a likely—homicide. One that we know of, at least. And to top it off, the dam itself is damaged. Structurally it's—"

"Bullshit. Structurally that thing will be standing here long after half the houses in this town have been torn down."

Rogers stepped closer, pressing Max (who was, dammit, a bit intimidated by the old cop). "That, Max, will be for the state engineer to decide. What you and I know about dams wouldn't fill—"

"I'm not canceling anything . . . not now."

Rogers started to talk, but Max raised his hand. "Not till the engineer's report, and if your people and the state police still haven't found out anything—"

Max could see his name now, in headlines, permanently linked to two dead people. No, he reminded himself, one dismembered person. The other—ha, ha—was still missing.

Rogers shook his head in disgust, then walked out without another word.

Next up, the chairman of the celebration was due in—and he had sounded mighty nervous on the phone, seeing his months of planning and balloons and parades go right out the window.

I'll need to calm him down, that's for sure. Calm him down and keep the ball rolling. By tomorrow all this trouble might be over. Tell him to go on and set up the platforms. Decorated, of course, with the red, white, and blue bunting, the tripod loudspeakers designed to carry the music and speeches all the way down to the plaza behind the dam. And the enormous sign, cooked up by the diligent housewives of the Junior League, proclaiming, KENICUT DAM—FIFTY YEARS with ELLERTON on one side and GOULDENS FALLS on the other.

And there was another meeting, just this morning. Someone interested in Ellerton—apparently with a good deal of cash to spend in town. He'd meet the businessman and then try to get back to running his own shop.

He looked at the guy's name—nice and Waspy. Martin Parks.

Sounded just like the kind of guy they wanted in Ellerton. Rich and Waspy.

"The dunes are 'forbidden territory,' you know," Leeper said. "Everyone worries about the precious beach, the nesting birds, everything, except your freedom to walk wherever the hell you want."

He led Dan down the twisting road, then along a makeshift path that cut through the phragmites and other tall grasses that swayed with the ocean breeze.

"I guess they're afraid of losing Montauk."

Leeper didn't laugh. "So they lose it. Nature's always changing things, anyway, blowing mountains away, washing out bridges." He looked right at Dan. "We're always pretending we're in charge. And that's a joke, a real joke. Here, head up to that hill there," he said, pointing. "I'd like to get some good climbing in."

He was strong, a squat, compact man not nearly ready to yield to old age. Dan felt the sand suck at his feet, causing them to slip. It was hard keeping up with Leeper.

But Leeper said he didn't want to talk about it in the house. Not about that day. He led Dan over a small hill, then down to a narrow depression, and over an oval bowl dug into the sand, girded by scrubby grass.

Leeper stopped walking.

"This here was made eight years ago. Hurricane Doris. Waves went right past the beach, over that hill there, and came down right where we're standing. Took the damn hill clear away, then the receding waves rebuilt the shoreline. This sinkhole stayed." Leeper looked around, smelling the air, breathing in the place. "And a lot of people lost their little beach houses." He gave a small laugh. "But they learned respect for nature, Dan. Respect for . . . power."

"So that's why your house is on a hill."

Leeper shook his head. "No. Not for that reason." His eyes were screwed into a permanent squint in the bright sunlight. "What are you scared of, Dan?"

He smiled, made uncomfortable by the strange question. And it suddenly felt like he was having this dialogue with the moon. "I don't know. My phone bill. My ex-wife—"

Leeper grabbed his arm and squeezed, hard enough to send a quick, painful jolt traveling to Dan's brain. "No, dammit, what are you scared of?"

The question was in earnest, and if he wanted anything from Billy Leeper—crazy or not—he decided he should answer.

"Bridges. It's a funny thing, but—"

"What else?" Leeper demanded.

"I don't know. Being trapped, not being able to breathe—"

"What else?"

And he remembered a day.

He was ten. Tension was in the air, wafting through his home like some kind of smoky fire. Building, building, until everyone—his mother, his two sisters—knew that something, something *had* to happen.

His father had lost his job—Dan never knew why—and had come home. He started drinking, talking loudly, walking from room to room, and the tension, the icy cold feeling in Dan's stomach, grew.

By the time Dan knew that it would be best to be out of the house, it was dark. A cold, dark November night, when the room lights seemed a poor replacement for the sunlight of a summer evening.

Dan's room was a mess. As usual it was filled with the

flotsam and jetsam of a boy's life. Rocks, soldiers, scattered coverless comic books, sneakers, dirty clothes. A real pigsty.

His father stormed into his room—on his random prowl—and then out again. (The voice now unrecognizable, loud, yelling his name. "Dan! Where the hell are you?")

He hesitated, but then he answered his father.

"Have you looked at your room, that goddamn garbage dump of a room? Just what the hell do you—"

His mom appeared, ready to intervene. (His sisters, one younger, another older, both had notice of storm warnings and had hidden away.)

"I'm so tired of you screwing up this house, so sick . . ." he said, lingering over the last two words.

And young Dan—prisoner—tried to explain. Which was a big mistake.

"Don't give me that crap, just don't feed me that line—"

And again Dan protested, then realized—too late—that he had pushed the wrong button.

His father's hand came flying out of nowhere, smacking him solidly across his face with a blow that knocked him sideways, off his feet, banging into a nearby wall and tumbling down to the ground (where his father looked even more powerful . . . more dangerous).

His mother yelled—a shallow, weak sound compared to his father's roar.

Dan saw something he never forgot.

Never.

His father wasn't there. For that split second his father, who took him to ball games, who played catch with him, who liked to take Dan to his Little League games, was gone.

Vanished.

Something else was there. Ready to hurt him.

Liking it—

And then, with the palm of his hand glowing red, his

father seemed to change. He looked at Dan. His lips moved, then, when no words came, he turned and left the house.

Leaving the smoky vapor of fear behind him.

What do I fear?

That thing.

That horrible, living rage that was in my father that day.

And it's in me.

He looked at Leeper, who nodded and started talking.

And Dan listened to his story. . . .

"Nobody found me that day. To tell the truth, nobody was looking for me. It was past midday, I could tell that from the sun. I got up, rubbed the bloody bruise on my head—I later found out I had a concussion—and started walking back to my house."

He climbed the dunes slowly now, following the natural rise and fall of the sandy hummocks.

"I didn't tell my parents what happened . . . not at first. I don't know what I said. Boy, when Mom saw my cut and got all excited, I broke down and started crying. Then I grabbed her arm and yelled—actually yelled—that Jackie Weeks was still down there. Still in the town."

Leeper reached down and picked up a crumpled, rusty Budweiser can. "Which was a lie."

"A lie? But he didn't come out with you?"

Leeper bent the can in half. "No, he didn't. You see, Jackie heard something inside the house, and he went in." Leeper laughed. "Jackie was always the brave one, a real adventurer. A good friend. He would have loved World War II." He paused. "But he didn't come out . . . so I had to go in."

"And?"

"Dan, the house was filled with people. *Filled.* All of them having some kind of party. Talking and laughing. In a few hours the water was going to come. At first I just smiled and stared at the whole thing, embarrassed, half expecting Jackie to come bumbling over."

"He wasn't there?"

"Oh, yes, he was there. I just didn't see him at first. I mean, it was dark in there. Dark, shadowy. No electricity, you know. It had been turned off. None. So I didn't see much. Then I looked down. The floor was wet, slippery, a real mess. I didn't know what it was . . . at first."

Dan could picture the scene perfectly, and he knew what it was.

"Blood?"

Leeper nodded. "Twelve years old, and I was standing in a pool of blood, all over the damn place. Then my eyes adjusted, and I looked at the table . . . the party table . . . where five or six guests were eating. And . . . and—"

His voice caught in his throat, and it lost its gravelly, rock-hard steadiness, quickly degenerating into a blubbering, whimpering sound.

"Jesus, I saw Jackie there. God, I saw him on the table, in pieces, strewn all over, while they picked at it, grabbed at the pieces . . ."

A gull screamed. And Dan felt his heart start to beat faster.

"I don't know . . ." he started to say mindlessly, searching for something to bring some normalcy to Leeper's words.

(We need some normalcy here.)

Leeper grabbed his wrist.

"Then one of them, a woman, held up a piece, and God, she grinned and offered it to me. Actually held it up and—"

He snorted and dug out a handkerchief.

His honking blow brought a momentary release from his story.

Is he crazy? Dan wondered. Lost in some kid's Gothic memory?

"One of them grabbed me, but I squirmed away—they

were all slipping on the floor. I ran as fast as I could . . . as fast as I could. Funny, Jackie was the real runner, the real bolt of lightning."

Leeper stopped, and Dan noticed that he was heading back toward his house. "And they found the house?"

"They found nothing. No one believed my story. Hysteria, I think the doctors called it. Too many Saturday matinees. By the time they started searching the house on Scott Street, there was a foot of water covering the whole town. But they found nothing. No blood. No Jackie. Just a boarded-up old brown house. They went on searching for days—and nights—all over the town. But I knew that he was gone."

Leeper led the way up the hill, climbing more briskly, as if eager to get back to his fortress.

"That's one hell of a story."

"It's not a story."

"I only meant—"

"Sure."

A few clouds were gathering in the east, dark clouds.

"And after that . . . what did you do then?"

"I went to school, lived with my family, tried to forget Gouldens Falls, Jackie, and the whole thing."

Leeper opened the door to his house and held it for Dan.

"And did you?"

Leeper smiled. "What do you think? You think I just put that little event out of my mind, went on with my normal life, and forgot all about it?" The smile faded. "You think that's possible?"

He walked over to the bookcase. His hand reached up to the top shelf and removed an old marble composition notebook. Its yellowed pages seemed loose.

"This is my first notebook on Gouldens Falls . . . and the dam. Started it in high school." He replaced it, then let his fingers trail over the remainder of the shelf, passing a dozen others overstuffed with paper. "My first notebook . . . leading to my last. A life's work, Dan. Crazy, huh?"

Leeper stood there, transfixed by a dozen notebooks, some bulging, fat with clippings.

"That's how long it took me to learn about it."

Dan stepped closer to Leeper. He was shaking.

"Learn about what?" Dan asked, in almost a whisper.

"The Club," Leeper said, turning away from the books.

"They call themselves the Club. I learned about them, about Gouldens Falls, and—"

He laughed, a hoarse, manic belly laugh that reminded Dan of some crazy shaman he'd once photographed in Kenya.

Talking to the moon, the interpreter had explained. The shaman was asking the moon for its help.

Leeper's laugh punctuated each word.

"And the—hah, hah—one that—oh, yeah—got away."

He pointed at the shelf. "They're all yours. The torch," he said with a grim chuckle, "is passed. Take them the fuck out of here. Today. Just don't tell anyone where you got them from." Leeper went to the window and looked out, at the darkening shadows on the beach.

"'Cause if you do, he'll come and get me . . . and I don't want to be got. Not now."

The old man—suddenly a scared boy—shook against the window.

"Now take them and leave."

TWELVE

James Morton liked to think of himself as a conscientious state employee. Though the life of an emergency safety inspector was none too thrilling, it offered a nice pension; regular, if small, salary increases; and, when he was lucky, the occasional oddity.

Like the Kenicut Dam.

While the phrase *they don't make 'em like that anymore* was an overused cliché, to his mind it certainly applied to this baby. In fact, he would have thought they didn't even build them this way fifty years ago.

First, it was done fast. Usually these small dams sank all the pumps and plumbing under the base of the dam, well into the ground. It was time-consuming, just like digging a caisson for a bridge, but it made the wall of the dam just that—a solid wall, really rooted to the bedrock.

But this dam was rooted to a solid slab of poured concrete, big, probably buried down fairly deep, but done too fast. And what made it worse, all the pumping stuff was inside the wall. Okay for a small dam, but this wall was holding back a good-sized lake.

How many hundreds of thousands of gallons of water? Pressing against the wall, day after day, year after year . . .

A fast piece of work.

Still, checking the wall as he walked down the metal stairs, everything looked in good shape. In fact, it looked reassuringly strong, with massive stone blocks on both sides of the spiral stairs leading down.

The lighting, though, was for the birds. Just a random bulb hanging here and there.

He began to worry as he neared the base that his tungsten lamp was fading, yellowing. He banged it, hoping to encourage a battery to a few more minutes of light. Just long enough so he could check the leak . . . if there was a leak.

"I'm getting a bit too old for all this climbing around," he said, grunting. He was comfortable talking to himself—an occupational necessity, he conceded. It didn't bother him to hear his voice echoing strangely around him, no one answering.

He kind of liked it, actually.

He let the lamp fall on the main heater pipes, snaking their way left and right. They looked in good condition. "No problem," he said, his yellowish lamp moving back and forth.

But he could smell the water.

Then he stepped into it.

"Shee-it," he said, allowing himself one of his infrequent lapses from his normally reserved speech. (Since discovering religion ten years ago, he'd become a pillar of his small Lutheran church. It was as much a part of his life as his thirty-plus years of marriage.)

The water—ice-cold—quickly soaked his right foot. He stepped back onto a higher, dry step of the staircase and looked around for a pole or something he could stick into the water to check its depth.

"Gotta be . . . something," he said, craning right and left, searching for anything he could use.

His light dimmed a bit more.

"Ah, c'mon," he pleaded. "Don't make me go all the way back up."

The fading light picked up a twisted piece of wire wrapped around a pipe. Not much, but he should be able to use it.

"Great," he said, leaning out over the railing. "Yeah, close enough now," he said, his fingers just about touching the wire.

He dug an index finger under the wire and yanked. It snapped off suddenly, and he tottered backward.

"Whoa, you almost went in the sink, Morton. There," he said, looking at his prize. "This'll do fine." He straightened the wire, crouched down—

And stuck it in the water.

The waterline went past his fingers, almost touching the sleeve on his New York State Public Works windbreaker.

"Oh, boy," he said. It was two feet at least, maybe a tad more.

A trickle yesterday, and now two feet of water.

"Not good, not good at all."

He stood up and started searching the northern wall for the source of the water.

He found it just where the site engineer's report said it would be.

Only it wasn't as described.

Massetrino reported a thin crack, barely visible, with a tiny line of water running to the ground.

That's not what this was.

The lamp blinked, and he gave it a quick bang. He could barely see the wall.

No, this was like a gash in the wall, a couple of inches wide, and who knew how deep.

And the water poured out of it like an open faucet, plopping down noisily onto the flooded floor.

"Oh, boy," he repeated. "This is going to take some heavy repair work."

He started up the staircase. "First I'll have to call Albany, tell Mr. Karl, get a time here on the double. Yes, sir," he said, climbing the stairs. His heavy boots held the water uncomfortably, and he thought, When's the last time a dam went down? And he knew the answer. Ridge Hill, Tennessee, 1954. Just a small dam designed to protect the watershed . . . to help flood control. It had been built in the twenties, and built badly. And when it went down, it went all at once.

A few people were killed . . . some kids, some people fishing. Some houses in the water's path washed away. Now you see 'em, now you don't.

But there was no town on the other side of that dam. No town, and about one third of the amount of water.

This?

This would be an entirely different story. Entirely different.

Then, only halfway to the top and the doors leading out, Morton's light died. He said his prayer—not the first of the day—as he finished his climb, guided only by the glow of an occasional naked light bulb.

The girl decided to go into the castle. Despite the fact that she knew they were waiting for her, planning to capture her the moment she passed the castle gates. Still, she was going in.

Because she had to. Had *to. The only way to save her family was to destroy the evil inside the dark, brooding castle walls.*

She started walking in, joining a group of peasants back from a long day in the fields.

Claire turned the page.

In that second of pause between pages of her fantasy novel, she heard something. Or rather, she didn't hear something. The TV was off—always a bad sign. Anything could be happening now. Once she found the brats investigating their parents' bureau drawers, dangling Mrs. Benny's frilly underwear in the air. It took her an hour to put it all back more or less the way it was. At least Mrs. Benny never said anything.

No TV always meant trouble.

And how long, she wondered, had it been off now? The book she was reading was so good, she was lost, drifting in this other world, struggling with the girl, sharing her fear, her courage.

"Samantha. Joshua . . ." she called, lazily sliding off the couch and depositing her book on the cushion, open and ready for her quick return. "What are you guys up to?" she asked, going downstairs to the now quiet family room.

"Why'd you turn the TV off?" she asked.

Claire walking into the sun-filled room.

Samantha was on the floor, surrounded by Barbie and all her slim and trim friends. (No fatties there.) There was Barbie's pink Corvette, her heart-shaped dressing table, her bicycle for two (for Ken, of course).

Yuck.

Right . . . I was supposed to play Barbie with her.

"Oh, yeah, I forgot," Claire said. "Sorry."

"I was just getting it all ready. I can't find her tennis stuff."

Claire smiled. "Her pink tennis outfit? I'll help you look, it's probably . . ." She looked around. No Joshua.

"Where's Josh?"

Samantha shook her head. "I dunno. He shut the TV off when Smurfs came on. He hates Smurfs. He says he'd like to blow the Smurfs up. Then he went outside."

"Stay here," Claire ordered. "I'll be right back." Claire walked over to the sliding door that led to the backyard.

She felt the air from outside filtering into the cooler family room. The door was open, just wide enough for a small body to pass through.

"Stay right here," she again ordered, tugging the heavy door open wider, her heart beating fast.

Damn my reading. It's just like my teacher says. I'm always lost in a never-never land.

But this was bad. Real bad.

She ran out into the yard, looking left and right, surprised by the peace and quiet. A bird chirped from a nearby tree. A gentle breeze rustled the willow tree just to her right.

But there was no sign of Joshua.

She yelled.

"Joshua!" Then, more insistently, "Joshua! Where are you? Come back here!"

Now, when there was no answer, she became really scared.

"Oh, no," she whimpered to herself. "Please, God, don't let this be."

"Joshua!" She looked straight ahead. And she knew where he had gone.

The woods, and then beyond. Down to the mesh fence and the reservoir.

("No matter what you do," Mrs. Benny had said, just about out the door, "don't let Joshua go down there. No matter what.")

She ran, feeling cold and clammy, sick to her stomach. This, she thought, was real fear. This was really how it felt. All sick and horrible.

"Joshua!" she screamed, "are you down here? Joshua!" And she began to wonder if maybe he went exploring in the other direction, toward the highway, crossing the street . . . just as some monster-sized truck with dozens of wheels came roaring down upon him.

An exposed root—a snaky, arch-shaped thing—snagged

her right foot and sent her down hard onto the leaves and twigs. Her knee was scraped, like when she used to fall skating down her driveway, but she popped up, not even looking at it. She started running again.

It was dark in here—only tiny pinpricks of light got through the leafy roof. It was a world removed from the bright green lawn and the gentle willow. And so crowded—leaves, plants, and hulking trees jumbled awkwardly together. Like some kind of battle was going on.

Then she came to the fence.

And no Joshua.

(Oh, please, where are you?)

The she heard him, just off to the side, crying quietly. She hurried over to him.

He was lying on the ground, rubbing his arm back and forth. It was the tail end of what had been a bout of crying, with the streaks of his tears dried into blotches on his cheeks.

She crouched beside him, fighting to hold back her fear and her anger. "What happened, Josh?"

He looked at her, and his tears picked up fresh energy. "I fell . . . off there," he said, pointing to the fence. "I climbed halfway up, then I slipped." He punctuated his sentence with a long swipe of his runny nose into the shoulder of his shirt.

"I told you not to go here, didn't I? And your mom told me that you were absolutely forbidden to—"

His eyes widened.

"You won't tell her, will you? Will you?" He was poised to begin crying again.

She paused, letting him dangle there a moment. Knowing, of course, that if she told Mrs. Benny, she would be the one in trouble. Baby-sitters were supposed to keep *some* kind of watch on the kids.

Claire gave his sandy-blond hair a light tussle.

"Deal."

He grinned in relief.

"We'll just say you bumped your arm on the climbing toy."

Joshua started to get up.

"What do you say we go back and dig up something for you on the tube. Some robot show or—"

"GI Joe!" he squealed.

GI Jerk, she thought, and groaned. "Yeah, maybe that's on."

She turned to go back to the house, glad that sick feeling was gone. When she happened to glance at the other side of the fence. Josh had already taken a few steps toward the house.

"Wait a minute," she said quietly. "Just a minute—"

From the fence, the ground sloped down to the water. The plants gave way to a small, narrow strip of mud beach. There was a boat in the water, not moving, and she could make out three people on it.

"C'mon, Claire, the show's probably started already."

"Hold on," she said.

But it wasn't the boat that made her stop. It was something else. The colors right in front of her. She'd read a book once with colors like that. A fantasy book, with strange creatures and plants. And the plants weren't just green but a whole rainbow of colors—dark purplish reeds and shiny orange blades of grass. Sort of like what she was seeing now.

She stepped toward the fence.

It wasn't so different . . . so strange . . . that most people would stop and notice. But it was there.

"Claire! C'mon!"

The grass had deepened past green to a rich, almost bluish, color. And the emerging stalks of the plants by the edge of the water glistened with a beautiful golden color that twinkled in the sunlight.

Almost beautiful. Almost—

Except for the blackish-brown puffles, ugly, dotlike things that seemed to be everywhere, thickest at the water's edge but seemingly spreading up toward the fence.

She looked down at her feet.

There were none there. And she was glad of that. But the grass was already darkening.

She saw a few blades sticking to the seat of Joshua's pants, and she quickly reached over and dusted off his fanny.

"Hey, cut it out."

She stepped closer to the fence.

She knew this place. Right here. The narrow, dark brown beach. Still water.

She knew it because she saw it every night (*every night*) in her dream.

(The same dream. All the time.)

But never with all the strange plants growing around, never with the bright colors spreading up from the water.

That was new—

"Let's go," she said, almost whispering. And she took Joshua's hand—hard—and led him back to the house.

Tom Flaherty tugged the top of his wet suit in place. He could see two children standing by the fence, looking out at him.

He was going to wave. But under the circumstances—diving for a body and all that—he thought it might be a somewhat inappropriate gesture. Besides, there were still people on the shore—not as big a crowd as last night but enough to make him feel their scrutiny.

"All set?" Ed asked him.

"Right."

There was no bantering that afternoon. No joking. The previous night had taken the wind out of all their sails, even Russo, who seemed to retreat to his dials, brooding over them like solid Ed—who seemed a bit pale when he showed up before lunch to do a check on their gear.

I wonder, he thought, *which one of us doesn't want to dive the most?* But that was no contest. Because, unknown to Ed and Russo, Tom had tried to get pulled from the job.

He actually had called the captain at the harbor patrol to plead a bad case of the heebie jeebies, He gave the captain a bunch of good reasons why he should send some other diver up to carry out the second day's search.

The captain bought none of them.

Since Tom knew the layout of the place, it was best, all things considered, that he go on working with Ed.

Then the captain hung up.

Tom thought he'd throw up when he put the phone down.

He just couldn't imagine coming across another body.

(No. He *could* imagine . . . that was the problem.)

He felt trapped. That's part of the problem with being a grown-up. Sure, you can get laid, drink beer, and order a pizza anytime you get an urge. But when duty calls, the rules say you gotta be there. You might be ready to crap in your pants, but hell, you got a job to do.

"Let's roll it," Ed said flatly.

"Okay," Tom said, moving to the edge of the boat, sitting with his back to the water. He was facing Russo, and he wished the writer was here.

(He'd probably had enough fun also.)

Dan had told them he had to meet someone . . . on Long Island, no less. *A likely story. Can't say I blame you.*

But he had a calm, reassuring voice under water. Not the shrill bleating of Russo telling them to go left or right, up and down like underwater puppets, sometimes forgetting all about them.

"Check your microphones," Russo said.

"Testing, one, two," Ed droned.

"Testing, one, two," Tom responded. He tapped his oxygen gauge—for good luck—as he usually did.

"Okay, gentlemen. Over you go—"

Easy for you to say, Tom thought, easy for you—

And he cantilevered backward into the reservoir.

THIRTEEN

"Yes, Mr. Morton. . . . I understand what you have to do. . . . Yes, I understand the danger—"

Let's overreact a bit, right, buddy? Same old story, Wiley thought. Give someone a bit of power, and all of a sudden everything's a crisis. Everything's a damn crisis.

Here's this guy wanting to close the roadway over the dam, prepare evacuation plans . . .

Dammit, evacuation plans! Unbelievable.

"But you just told me that you can have a crew in there tomorrow, pumping the water out, patching it up, so why can't—"

But it was brick-wall time.

"The procedure's very clear, Mr. Wiley. The area is to be closed off, pending the repair and reinspection."

"Even though by tomorrow afternoon—tomorrow afternoon, for Pete's sake—everything might be okay?"

"Might. The operative word here is *might,* Mr. Wiley. Meanwhile you should immediately consult with your local police about evacuation routes . . . notify anyone in the affected area. It's only a precaution."

Only a precaution. Nothing less than a full-scale alert, trashing everything because of some small leak—

"Look, Mr. Morton," he said, forcing himself to smile diplomatically, "I want to cooperate as fully as possible. But please understand we have been building to this week for more than a year." He stood up. "So how about this . . . we'll clear the roadway, set up a phone chain—internally, that is—so that we can notify anyone living near the place. I mean, I'm sure you people don't want any panic."

"No, of course—"

"But let the plans for the celebration go on . . . putting up the banner, setting up the speaker's platform . . . so that if everything is fixed by tomorrow, we're still ready. Now isn't that fair enough?"

C'mon, you old bastard. He knew that if he wanted to, Morton could declare the whole area off-limits.

"Well, I guess that'll be okay. Just see that your workers stay clear of the engineers who'll be coming."

"No problem."

"And make sure the police know what's happening."

"I'll do it right now."

"Okay, then. I'll call and let you know when they're done . . . if you'll tell me where I can reach you."

Wiley scrawled a number down on a piece of paper, passed it to Morton, and then happily, with a big grin, ushered him out of his office.

It's still manageable, he thought as the door closed. Get the stupid leak fixed, find Tommy Fluhr's body (write him off—hey, accidents happen), and keep Rogers from going nuts over Massetrino. (Though that little event disturbed even him. He knew what murder could do to a small town. A few summers ago the river town of Harley-on-Hudson had become hostage to some maniac. It's bad for business.)

He could still pull it off, he thought, and launch his congressional campaign.

The festivities would all start the next day . . . well away from the dam. The Kiwanis and Embassy Clubs were sponsoring a big gala costume ball at the Stone Hill Country Club. Lots of money there. Lots of it. And he planned on letting his political aspirations slip a bit early to some of the high rollers.

Inside information.

Just between me and some of the county's fat cats. Get the old bandwagon rolling real soon.

The town clerk buzzed him. "Mr. Wiley . . ."

"Yes." He was eager to wrap it up early, maybe meet Jamie later. Work off some of the pressure.

"Your next appointment is here . . . a Mr. Parks. Shall I send him in?"

Martin Parks. He'd described himself as a businessman—worldwide holdings, he had said—seeking to open up an East Coast office. Couldn't find a better small town than Ellerton, he had told him. No, sir.

"Send him in."

The notebooks sat in the backseat, filling two torn and musty boxes Leeper had dug out of a closet.

"Take care," Leeper had cautioned Dan. "They're getting old and brittle. They won't stand up to much rough handling."

It seemed to Dan, as he took the Long Island Expressway back toward Manhattan and the bridges to the Bronx and Westchester, that he was bringing Billy Leeper with him.

His life's work, certainly. Year after year, page after page, devoted to finding out *everything* about Goulden's Falls . . . and the dam.

He still wasn't sure he swallowed the story about Leeper's boyhood friend, Jackie Weeks. C'mon, Dan thought, that just had to be some kid's wild imagination. Dark old houses could work wonders. Or maybe it had been embellished by years and years of reliving that moment, reliving the fear. Exaggerating it.

Not that there weren't strange death-cult stories that had some basis in fact. There was that Wisconsin guy, Ed Diefenbaker, who made a habit of snatching passersby, filleting them, and storing them in his homemade freezer. They never proved that he ate them, but nobody could guess where all the meat went.

Then there was the Mogue family. A whole tribe of maniacs, mom-and-pop mayhem that operated out of their ramshackle Southern California desert home, luring over a dozen people to their familial gatherings. Even after they were all arrested—the adults in jail and the kids in juvenile homes—there were reports of the family still prowling around.

Still loose.

Dan smiled. Teenage kids and all their slasher videos. *Friday the 13th, Halloween* . . . just cheap thrills for them. But suppose they met a real slasher?

Why, it had to be like being on another planet, some dark, horrible world where all the rules of humanity were suspended, gone.

The Amazon tribes he photographed the year before were almost a model society in comparison. They don't even have a word for *murder* in their vocabulary.

And what of Gouldens Falls? Something was going on, that's for sure.

But what? Would Billy Leeper's notebooks tell the story, or just add the rumor of his own crazy imaginings?

He saw the sign announcing the Throgs Neck Bridge, and he dug out two dollars for what he regarded as an exorbitant toll.

With his ever dwindling money supply, everything seemed priced much too steeply. Dinner at Susan's would be welcome in more ways than one.

"Gouldens Falls . . ." he said aloud, as if it were an

incantation, as if he could summon a picture of the town in those last few weeks before it disappeared.

He just hoped that picture was in the notebooks.

"Same spot, fellows. Just head down and we'll pick it up from where you left off."

Right, Tom thought. Just like it was an underwater scavenger hunt. Body, body, now who's got that body?

A small squad of pumpkin seeds flurried by, swimming away from the bottom.

Where are you going, girls?

His light made their iridescent belts of yellow and orange glisten in the water.

At least the "roof" is lit, he thought. It was reassuring to look up and see the dull blue glow of the sky. Better that than just more darkness . . . much better.

He and Ed swam close together now—no more solitary exploring.

"There we go, Tommyrot," Ed said, aiming his light straight down.

Sure, Tom thought, that's the place. The backyard. The tree stump. The stockade fence.

Home sweet home.

"Where to now, Russo?"

"Due north . . . you can cut back and forth. Use your lamps this time, Flaherty. No more bumping ass-backward into things."

"Right, Chief. I had planned on doing that myself."

They swam, strangely silent, north, over other yards, past another excavated hole, left by someone who had taken their house with them. They both hovered low over it, letting their lights go back and forth.

"Nothing," Ed said, kicking quickly away, giving the site only a cursory glance.

The old boy's nervous. Never thought I'd see the day.

They passed another block.

"Damn," Ed said. "Will you look at that?"

Tom brought his light up.

They were suspended before a tall, splintery steeple of a church. It was pockmarked with holes. A fish darted out of one, startled by their lights. The cross was gone and the point was broken, worn down to a stubby nub.

Needs sharpening.

Below, Tom could see the name of the church, the raised letters on the sign only barely visible. He read it slowly: THE FIRST LUTHERAN CHURCH OF GOULDENS FALLS, REV. DUNCAN PASSWORTHY, RECTOR.

Funny, it was reassuring seeing a church here.

Place can't be all that bad.

Ed kicked ahead—the first time he left Tom's side.

Past the steeple and then down.

"Hey, man, wait up. I thought we—" Tom hurried to catch up.

He passed behind the church and nearly bumped into his partner.

"What's that?" he said, looking just ahead.

"You guys find something?" Russo barked.

Ed aimed his light down, at something on the ground. The skeletal remains of a tree lurked off to the side.

Ed's light picked up a grayish cluster of tombstones.

"The graveyard, Tommyrot. I would have thought they moved 'em all."

"Buried at sea," Tom said, joking.

Ed didn't laugh.

Tom went a bit closer. "Cletus Finch, 1806–1882. Beloved father of Anna and—looks like—Johanna. Devoted husband to . . . can't make it out. It's all crusty with algae and shit."

"Let's go," Ed said. "We've enough air for another sweep. Okay by you, Russo?"

"Sure . . . just go east about fifty feet or so, then head back south. I'll try to center the boat over you."

The shoreline couldn't have been more than a hundred feet or so away. No Tommy Fluhr. Not yet, anyway.

(And just what happened to Fred Massetrino? Yes, the big question was—ta da!—did old Fred get chopped up before or after his swim? That was the question, but Tom wasn't too damn sure he wanted the answer.)

"Hey, Tom, look over there . . . quickly."

He spun around and aimed his light in the same direction as Ed's.

"What have you got?"

"I thought . . ." Ed said.

Easy, boy. I'm supposed to be the nervous one. I tried to get out of this gig, not you.

(Or did you call police headquarters too?)

"You see something?"

"I thought I saw something, over there, toward the shore. Could have been a shadow or something."

"I'm right over you guys," Russo said, sounding almost human. "Could have been the boat's shadow." Probably getting a bit worried they were losing it. "Want to come up? Take a break?"

Ed looked at Tom . . . a subtle shift of power.

Tom shook his head. "Let's get it over with, Ed. Finish this, and then we can go home today. They can get another team if they decide to scour the whole lake."

Ed nodded. "We'll go on, Jack. Are we still heading okay?"

"Sure. You're almost at Scott Street again. Another fifty feet past that should do it."

They swam quickly now, not really caring whether they found anything or not.

No, that wasn't exactly true.

Not *wanting* to find anything.

Mechanically their flippers moved almost in unison, while

their lights moved back and forth, catching the top of the house, then the water-bloated branches of a long dead tree.

Jeez, how long does it take for this stuff to rot?

And he thought of all the people who drink this water. It was enough to make him gag.

"Okay, this is the street," Ed said. "Let's just keep moving."

But Tom saw something. It was just another house, big, brown. Just an ugly hulk down here, away from the light, but he could imagine on a hot summer's day people dressed in white shirts sitting on the oversize porch drinking lemonade.

Then he saw something else. Just a small detail. Worrisome, the type of thing one would like to wish away.

But unfortunately he couldn't.

The front doors—two heavy-looking pieces of wood—were wide open.

"Ed," he said, but Ed continued swimming, across the streets. "Ed!"

His partner stopped.

"What's up?"

"The damn doors are open. To that house there. Do you think we should—"

He watched Ed examine the doors at a distance, his light just barely picking them up. Was it his imagination, or did Ed's eyes seem kind of funny, wide open?

"No big deal . . . probably the wood just rotted away around the lock. No, we'll just keep—"

"Better take a look," Russo said.

(Easy for you to say, fucker. Get your ass down here and see how you'd like to—)

"Why?" Ed asked angrily. "You think the kid went swimming into the house? It's a couple of hundred feet down, for Pete's sake."

Russo yelled right back. "And how do you know what

kind of funny currents are in the water? Could be the body ended up right inside. At least you can take a look."

He looked at Ed. Whatever he said, he'd stand by. Look or leave, Tom knew he'd do whatever Ed said.

But he sure hoped he said to hell with it.

"Look, Russo, how could—"

"Remember Fiscetti?"

Tom remembered Fiscetti, and he knew Ed did too. He was a two-bit capo who was playing ball with the Kerner Commission, secretly testifying, wearing a wire. But the mob finally got wise to him and dumped the body, all tied up and weighted down . . . but not in the East River.

No, they threw him in the bubbling stew called Spuyten Dyvel—the spitting devil—where the East River and the Hudson River meet the brackish waters from upstate.

It could be rougher there than in the ocean.

Someone called in a tip—laughing—that Joe Fiscetti could be found—hah, hah—swimming with the fishes there.

But after two hours of searching they had found nothing, except every kind of garbage from shopping carts to the rear axles of Camaros.

There was a small indentation—a cave, almost—that they had passed . . . illuminating it as someplace to search. So they finally went back to it, swam in, and found Fiscetti's body, wedged there by some kind of strange current that kept all kinds of crap pushed into the hole.

He had a D'Agostino's bag over his face.

"Yeah," Ed said, "I remember Fiscetti."

"So," Jack said, "maybe the same thing's happening here. Maybe the body got pushed in there . . . maybe—"

Ed tapped his head to register his opinion of Russo's brainstorm.

"Okay, okay, we'll go."

And Ed waited, Tom knew, for him to offer to go in.

One man always stayed outside any underwater structure—in case of trouble—while the other went in.

(*Stay here, Ed. I'll check it out. Okay, pal?*)

But he couldn't say that. And he knew—knew, damn him—that Ed would have to offer to go. Age, seniority, and a whole stupid macho code.

"Well, I guess I'll take a look, Tommyrot. Just stay nice and close in case . . . in case I get hung up on something."

"Sure," he said, trying to keep the relief from his voice.

Ed turned lethargically and began swimming toward the door. He followed a few feet behind.

"Just give it a quick look inside, Ed. It couldn't have gone in far . . . if at all."

Ed said nothing.

He swam over the porch.

(Lemonade, sir?)

Paused at the entrance.

And then went in.

"See anything?" Tom asked.

"Hey, they left their furniture. Do you like—"

"Like what?"

But Ed didn't continue.

"Like what, Ed?"

Again, there was only silence.

(Oh, damn, he thought. What's wrong now? Is the radio all fucked up? Something causing interference with the system. It's supposed to work for a good half a mile. Through walls, debris, anything . . .)

Tom moved closer, under the overhang of the porch.

"Jack, I've lost Ed. Can you hear him?"

"Just you, Tom. Where are you?"

"At the door." C'mon, Ed . . . c'mon. Don't do this to me. Just get the hell out.

"Ed!"

He inched closer to the door, all light from above now cut off by the porch.

He pointed his light in, the darkness gobbling up the glow, catching just the faintest outline of the inside steps leading upstairs.

I'm not going in, he told himself.

I can't go in.

"Ed, man, if you can hear me, come on out. C'mon, dammit."

Again, nothing.

Help, he thought. *I'll get help. Go up . . . get someone to come down with me . . . or maybe it's just his radio not working.*

But I'm not going in there.

No way.

He gave a small kick back with his flippers. Just enough to edge away from the door.

He didn't move. There seemed to be the smallest current moving around him, into the house. He kicked again, harder, waving his hand to give himself a good push.

He didn't move away. In fact, he seemed to slide closer to the entrance, just a few inches but closer.

Now he kicked madly, swimming full out, using his lean, muscular body to swim quickly and sleekly away.

And he drifted yet closer to the door, feeling it sucking on him now, like a small piece of meat being squished down with a gulp of water.

"No. Oh, God, no. Russo, I'm—" he started to say, but he let his lamp fall and reached out, grabbing at the open doors, his fingers closing, viselike.

He held tight, and for a moment he didn't move.

"What's wrong, Tom? What's the problem?"

"I . . . don't . . ."

He held, then the pull grew stronger. But this was no current pushing him in.

That had been an error.

No, this was suction, from behind. From inside the house. He held for another moment. Then it became even stronger, and stronger, the water rushing past him, dragging chunks of wood, twigs, a stray fish, whose terrified eyes looked so familiar.

His fingers began to slip.

"Oh, God, no!" He tried to tighten his grip. But it was no contest.

His legs were back now, sucked into the inside of the house, with only his hands outside. They slipped another fraction of an inch.

His light was on the ground, pointed out into the dark reservoir.

He felt something in the back, in the darkness, touching his flippers . . . gentle touches . . . then moving up the rubber ridges to the small, cut-out spots of exposed flesh.

"Russo!" he screamed.

But he heard nothing.

And his hands pulled away, and he flew backward into the darkness, into the house, screaming as he slid giddily down the hall.

His abandoned light outlined the twin oaken doors as they slowly shut.

FOURTEEN

Wiley tried to make himself comfortable in his own office. But despite his best efforts—squirming in his seat, crossing, then uncrossing his legs—all he could think of was getting the hell out of there.

And in spite of the steady drippy hum of the antiquated room air-conditioner, it felt close in the office, as if there just weren't enough oxygen in it.

The visitor, though, seemed perfectly at ease. He sat—no, rested was more like it—with an ever so cool grace on the hardwood chair. His suit, a summery pale gray, was immaculately tailored. As he talked, his eyes were riveted on Wiley—perfectly relaxed and ignoring his discomfort.

Whatever this Martin Parks claimed his credentials might be, Wiley believed him. Tall, thin, with an angular face that seemed all lined in edges, he looked like a man who meant what he said.

Totally.

"So," Parks said, "we're looking for just a small piece of undeveloped land, for a block of offices. A small warehouse.

Nothing too big. Just something nice and quiet for our U.S. office. You understand."

He was in his early forties, maybe even a bit younger, with a tan complexion that spoke of leisurely weeks cruising the Mediterranean.

"I understand," Wiley said, "and I'm sure that our Chamber of Commerce would be more than glad to help you . . ."

Parks's face registered disappointment.

"Oh. I was hoping you could take a personal interest in our small proposal. You know, perhaps running interference for us." He smiled. "In fact, if you can help us," he said, reaching into his inside coat pocket, "we'd be most appreciative." He removed an envelope and slid it toward Wiley.

It was fat, bulging. And he saw it wasn't filled with singles.

Parks's grin broadened. "Consider it a retainer for your 'consulting services.' Perhaps you can use this in your"—he paused—"upcoming campaign."

He looked right at Parks. How could he know of his plans? No one in town knew, certainly not a stranger. He started to shake his head. "I . . . I don't know."

Parks stood up. "Call it a friendship offering. From a new business partner."

Wiley let his hand close around the chunky envelope. Still confused, he blurted out, "Perhaps you'd like to come to a dinner tomorrow night. It's at the country club . . . for the Kenicut Dam celebration."

Parks nodded. "How thoughtful of you to invite me. Why, I'd be delighted."

"It's a costume—"

"I know," Parks said, interrupting. "A costume ball."

Wiley saw Parks's expression shift, and he wondered, Who the hell was this guy? Some mafioso front man?

Parks took a step closer to him. "I do hope your celebration goes off smoothly," he said. "Some of my associates were planning on coming to town. I'd hate to disappoint them."

"N-no," Wiley said, stammering. "I'm sure there'll be no—"

But Parks was already moving to the door.

"I'll see you tomorrow night, Mr. Wiley. In costume, of course."

He let himself out while Wiley stood there, breathing hard . . . remembering his childhood asthma.

Playing with the big boys, he thought. That's what this is. Whatever business Parks is up to, it's no good.

He walked over and shut the office door.

He opened the envelope and started counting the thick stack of hundred-dollar bills.

"Anybody home?"

The voice startled her, carrying over the hum of her ray-gun-shaped hair dryer. She hurried out to the living room.

Dan was at the screen door, holding it open and sticking his head in.

"Oh, sorry, I didn't hear the buzzer over my dryer."

He gave a hearty sniff. "That's the mighty aroma of garlic, if I'm not wrong. Smells good."

"Chicken Provençal . . . from my limited repertoire of French dishes. You'll love it."

He walked in, and she felt again how dangerously attractive he was. And all wrong for her, she had tried to tell herself all day. *You just can't let yourself fall for some good-looking, interesting, and intelligent hunk.*

What the situation requires is some calm, settled, and wealthy businessman, ready to love and support her and Claire. Dull but reliable.

Not Indiana Jones with a camera.

Except that she had left work early to come home, putting

on makeup and a new summer dress—perfect for moonlight walks, and, of course, a knockout dinner.

"Drink?"

"Sure," he said with a grin. "Bourbon, if you have it."

She talked as she opened the just purchased bottle of Jack Daniel's. "So how'd your visit with Billy Leeper go?"

Dan had plopped down onto the couch. "Ask me tomorrow. I've got the past fifty years of his life in the back of my car." He told her about the notebooks as she handed him his drink. "Tonight I'll hole up in my motel room and see just what the old buzzard learned."

"Eat and run, huh?"

He smiled, a big, generous grin that was light-years away from the tight-faced looks of the long gray line of anxious commuters trooping down to the train station in New York. Dan Elliot certainly didn't belong in this town.

"No, I'll stick around a bit . . . maybe we can take a walk after dinner."

"I'd like that," she said, looking right at him.

And for a moment they were both quiet.

She heard a car pull up outside.

"Oh, there's Claire. She baby-sat today. . . ." The spell was broken, and she felt almost relieved as she went to the door.

"Hi, honey," she called. Claire walked up to the house slowly. "How'd things go?"

But it took only a brief look at Claire to see that things hadn't gone too well. Her daughter's face was locked, masklike, into some fretful grimace. Lips pursed, her brow knitted.

Obviously it hadn't gone well at all.

"Baby, is there anything wrong?"

Claire's entrance was punctuated only by the rude slap of the screen door.

"Claire?"

"I don't want to talk about it." She looked over and saw Dan.

"Hi, Claire," he said.

"Hi," she said flatly.

Dan looked at Susan. "Perhaps I'd better go?"

Claire continued walking through the living room, past the kitchen, down the hall to her bedroom.

"No, please," Susan said, not very convincingly, "the dinner's almost ready. She gets in these . . . snits all the time. I just— Will you excuse me just a moment, until I find out what's wrong?"

"Sure, go ahead."

Susan turned from him and hurried down the hallway.

It's always children, she thought. They come first. All the time. Your job, your social life, everything is secondary. And lately, with Claire's terrible dreams growing worse, she was beginning to worry.

Was there something really wrong, something big, something more than just a little nightmare?

Her teachers always said she was a bit of a loner—standoffish, lost to her books. Was there a real problem, and was it her fault? It's the kids who pay in a divorce, that's what her mother always told her. And despite her best efforts to be a supermom, maybe she was actually blowing it.

"Claire." She turned the door handle to her room, but it was locked.

"Claire, can we talk?"

"Later," Claire said in a surprisingly firm, assured voice.

Susan debated forcing her to open to door.

"Okay, honey, we'll talk later."

She went out to Dan, and the dinner she no longer had an appetite for.

Dan had eaten heartily, while Susan had simply moved her food around, mostly munching on chunks of crusty bread, dipping it into the garlicky wine sauce.

Twice she tried to get Claire to come out and join them,

but Claire quietly balked. She was relieved when Dan again suggested a walk around the block.

"I'm not used to sidewalks," he said, joking.

The sun wasn't quite down yet, but the trees and homes had the bluish tinge of twilight.

"We bought this house here because, well, it looked like a good place to raise kids."

"We . . . you mean your husband and you?"

She nodded. "We had this quaint *Our Town* image of our life, a nice quiet block in suburbia. A safe place for the me generation to raise their kids."

"Yeah." Dan laughed. "I tried that too. Fortunately none of the ladies I did time with wanted to have a kid with me." He looked right at Susan. "Can't figure out why, can you?"

She laughed. "I guess most of us need, I don't know, security, stability—"

"Go ahead, focus on my weak points."

They turned the corner, walking past well-kept lawns. She saw old Samuel Jones—watering his lawn in a tank top and Bermuda shorts. He waved at her.

"So, what was your problem, Ms. Sloan?"

She took a breath. "I made the mistake of marrying someone older. Older, wiser, and, it eventually turned out, all wrong. He was a publisher, just divorced, and I wanted to write. His fifteen-plus years on me didn't seem to matter. And despite his teenage daughters, he wanted to start another family."

"So what happened?"

"Everything. And fast. I discovered that one of his peccadilloes was seducing would-be authors . . . just like he had seduced me. His weekend jaunts to book conventions became a regular feature of our life together. As soon as I was pregnant, he seemed uncomfortable with me. I became a dull housewife, cooking meals only to be reheated when he came home late, growing fat with the baby, while I knew he was still running around. Shortly after Claire was born, he split. Said I had become just like his ex-wife. I was so relieved, I didn't try to nail him. Just support money, and the harrowing life of a single parent."

"Sounds like it made you grow up fast."

"Oh, sure, there's nothing like taking care of a kid all by yourself to make you feel grown-up. I started writing. Fillers for the local paper. Graduating eventually to feature stuff, until"—she sighed—"I became the sparkly, happy, successful person you see now." She gave Dan her best self-deprecating grin, scolding herself for letting herself go all maudlin and bitter on him.

"Hey," she said, "I'm sorry that I—"

He reached over and took her hand.

(*Yes,* she thought, *I need that. Some assurance that I'm still human, still—*)

"I should get you back so you can talk to Claire. I like her, Susan, really like her. She doesn't miss a trick."

They stopped at the corner, ready to turn back. It was dark now, time when people outside became pale, shadowy outlines—the colorful mishmash of their summer outfits gone.

"You're right," she said, looking at him.

And she leaned up, impulsively, to kiss him. His arms went around her, powerful arms that squeezed her close. He kissed her back, hard, and it was over.

"C'mon," she said. "You've got a lot of reading to do."

When Dan had left, and she'd gotten back to the house, she found Claire sitting at the kitchen table, eating Oreos and drinking a glass of milk.

"Hi, Mom," she said quietly.

Herbert Blount had been tempted to sell his house. After his wife left, taking the kids, it seemed, at first, to be too big and filled with too many memories.

He didn't like memories.

The fights with Myrna, her threats: "I'm disappearing, you bum. You'll never see me and the kids again! Never!"

To which he'd mutter, "Go ahead. Nothing would make me happier."

Nothing.

Except they'd been gone for—what—four months? And his life had certainly changed. It was like it was filled with all these holes, holes he had to fill . . . watching Mets baseball (with not as many free games now that they were on the sports channel), drinking beer, sitting on his porch, as the neighbors ignored him.

A real-estate agent had even called to ask him about selling the house.

But he said no. Not now. Maybe never.

He walked onto his porch, no lights on, and sat down on the splintery wooden Adirondack chair.

It faced the plaza—three large circles of green grass surrounded by walkways and marigolds—and then beyond, the dam.

No, he didn't want to move. Not with this view.

He took a sip of his beer.

Before returning to his motel room, Dan stopped and picked up a bottle of Jack Daniel's.

It was going to be a long night.

He noticed that the Ellerton Motor Inn seemed to be picking up more customers. Most of the parking spaces were filled. He had to park his Rover off to the side, near a desolate-looking field, and then carry the two heavy boxes of notebooks over to his motel room.

As he crossed the lot another car arrived, its lights on. Long and black, it slid into the lot like it owned it.

The headlights glared in Dan's eyes. The car paused, watched Dan cross. And he hurried to get out of its path.

He looked at it as it passed, but he couldn't see the driver. He plopped the boxes down, dug out his room key, and opened the door.

"So what's the story?"

Claire gingerly dipped one Oreo halfway into the milk, something she had done since she was five. "Nothing," she answered.

"Right," Susan said with a nod, "you always come home and lock yourself in your room. Dan would have liked to spend some time with you. He likes you—"

"I know. I like him. A lot. It's just that . . . just . . . oh, forget it."

"Tell me, Claire. Tell me what happened."

She looked at her and her chewing stopped, and she could see that Claire was on the verge of crying. "Something with the Benny children?"

Claire put down her half-eaten cookie. And told her everything. About Joshua, the fence, how she finally saw the beach from her nightmare.

"And there were these plants all over the place, plants like you never saw before, and—"

Susan cupped a hand over her daughter's hand. "You were scared, that's all, honey. And believe me, there are plenty of strange plants . . . plenty of weird stuff. That's all you saw, just—"

"But, Mom—" Claire was having trouble keeping calm. "These weren't anything normal. The grass looked blue, the reeds sort of glowed, and—"

Susan smiled. "Maybe it was the light, sweetheart." She feared her daughter's imagination. It seemed almost dangerous, churning up images, dreams, now this. "Maybe we could take a look sometime," she said, trying to soothe her. She stood up, ending their talk, and started to clear the dishes, bringing an air of routine back to the house.

"But," Claire said to her mom's now empty seat, "there's something else."

Susan rinsed off the plates and lined them up in the dishwasher. "What's that?"

"Something wants them," she said quietly. "Joshua, Samantha, me . . . you . . . everybody. I felt it. Something in the water. Standing there."

She turned around and ran a hand through Claire's ultrafine hair. She probably knew about Tommy Fluhr, she figured. Maybe—my God—even Fred Massetrino.

"No, Claire, it's just a lake," she said, sighing. She'd have to start watching what Claire read. Enough fantasy stuff for now. "Now, lazy bones, come on and help me clean up this dump."

She went back to finish filling the dishwasher.

The first notebook was filled with old newspaper clippings. There were photos of the town, showing exactly where the new reservoir would lie. And there was a sketch of the proposed Kenicut Dam. Then there were pages and pages of progress reports, records of town meetings, plans to relocate stores, buildings, and homes to neighboring Ellerton.

And there was also a story on the buildings to be left behind. Some too old to be moved, too big, many homes and stores to be left.

Dan took a sip of his drink.

Nothing much exciting here, he thought. There was a funny story of a cow that ate some dynamite, and then later a story about how two workers died when the concrete base was being poured.

(And where were they now? he wondered. Part of the cement bedrock of the dam?)

He finished the first notebook, feeling that Billy Leeper's magnum opus might not have any great secret to reveal.

But that feeling all changed when he opened the second notebook.

It contained jottings from Leeper—written in a scraggly hand. There were comments in the margins and written underneath the clippings.

Now all the material was taken from the years before the dam was built. Pictures and stories from Gouldens Falls in its salad days. There was a picture of the Lakeview Hotel, a squat pillbox of a building with an elegant front porch and stairs leading down to a dirt road. The church, with its elegant steeple. A firehouse on a hill overlooking the town. A photo of Main Street with its mixture of cars and carriages. But Leeper had circled someone standing in one of the pictures, right next to a roadster parked beside the hotel.

There was a name scribbled in the margin. "Thomas Raine," Dan said, reading aloud.

Then he flipped to another yellowed page from the paper. Jonathan Reynolds was announcing the annual October Harvest Festival. Behind him there was a stack of pumpkins that stood over ten feet tall.

Mighty big pumpkins.

Who are these people? Dan wondered. Why had Leeper tracked down their photos?

Then a doctor, holding twins. Dr. Samuel Hustis, beaming as he cradled the twins, one in each arm. And a storekeeper, personal photo here. A curling black-and-white Kodak print of Mr. Wallace Pfister, who stood smiling behind the counter of a store that looked like it sold everything from sausages to sneakers.

He turned another page.

There was a space for another clipping, but it apparently had come loose . . . slipped away.

"Probably in the box somewhere," Dan said to himself. He reached over and tipped in a few more fingers' worth of the Kentucky bourbon.

And underneath the space, scrawled twice as big as any of the names, was a large question mark and a circle.

A question mark. Four names. Five photos. One question mark.

He was thinking about this, as well as he could after a couple of belts, when the phone rang. He shook, startled by the brash ring.

It rang one more time and he picked it up.

FIFTEEN

She so hated being alone.

Even with the TV on in both the bedroom and living room, Sharon Benny felt abandoned by her husband. Of course, she never let Bob know that. She supported him completely, doing her best to keep their modern, split-level home running along smoothly. The last thing he needed was her getting all fidgety about being by herself two or three times a month.

To be sure, she trusted him totally. He just wasn't the type to use his jaunts for affairs. And he always came home all worked up ("hot and bothered," she called it), eager to get the kids to sleep and spend time alone with her.

She guessed she was happy.

This seemed to be everything she wanted out of life. A beautiful home overlooking the lake (even if they never could get close to it), two reasonably well-behaved children, no more obnoxious than the other kids she saw her friends coping with. A devoted husband— something of a rarity, to hear her friends talking. Still, sitting in the living room, just cleaned today by Esther (another find!), she couldn't help feeling oddly dissatisfied.

Dissatisfied and disturbed.

She thought she'd like this house, all off to itself, surrounded by heavy oak trees, well away from any neighbors.

But on a night like this, with Bob in California, she felt a prisoner. The kids slept peacefully, but she tended to stay up late—too late—tossing, turning, listening to the breeze from the lake rustling the willow trees, an eerie whoosh. More than once she was tempted to go to Dr. Rheinman and ask for a sleeping-pill prescription (just like her mother, she thought, who progressed to regular doses of Valium "for my nerves" until the medicine cabinet looked a display at a pharmaceutical museum of horrors).

So she just roughed it out . . . like she would tonight.

She pushed the remote-control button and the picture tube blinked off, leaving the filmy afterglow of a sandy-blond newscaster.

She left the living room light on.

It's worth the fifty cents or so of electricity, she thought. She turned on the security system, first for the downstairs, and, when she had reached the bedroom, for the upstairs.

It should have made her feel better—more protected.

But it didn't.

"Slow down," Dan said on the phone. Susan sounded excited, overwrought. He looked at his watch. It was nearly eleven P.M. "Now, what happened?"

"Allan, my editor, called about an hour ago. The divers are gone, Dan. gone! They were supposed to finish their search, but they went down a second time and never came up."

Dan looked at the notebook on his bed—open to the page with the missing photo and the question mark. He thought of the divers—Ed, a tight-lipped Clint Eastwood type who seemed totally unflappable; and Tom, who seemed to have been developing a rocky set of nerves.

And now they were gone.

(What's going on here?)

"What do the police know?" he asked.

"According to Allan, nothing. The guy in the boat . . ."

"Russo."

"Yeah. Well, he stayed out there, going back and forth for hours, calling for them on the radio. He had to be ordered to come in. Maybe they got hung up on something, maybe one of the old buildings collapsed on them—"

Wrong. There was no way that two divers with their experience could have let that happen.

"So what's everyone doing?"

"The police aren't saying anything, though Allan said that the New York police were notified. State troopers are already here. Another diving team might be on the way, but it's just speculation. I'll know by tomorrow."

"Oh . . . how will you know tomorrow?"

"Allan said I'm to can everything else and just stay on this story—the dam, the missing people. It's the biggest story to hit Ellerton since—"

Dan turned toward the door. He thought he heard someone walk by outside it. Footsteps on the poured concrete. He could have sworn they paused a minute, and then moved on.

Easy, boy, he thought. Wouldn't do getting all paranoid.

"Susan, I don't think that's a good idea. You don't know what's going on there. I—"

"C'mon, Dan. I'm a reporter, a writer like you. It's a story, a big one, too, and I'm not going to go diving." She paused, her irritation at his concern obvious. "I'm a big girl, and there's no reason why I shouldn't cover this story."

He tried to put his feelings into words, to find an argument to convince her to stay away.

"Don't go there," he said. "Just don't go anywhere near the dam and the reservoir."

She was cool now, her voice turning flat and professional. "I have my job to do. I just called 'cause I thought you'd be interested. I'm sorry you're not. I have to get some sleep. It's going to be an early morning. Bye."

Susan's receiver clicked rudely in his ear.

So much for that blossoming relationship.

But as he went back to the open notebook, something seemed to stick in his mind.

The picture of Claire walking into her house.

It's almost as if she knew the bad news first . . . before anyone.

He looked over at his diving gear, sprawled on the floor around the squat dresser that he hadn't used, preferring to live out of his two suitcases.

The air tanks were all filled, ready for a nice dive into the Kenicut Reservoir.

Except suddenly he wasn't so eager to take that dive.

Sharon Benny had been asleep.

She was sure of it.

But then something woke her up.

She looked around her bedroom. The digital clock read 12:01. She listened. She heard her own breathing, irregular, as if she were taking random gasps of air. The pillow rustled noisily in her ears as she turned her head from side to side.

No sound now. *It's okay,* she thought. *I can go back to sleep.*

(*Try* to go back to sleep.)

She curled around, hugging Bob's pillow close, hating him now for not being here. She closed her eyes tight, making an iridescent pattern of crisscrossed lines appear before her eyes.

She heard something.

A sound from downstairs, down near the family room.

At first she knew, just knew, it couldn't be anything wrong. The security system was the best money could buy. Any attempt at entering from the outside would trigger the motion detectors.

Alarms all over, and a gaggle of rent-'em cops ready to come to her home within minutes.

(She knew that because they had tried it out. "Just a mistake," Bob had explained to them. But it really had been an experiment. The system was worth its yearly maintenance fee of two thousand dollars.)

She sat up a bit, again trying to listen. Mice, maybe? (If she wasn't so allergic to fur, they would have invested in a cat a long time ago.)

No. It sounded like—

(Her heart started a strange tattoo. Gooseflesh—always quick to rise on her—popped out.)

The sliding door being opened.

But why no alarm? Unless . . .

If it's opened from the inside, it automatically neutralizes the alarm. ("Keeps your kids and pets from driving you crazy," the sleazoid salesman had explained.) She sat up quickly, pausing just another second before making the inevitable decision.

She got out of bed, ignoring her robe, and whirled into Samantha's room. Her daughter was asleep, curled up near the top of her bed like she always was, her arm around her Alf.

She started to feel a bit relieved. Samantha sometimes got up, took a pee, and decided to dig around for some goodies to eat in the middle of the night. Joshua, though, was dead to the world until sunrise (at which point he always found some reason to wake everyone up).

She went into Joshua's room.

For a moment she saw him there, wrapped up in his tangle

of sheets and blankets. But the room was dark, and she looked more closely. He wasn't there. She patted the sheet, the blanket, the pillow, groaning as her hand felt only the softness, and no little boy's hard and bony body.

"Oh, God," she said, and she ran out of the room, throwing the hall light on, already creating explanations for where he was.

He woke up . . . went and got a cookie . . . maybe tried to find some cartoons on TV, sure, that's all—except she had heard the heavy door slide open.

She went down the stairs quickly and reached for the light.

The family room was empty.

The red light—indicating that the security system was on—was dark. Shut off.

And the sliding door was open to the moonlit night.

A pattern began to emerge.

But Dan hadn't the foggiest clue as to what it had to do with the reservoir.

There was one whole notebook filled with "human-interest" newspaper clippings from Gouldens Falls. The Johnson baby's remarkable recovery from a horrible illness. Despite the drought of 1935, Mr. Patterson reported a bumper crop of corn. ("We did some irrigating," Patterson was quoted as saying, a big smile on his face.) Donnelly's Hardware—most of its stock destroyed in a fire a month earlier—reopened with a gala celebration, and an even large selection of items. ("The insurance really helped," Joe Donnelly told reporters.)

Page after page, until it looked like Gouldens Falls had become the garden spot of the world, a place where only good things happened to nice, God-fearing people. The rest of the country might have been in the middle of a hellish depression, but Gouldens Falls was prospering mighty nicely, thank you.

He finished the notebook, seeing that the only thing Leeper had written down was the names of the people in the stories.

"Like some sort of scorecard," Dan said aloud. He began to think that Leeper had done more than just bang his head on that rock that day.

He started the next notebook.

It began in 1936, and now all of a sudden there were different stories . . . tragic stories. Patterson's prizewinning mare falls down dead—a heart attack, the vet said. And a toddler—little Annie Martin—falls victim to a particular nasty strain of the flu. The parents move away. A house burns down. A young man has a stroke, falling into a coma.

Again, there was a list of names in Leeper's hand. And Dan sensed what should have been obvious. Some of the names are the same. It was as if they'd had a stroke of some incredibly good luck, and then, later, something went wrong. Not to all of them. But according to Leeper's records, many of the names were the same.

He poured himself a drink.

He rubbed his eyes. Eight notebooks left, and who the hell knew what kind of story was coming out. He was tempted to look at the last one.

He reached over and fingered its shiny metal spine.

He heard a car outside. No, he thought, listening, not a car . . . a deeper rumble from its engine. From a pickup, or maybe a small truck.

It entered the lot slowly, and Dan heard it pause by his room, as if someone were checking out the numbers. Probably some guy four sheets to the wind trying to make the room numbers stop going double on him.

I know that feeling, Dan thought.

He picked up the next notebook. And he thought it was a mistake. More clippings, of course, with the dates circled and the locations written in by Leeper. But they were from all over.

Missing people. From nearby New York City. From upstate. From Boston, Philadelphia.

There were copies of announcements—brown and hopeless with age, all faded—asking if anyone "knew the whereabouts of," and then a name. Dozens of them. From 1936, 1937, and 1938. Why were they in this book? As if Leeper had tracked down every missing person from those years.

Every unsolved missing person.

He stood up, letting the notebook slide to the bed. He shook his head. *What is this? What's going on here? And maybe it's time I got out of it.*

He looked at his AMF diving suit—not the most modern, easily out-of-date by a good five years—hanging in the closet. His knife, a mean, jagged-edged item that he kept razor-sharp, was draped over the coatrack.

He thought of Tom and Ed.

(Supposedly it's not so bad dying by drowning. The air gives out, and you start sucking your own carbon monoxide back in. Your head starts to spin. You black out. Not so bad. Supposedly.)

If that's what had happened to them . . . if somehow they'd been pinned under the water.

(But Dan remembered being trapped in his car, feeling the icy water shooting in, sitting there watching it fill the car. He wouldn't let himself go through that again.)

No matter what.

But this . . .

This was growing stranger by the minute, and for the first time he thought he'd pick up all his gear, throw it into the back of his Land Rover, and get the hell out of there.

"What's a couple of thousand dollars?" he said, trying to convince himself to give up the article.

After all, it's a bit late in life to become a materialist.

He heard something outside again.

Steps, slow, tentative, coming toward his room.

Probably the late-night rummy on his appointed rounds. Trying to get a closer look at the room numbers.

But the steps were steady, assured, until they came to stop just outside his door.

Dan looked at the door. He half expected the doorknob to twist back and forth ominously.

He looked over at his knife. (Easy, boy.)

The late-night visitor knocked. Once, gently. Then harder.

It felt cold in the air-conditioned room.

He went to the door and opened it.

Claire could still feel it. Lying on her bed, eyes wide open.

As if she could smell the reservoir here, touching everything.

Her mother hadn't believed her. But she understood that, really understood that. You couldn't have moms running around believing in their kids' crazy fears, now could you?

It just didn't work that way.

Kids get scared, and the grown-ups make it all better.

Except that this was different. (She should have known that a long time ago.) The dream had been a warning from . . . from . . .

Somewhere. Trying to tell her about what was going to happen.

(Her mother made a sound in her sleep, a little grunt, and it made Claire feel weird to hear it, like she was in charge, watching over her mother or something.)

And maybe she was.

She thought now, too, of the Benny kids—not that she liked them; they were too spoiled for that. But still she worried about them, in that nice new home so close to the water—

(And the plants, and the funny black things growing in the ground.)

When she closed her eyes, she could also hear them growing, like toadstools popping out of the ground, the grass going to seed, waving in the breeze. And the water.

God, yes, the water. Not just sitting there nice and still, but jumping around in the moonlight.

Excited.

She pulled her blanket closer.

Didn't anyone else hear it, she wondered, or smell the way the air was damp and heavy? Reaching everyone as they slept, filling their lungs with the moist air from the lake.

Everyone who slept.

But not her. She wouldn't sleep tonight. No way. She'd keep her eyes wide open, listening, waiting . . .

Until everyone heard it and she wasn't alone anymore.

If only it wasn't too late.

SIXTEEN

At first she didn't call out his name, as if breaking the silence of the night would somehow confirm that there was, in fact, something wrong here.

She didn't want to admit that.

Her Joshua just went outside. That's all. Her explorer, her adventurer, saw the moonlight (so bright tonight) and went out . . . to see it.

But as soon as she started running across the milky white yard down to the woods, she knew that this, her backyard, had changed. Now it was an eerie, alien place where she had no right to be.

So she yelled out his name, listening to her voice carry so clearly in the night air.

"Joshua!" She heard a truck, miles away. Then a gentle breeze pressed her thin nightgown against her skin. Leaves rustled.

But no one answered her call.

Now she ran, full out, single-minded, into the woods.

The lake was all he talked about. He loved the lake.

("Why can't I fish there, Mommy, and why can't I swim

there? And why can't Daddy buy us a boat for the lake? And why is there a fence around it? Why, why?")

The lake was like a lurking stranger.

Luring her child with the promise of play and excitement.

Every few steps she yelled out his name.

Once she thought she heard his answer—or maybe it was just the sound of her own voice echoing off the sheer cliffs across the water.

She reached the fence, and even though the moonlight made everything almost dazzlingly white, she didn't see much. The trees went right up to the fence line, arching over it, covering it with shadows.

She looked around, confused, as if she expected Josh to be there, standing beside the fence, wearing his mischievous grin.

("Sorry, Mommy.")

But he wasn't there. She went to the fence and dug her fingers into the mesh, looking left and right.

(Now she doubted herself. *Maybe he's still at home, maybe he opened the door, took a quick look outside, and went back to bed or to the bathroom. Sure, I probably missed him, and—*)

Such hopeful thoughts rambled through her mind, then she saw there was an opening, at the bottom of the fence. It was like someone had dug at the bottom of the mesh and yanked it out of the ground, pulling it up and out like the flap of a cardboard box.

Could Josh have done that? Just big enough for a boy to crawl under.

"Oh, no," she said, moaning. And again she made a pitiful, hopeless sound. She knelt down.

(Ignoring the tiny popping sound of whatever was growing on the ground.)

She crawled under the opening. It was so small, just boy-sized, but she might just be slim-waisted enough to go under it. She pulled on the mesh, gaining another few inches to move, pushing away the nasty metal barbs at the base. She stuck her head through the opening.

Now she inched forward, her bare legs digging into the dirt, mashing down whatever was growing there while her arms snaked their way through, her fingers digging into the mucky soil, pulling, pulling . . .

She could see that Joshua wasn't directly on the other side, just opposite the opening. But the shoreline weaved in and out, dotted with old oak and maple trees. He could be ten feet away and she wouldn't see him.

(The other thing she didn't let herself think. No, despite the noisy sound of the water sloshing nearby, she didn't think of Joshua walking into the water . . . falling in . . . calling for her once, twice, before disappearing forever.)

No. He was here. Or back at the house.

She admitted no other possibilities.

She dug her knee into the ground and moved forward with a grunt. A strong barb caught her shoulder, digging deep.

"Ow," she said, whimpering. She tried to lower her body to free herself from the barb, but it seemed stuck. She brought her left hand back and reached behind her. She grabbed the mesh, and seeing no other choice, she pushed it away. The metal spike pulled through her skin, tearing it. She felt the blood trickle down her side, tiny rivulets dropping to the ground.

Then forward again, until she was almost free, almost on the other side.

She felt something move.

Below her.

A tickling sensation at first, almost pleasant. A gentle vibration under her prone body. She heard more popping sounds, quiet noises, like the sound summer puffballs make when you squeeze the bulbs, releasing thousands of spores into the daylight.

The popping seemed to pick up intensity, and she started moving forward.

Then the tickling turned into a rougher movement, something snaking out from under her. She looked at her left hand.

It was lying flat on the ground, palm down, surrounded by the tiny blackish fungi, ugly dotlike things. She watched them pop open then, and after a pause snaky tendrils came out and crawled over her hand. Then along her arm, and her other arm. She raised her head a few inches above the muck and looked to her left and to her right.

The ground near her was filled with thousands of them. She watched them open up—dozens of tendrils waving in the air, hesitating for a moment before falling onto her face, her neck.

(And, sweet God, all along her body.)

"Please," she prayed. She tried to move backward, out from under the mesh. But her struggling did nothing.

The tendrils landed and pulled her down to the ground, real close. And the popping went on, until the noise grew horrible and the tendrils crisscrossed her face in layers, and all her horror-struck eyes could see was a tiny chink in the weblike lattice that now covered her face.

She moaned. She tried to scream, but the tiny vines that covered her mouth congealed, growing into a rigid cast that reduced her to inchoate mumblings.

One nostril was still open enough to suck in desperate snorts of air. Then more tendrils landed, and there was nothing.

Her muscles quivered against the ground. Her legs, arms, chest all spasmed uncontrollably.

The tiny black threads tightened just a bit more.

Then all was still again.

Dan went to the door. The minuscule fish-eye lens gave him a distorted fun-house view of the parking lot. Whoever was there stood to the side, just out of sight.

He took a breath and opened the door. And saw Billy Leeper.

"Hi, Dan. I hope I didn't wake you or anything."

Dan let his breath out. Leeper stood in the yellowish glow of the motel's parking-lot lamps. Big winged moths, not deterred, darted around the doorway.

"You gave me a start, Bill. I'll say that." Dan opened the door all the way. "I've been plowing through your notebooks. . . . I guess they're getting me a tad edgy."

Leeper walked past Dan into the room, looking at the notebooks on the bed, then at Dan's diving gear. "That's why I came. Believe me, I didn't want to."

Dan shut the door. "I was just beginning to wonder if I'd ever get the story pieced together."

Leeper nodded.

"Drink?" Dan asked.

Leeper smiled. "Never touch the stuff." He tapped his skull. "I like being aware all the time."

"Sure," Dan said, pouring himself another drink. "Me, there's plenty of times I'd prefer not being aware. Have a seat," he said, gesturing to an ugly green chair standing incongruously near his diving gear.

He saw Leeper dig into his shirt pocket and pull out a crumpled photo. "I'd prefer to stand, thank you. It's been a long drive from Montauk, sitting on my behind. I found this . . . a couple of hours after you left. Must have come loose, slid behind the shelf." Leeper handed him the photo. "Maybe it was fate," he said, laughing.

Dan unfolded it. It was a professionally done portrait of a young man—thirty, thirty-five years old, dressed in a gray pin-striped suit. His dark hair was slicked back, and a cigarette was held for effect. The man in the picture had a confident, powerful smile as he looked right at the camera.

"Nice picture. Who is it?"

Leeper walked over to the bed and picked up one of the notebooks. He flipped it open to a page and pointed.

"The photo belongs right here." He pointed to the page with the question mark.

"The fifth man," Dan said. "I was wondering what happened to it."

Leeper was nervous, pacing the room with the notebook held tight in his hand. "The fifth man." He smiled. "You know, for a long time I didn't know who the hell he was. He covered his tracks real well. Records removed, editions of the paper missing, but I found out, years later, of course, who he was."

(Once again Dan wondered about Leeper's sanity. He was a man obsessed, completely absorbed.)

"And?"

Leeper grinned proudly. "Why, he's the one that got away, Dan . . . a lawyer, wouldn't you know it. Mr. Martin Parks, Esquire."

Dan sat down on the bed. "I'm afraid you're losing me, Bill. I've another eight notebooks or so to go, and although I feel something strange going on here, I haven't a damn clue as to what it might be."

"Tired?" Leeper asked.

Dan shook his head. "Not at all."

"You know, I probably knew all along I'd end up here . . . as much as I didn't want to. Sometimes there are jobs you just gotta do . . . no matter how much you want them to go away."

He paused and walked over to the picture window. He pulled back the curtain.

"So that's why I'm here. But if I'm going to tell you the story, Dan, I'm going to tell it to you on the move. C'mon, let's take a drive."

"Now? I'm not so sure I'm in any condition to—"

"I'll drive. You just listen. But no more drinking, friend. Your turn comes later." Leeper walked over and pressed a hand on Dan's shoulder. "You see, you, too, got a job dropped in your lap, Dan. And I'm afraid it just won't go away."

It was Thursday morning. Two A.M.

Joshua curled up tightly, pulling his Popple—half basketball and half furry alien—sleepily to his face.

For some reason the hard floor felt comfortable. He had climbed down from his loft bed and had arranged the sleeping bag over his body like a tent.

He hadn't heard his mother come into his room, pat his bed, then quickly run out. So he slept peacefully here, in the dark, in the corner of his room, till dawn.

"It started, hard to believe, as a club."

They were in Leeper's jeep, a shabby-looking relic that moved along the Taconic Parkway, heading upstate with surprising speed.

Dan sat back in the passenger seat, his window wide open.

"There were five of them . . . pillars of the community and all that. I don't know how it actually started, but they got together to talk about the future of Gouldens Falls. At least that's what they did at first."

Dan looked at Leeper, his eyes on the road, but also looking beyond, out to something else.

"Just a bunch of town boosters they were, Dr. Samuel Hustis, Thomas Raine, Jonathan Reynolds, Wallace Pfister, and the fifth man—Martin Parks. Took me a while to find him. They were sort of like the Kiwanis or something."

"Sounds pretty harmless." There was no real traffic on the highway, only an occasional car heading south. The full moon gave shape to the gentle curve of the hills.

"And it was. Until 1934. That's when Dr. Samuel Hustis

met some doctors in Manhattan, wealthy society doctors studying some new methods in medicine, some kind of mental-healing mumbo jumbo. Dr. Hustis got involved with them. And through them he met Aleister Crowley."

"Crowley? That rings a bell. Should I know him?"

"That depends, Dan. Crowley was the world's authority on black magic and the occult in the twenties and thirties. His nickname was the Great Beast."

"Oh, brother."

Leeper looked over to him. "He was a master of the 'dark art,' as Crowley called it. He was considered—still is, actually—to be a harmless crackpot. He wrote a lot of books, sacrificed some goats with his jaded London followers. When he died, he was a quaint relic of a more gullible era."

"So how does he connect with the Club?"

"Dr. Hustis met him, read his work, and then went further. He was a brilliant man, and he tried things Crowley only talked about. He spent a summer in Europe researching books only rumored to exist, and when he came back, he started talking to the Club. They became interested in his strange pursuit."

"They bought all that stuff?"

"Not at first. Who would? But he did something that convinced them."

"What?"

"It's in the third notebook, June 8,1934."

Dan tried to remember—so many yellowed clippings. "I don't—"

"Parker Finney. Town drunk. Accidentally shot himself. The wound was fatal, and he should have died in minutes." Leeper paused. "Only Hustis got to him, and whatever he did, it saved his life and convinced his friends to devote themselves to this new 'science.' "

Dan laughed. "I don't know. It seems a bit farfetched. More strange tales from the Hudson Valley and all that."

"Let me finish. At first the Club used their new toy—whatever it was—to help people. Farmers prospered, babies recovered from the flu, boom time for Gouldens Falls. But there was a price for all these good things, and slowly some of the townspeople became aware of that price."

"Price? What kind of price?"

Leeper shook his head. "I don't know. Not for sure. All I could find out was that some of the townspeople just disappeared. Dozens of lifelong parishioners stopped going to Reverend Passworthy's church. Then some Gouldens Falls people, Arnold and Jim Browder, were arrested in Pennsylvania. They had a young couple tied up with ropes and gagged in the back of their truck."

"What the hell for?"

"The papers didn't say anything . . . didn't even speculate. They just treated the Browders as a pair of crazies on some kind of rampage." Leeper pulled off an exit ramp. The sign read SHOOTERS HILL ROAD, and it ended in a dark crossroads with only a boarded-up house perched on a nearby field.

Too damned strange, Dan thought. Driving along this deserted road, the moon looking positively alien, and mad Billy Leeper ('cause Leeper might just actually be crazy) talking about weirdness from the thirties.

Leeper stopped the jeep. Then he killed the lights.

"Don't want any state trooper bothering us. Just need a break before I take us back." Leeper looked up at the moon. "So I went to get the police report from the Buck Hill County police records bureau. It cost me a hundred dollars under the table," he said with a laugh. "But it told me more than I wanted to know."

Dan heard a car approaching from behind them, the hum of its engine rising as it reached them, then falling off quickly as it streamed off.

"The Browders babbled out some crazy story about the Club, something about the city paying them back. The report said they seemed more scared of Hustis and his friends than the police."

"And what did the police do?"

"They notified the Gouldens Falls police, of course, and locked the Browders up. Three days later the brothers hanged themselves—side by side—in the same cell."

Leeper fiddled around in the glove compartment of his jeep and pulled out his pipe.

"It's all in the notebooks, Dan. You could read it yourself . . . if there was time. Even after that I still didn't know what was going on, not really, and how it would end."

He filled his pipe with some sweet-smelling tobacco and lit it. Pungent smoke filled the small cabin of the jeep.

"For that part of the story I had to track down Reverend Duncan Passworthy." Leeper looked right at Dan, his eyes glowing now. "He was on my list of old Gouldens Falls people—the ones still alive—to speak to. I didn't know if he was living. I found him in a Lutheran nursing home in northern New Jersey. At first he wouldn't talk to me about the town, the dam, anything. When he found out who I was, he told me just enough to scare the hell out of me."

Leeper paused. "It was the worst thirty minutes I ever spent with anyone."

Dan licked his lips.

"Passworthy said the Club owned the town. Completely. What started as a friendly group soon bred fear and terror in everyone. Those who didn't do as the Club said, had unfortunate 'accidents.' You've seen the clips. Passworthy's church became a ghostly shell. Nobody would risk coming. He feared for his life. Slowly Passworthy started meeting with a few other people . . . a handful of brave souls. They had secret meetings, with each of them deathly afraid that the Club would find out . . . and afraid of what the Club would do to them."

"Nasty group."

"There's more. Passworthy said that Gouldens Falls was supposed to be the first town . . . the first of many."

Dan stuck his head out the window a bit, gulping in the fresh air. "And Passworthy and his friends stopped them?"

"Yes. But he wouldn't tell me how. He only said that the reservoir was planned to bury many things . . . many things. They convinced the governor in Albany to help them, and he ran the project through all the red tape."

"Did they kill them, the Club?"

"He told me only two more things, two things I'm going to tell you now, Dan." Leeper puffed on his pipe, the bulb glowing a fiery red. "He said he put his story in a diary—telling everything. Underneath the nave of his church. Buried with the town. With everything. It's under the third stone from the north wall."

"Not exactly a handy location, under a couple million gallons of water."

"And Passworthy said something else. He said that they failed. That they didn't end it. Because. Dan, one person got away. Passworthy said if he ever came back, it would start all over again. Maybe worse than ever before."

Leeper started the jeep, startling Dan. He edged it forward, turned left, and took it onto the ramp leading to the Taconic Parkway south.

"He's back, Dan. The last member of the Club. Martin Parks. And that's why all this is happening. And," Leeper said, giving him an uncomfortable grin, "I'm afraid you'll have to get that diary."

SEVENTEEN

Sometimes, Dan thought, you get your wish.

After all, he actually wanted to dive down to the sunken town— yeah, because he wanted the story behind its inundation.

Now his wishes had been granted. And what better story than some mysterious diary buried for fifty years under a lake?

He lowered his battered tanks gently into the back of his Rover. It wouldn't do to go waking up his neighbors in the motel. Leeper sat inside Dan's room, on the bed, sketching an old map of the town, indicating just where the church was.

It was all so strange. Like giving directions to Aunt Mathilde's. Just make a left at the drugstore and keep on going until you see a graveyard. Can't miss it, chum, even under a couple hundred feet of water.

The moonlight made his scratched-up yellow tanks look iridescent. He would have liked to have been using Tom and Ed's gear, top-notch stuff. And the radio—damn, that would have made him feel a whole lot better.

(After all, we're talking about a lake that has a penchant for making people disappear.)

But at least he had Russo.

That was an amazing stroke of luck. The police had told Dan that Russo was staying at a friend's house. They gave Dan no trouble about giving him the number. He knew that Russo had taken Ed's and Tom's drowning's bad. Susan said Rogers had to order him to stop patrolling the waters looking for a sign of them.

So it didn't take much for Dan to convince him that it was worth their while to go out, before dawn, and continue looking for them.

The cops on the shore probably wouldn't question Russo. After all, they had already seen Dan with the other two divers.

He didn't, to be sure, tell Russo anything else—not a word about the Club, the diary, and the other ravings of Billy Leeper. That would have been a sure way to lose Russo's help. Let him think that they were just going to look for the now surely dead divers.

That's all.

As for the other stuff . . . well, even he wasn't sure how much he believed. It wouldn't be the first time a group took over a town—conservative businessmen do that all across middle America. And Dan knew that interest in cults became something of a fad in the twenties and thirties.

But even if one of the leaders of the cult got away, how could it have anything to do with this?

Dan wanted to doubt, wanted to look at it as if it were just another weird tale, a new folk legend from the misty hills of the Hudson Valley.

More likely there was some kind of current—a freaky, periodic swirling movement in the water. A whirlpool that pulled down Tommy Fluhr, then the divers, pinning their bodies somewhere . . . down there.

(And what of Fred . . . all chopped into sections? How does he fit that theory?)

No theory is perfect, he told himself.

He checked that the tanks were securely positioned on the small, flat bed of the Rover, and he walked back into the room.

"All set," he said.

Leeper looked tired and shaken. He handed Dan the map. "Let's go over it," Leeper said.

It was five A.M.

James Morton stood in the roadway of the dam, looking and listening for the sound of a truck. The repair crew had been due fifteen minutes ago, and he hoped that his directions hadn't been too confusing.

His wife always said, laughing good-naturedly at him, he'd have trouble giving directions to go around the block. Just a darn tendency of his to mix up his right and left. Ambidextrous, he called it.

Just as he was about to go look for a phone and call his office, he heard the truck. They stopped at the police barricade with the sign announcing that the roadway was TEMPORARILY CLOSED DUE TO CONSTRUCTION and flashed their lights at Morton. He gave them a wave, ran over to the gray New York State Public Works truck. The crew consisted of two long-haired young men dressed in T-shirts and jeans, and Stu Schmidt, completely bald, built like a wrestler, and dressed in an immaculate olive uniform. His voice was jarringly loud and assured for such an early hour.

"Had to wait for one of these young fellows to get his ass out of bed," Schmidt said. He stepped down from the cab and stuck out his hand to Morton. "Good to see you again, Jimmy. So what do we have there?"

The two young men sleepily unloaded pipes and hoses

from the back of the truck, laying them out carefully on the road.

Morton led Schmidt around the barrier, toward the roadway, and down to the dam's interior.

"It's a bad leak, Stu—a couple of feet of water at the base, with an additional fifty gallons an hour pouring in."

Schmidt whistled. "That's no little drip."

"Fortunately it's easy to get to, and the dam still has electricity all the way down."

"Good thing." Schmidt gestured at the platforms in the roadway. "What's all this crap?"

"The town's celebrating the dam's construction this week, if you can believe it. Speakers, fireworks, picnics, all that stuff. You see, you're sort of the cavalry coming to the rescue."

"What else is new?" Schmidt laughed. "Well, we'll do our best, Jimmy. The cement trucks will be here around noon. If all goes well, we'll be able to give your dam a clean bill of health by Millertime."

"Good," Morton said. Then he hesitated a moment. "There's one other thing I should tell you . . . though it's not really a factor now."

"And just what might that be?"

"They had an earthquake here Monday . . . about a five or six on the Richter scale. Might have shaken things up a bit down there. I thought you should know."

They reached the heavy metal door leading inside the dam wall. Morton unlocked it and pulled back on the handle.

"Well, thanks for that bit of comforting information, Jimmy. You won't mind if I don't tell my boys about that." He smiled "They tend to get fidgety enough as it is."

Morton grinned back and led the broad and burly Schmidt through the narrow doorway.

Dan loaded the small police boat, feeling a bit like a school kid playing a prank. Russo's no-nonsense attitude certainly helped them bulldoze their way past the two cops on duty. One cop wanted to tell Chief Rogers, wake him up and check out if it was okay. Russo simply gave him a withering stare and shrugged.

"If you want to wake your Chief up just to see if we can help look for my partners, you go right ahead. Don't blame me if he rips your head off."

Russo knew he technically outranked them, and they both remembered seeing Dan on the first day.

"Okay," one of them said, hedging. "We'll check later."

"In the meantime we're going to do some searching," Russo declared, pushing past them.

Dan saw some workers on the roadway, unloading heavy equipment from the back of the truck.

About time they got to that leak. And he remembered Fred leading him down the dungeonlike stairs.

"Let's go," Russo said in a voice that brooked no disagreement, and he helped Dan finish loading his diving equipment into the boat.

Billy Leeper stood there oddly frozen, just watching them and looking at the lake.

Dan looked over at him, curious at Leeper's sudden, strange silence. "You okay, Billy? Anything wrong?"

Leeper shook his head.

Than Dan recognized the obvious. Something he should have known. *It's the first time Leeper's been here in fifty years.*

Fifty years. And he must feel like the boy he once was . . . scared, oh, so scared.

"Bill . . . you all right?"

"Yes. It's just—you know—strange."

Dan nodded. He bet it was. Down there was his hometown . . . down there was Jackie Weeks . . . down . . . down . . .

Leeper turned away. Dan thought he heard something, a sound like crying. He stepped out of the boat and went to Leeper. He put his arm around him and, in an unnatural gesture for him, pulled the old man close.

"I didn't expect this," Leeper said, looking out at the lake. "The feelings, the memories. It's all too much. I shouldn't have come."

"I don't know about that. Without you we'd know nothing."

"Let's go, Dan," Russo said.

The sky had faded to a lighter gray. A faint tinge of pink in the east signaled sunrise. Dan wanted to get going before someone showed up on the scene to stop them. "Okay," he said.

Leeper turned and stuck the map in his hand. "Take another look at it before you go down. It's going to be mighty confusing."

"I bet."

Dan got to the boat, and Russo quickly untied it. The small inboard motor broke the early-morning quiet. He brought it to a spot only a hundred yards away from shore.

"How about a bit farther out, Jack, a bit north?"

Russo had stopped the boat and flipped on the sonar. He'd been a pretty somber fellow before, but now, Dan thought, he was absolutely morose. "No. This is where I lost contact with them. If we're gonna look for them, this is where we'll start." The small sonar screen came to life.

"Yeah, but if some kind of current got them, I thought it would be good—"

Russo shook his head. "We'll start *here*."

Okay, Dan thought. It's your boat.

He peeled off his T-shirt—gooseflesh rising—and pulled on his wet suit. There were a few cracks in the rubbery suit that exposed his skin to the water. The fins felt slimy, almost lizardlike.

"Give me a hand with these tanks," Dan said.

Russo picked up the twin tanks and held them while Dan put his arms through the straps.

"Good," he said, and he pulled the straps in front of him, making everything tight before buckling it. He reached down and picked up his weight belt.

"Wish we had that radio," Russo said.

"You and me both." Dan put his face mask on his forehead and gave his regulator a test by sucking on it.

"All set?" Russo asked.

Dan nodded. He slipped the mask down and sat on the edge of the boat.

(*Fool. Why the hell am I doing this? Never was one for good judgment.*)

He glanced over at Billy Leeper, standing on the shore, looking suddenly so all alone. The two cops were in the roadway talking to the crew working there.

And he was *worried*. But not for himself.

For that old man who shouldn't have come back here.

He flipped himself back, curling sleekly into the water.

Joshua woke up all in an instant and did what he did every morning. He left his room quietly, moved even more quietly past his mother's bedroom, and walked down to the family room. And the TV.

If he did it all quietly enough—just like a mouse—he'd get to watch cartoons, maybe two shows before his mom woke up. *Thundercats,* then *GI Joe*—his favorite.

Except his mom hated the show, actually told him that. "I hate that program. It's just a bunch of stupid violence."

He didn't know what violence was, but if it was what made *GI Joe* so super, he was all for it.

He sat Indian-style in front of the TV, enjoying the toy and candy commercials almost as much as the program.

It wasn't until *Thundercats* ended that he noticed that

the great sliding door leading to the backyard wasn't quite right. No, for one thing, the funny red light was off. Usually his mom did that, flipping it off as she said, "No more TV, mister."

And the door was open. Just a crack. But the light showed green.

A few thoughts ran through his head. Was his mom up already? Or maybe his sister was up? Or . . . or . . .

But then *GI Joe* began with the Joe Team blowing up one of Cobra's sky tanks, and Joshua gave up on the problem.

When *Joe* ended—and he still hadn't heard his mom walking around upstairs—he became a little curious. He got up during a *Jem, Queen of the Teenage Rockers* commercial—yuck!—and walked over to the sliding door. Outside, it was foggy and misty, like in one of his dad's spooky movies that he wouldn't let Joshua watch. He could barely make out the trees, and the backyard looked cold and wet.

He put all his weight against the door. It didn't want to move, but he dug his small feet into the tightly woven rug and pushed even harder. It jerked forward an inch or two.

But it wouldn't close.

And all of a sudden Joshua wanted to find his mom. He ran upstairs, calling her name, his voice growing louder with each step.

(All the time expecting her to just be there, a frown on her saying, "Josh, what have you been watching?")

"Mom!" He reached the hall and ran to her room. Her door was open and her bed empty. She's up real early today, he thought. Real early.

"Mom," he said now, quietly. "Mommy?"

The house was still.

Then he heard voices from downstairs. He took a step out of the room. Right into someone.

"Josh, what's all the noise, for Pete's sake? You woke me up."

"Where's Mom?" he demanded of his sister.

"Mom? You probably woke her up, you ding-dong. Mom?" she said quietly, peering into the empty room.

Samantha looked at the bed, then at Joshua. "You're going to get it from her, buster." She turned sharply around and walked away from Joshua.

He watched his sister enter the kitchen, throw the light on, her voice now calling out loudly, "Mommy!" When no one answered, she turned back to Joshua.

He walked down the hall slowly, the TV's voices from downstairs growing louder.

"The door downstairs was open," he said, biting his lower lip, not liking the way his sister's face looked. "It was open, and the red light was off."

Samantha came close to him, and he was glad.

He looked up at her, not really so much taller despite her two years.

"We should," he said slowly, "go look for her."

Samantha took his hand.

Claire was up early and in her mother's room, negotiating even before her mother had her eyes open.

"Mom, I won't be any problem. I'll bring along tons of books and I'll sit in the car if you want me to and . . ."

Her mother crawled out of bed, looking past Claire as she made her way to the bathroom. She shut the door, and Claire came behind it and raised her voice a bit to get past the wood.

"So what do you think? Can I go with you today? Skip camp? Huh? Huh?"

"Claire, can't I pee in peace?"

"Sure," Claire yelled back. "Sorry, Mom."

She backed away from the door a token few feet and waited for Susan to come out again. She heard the toilet flush, then the sound of water running in the sink. After an eternity or two, her mother came out, her eyes now open and staring right at Claire.

"Not today. Besides, I paid a lot of money for that camp, which I'm not about to see wasted."

Her mother breezed past her and rattled around the closet for some clothes. Claire never tired of watching her mother dress—the way she went from some crumpled, hot, frizzy-haired sleeping monster into someone beautiful.

I'll never be like that, she knew, *no matter how many times I watch.*

And she knew she wouldn't tell her mom the reason—the real reason—why she didn't want to go to camp. That worried look was in her mother's eyes a lot lately, whenever they talked of Claire's dreams.

How could she tell her this, that the lake at the Kenicut Reservoir was the same lake? The same lake from her dream! And that she knew, really knew, that it was dangerous.

(Did she sleep last night? she wondered. Did it touch her as she slept?)

She didn't want her mother going there alone. No, she was wise to the lake and its tricks now . . . the way it had almost snagged Joshua. The way it had probably snagged the others.

And it wasn't going to get her mother.

No way.

"I'm sorry, Claire, but I'll be talking to people all day, the police, other people. It wouldn't be right."

Claire began to perform. First a simple tear formed and rolled down her cheek. Then it became easier. "But . . . but I'll be scared to be away from you. I'm so scared by my dreams, Mom. Please don't make me go to camp."

Her mother took a step closer and ran her hand along her daughter's cheek, catching a tear. "Claire, baby, don't. They're just dreams . . . just silly—"

Claire threw herself at her mother. She clutched her tightly, sobbing now, on cue. *She'd have to be the witch from "Hansel and Gretel" to send me away now.*

"Stay home," Claire pleaded.

"I . . . can't, honey. I'm writing a big story."

She looked up at her mother's face. "Then take me with you."

Her mother looked right back, her eyes filled with a funny pain. They were all milky and confused. She ran her hand through Claire's hair.

"Okay, sweetheart, you can come." She pulled Claire tight, squeezing her in a great bear hug. "You can come," she held Claire away. "But I warn you, it's going to be mighty boring, and you'll be stuck inside the car a lot."

"Well, at least we can do lunch together," Claire said, permitting herself a small grin.

Her mother smiled back. "Yes, we can 'do lunch.' Now go pick out something nice to wear."

"I'll be back in a few minutes," Claire said, running to her room.

There, she thought. For the first time she could breathe almost normally. *There. At least I'll be able to save my mom.*

It was everyone else that was in danger now.

Herbert Blount was an early riser. In fact, on the regular mental-health days he took off from his job, he'd often sleep in until eleven, or, God, even twelve.

So now why the hell was he up at seven A.M.?

He stepped out onto his porch. He sipped his coffee, stronger than his wife would ever make it. Just a small sip, savoring the warm, burning sensation on his lips, his tongue, and then down his throat. It was nice and hot.

And that's when he noticed it.

Not the dam, though they seemed pretty active up there for so early an hour. The banner was nearly completed. (Just the word FALLS was missing, the year 1989, and the last few letters of the word CELEBRATION. Then it would be all done, as big as a building.) And there seemed to be workers moving stuff from a truck onto the dam.

More paraphernalia for the celebration, he figured.

But that's not what he found, well, peculiar.

It was *cool.*

Sure it could be a little cool, up here away from the city, on a midsummer's morning. It happens. But by seven the sun—even through the clouds—usually had things warmed up a bit. And the weather report for Westchester, which he watched every night on the Weather Channel, was for a real hot, muggy day. Overcast and humid.

Except that it seemed damn cool out here, standing on his porch. He almost could use a sweater.

But despite the chill, he just sat down on his Adirondack chair, sipped his scalding coffee, and watched the curious activity on top of the wall of the Kenicut Dam.

PART THREE

EIGHTEEN

"You haven't eaten a thing." Edith Rogers sat down at her small butcher-block kitchen table, facing her husband. "It's just not like you to skip breakfast."

Paddy Rogers pushed his chair away from the table, away from his I-can't-believe-it-'s-not-buttered toast, melon, and bowl of Special K. He took a sip of his coffee.

"Just not hungry. Not today."

He hoped his wife would back away, just let him sit there a few more minutes, think about things, try to figure something out.

She had a napkin all twisted in a knot around her bony, wrinkled hands—once so soft and beautiful, now ravaged by arthritis that she rarely complained about.

She'll always be young and beautiful to me, he thought. *Always.*

But now he needed just to sit and stew.

"I've got no appetite," he said, managing a weak grin. "Don't worry, I'll make up for it tonight."

She smiled back, but her napkin made another loop

through the web of her fingers. "Then take your vitamins, at least."

He nodded and picked up the assortment of containers, popping down the chunky megavitamins. "I don't like to see you so . . . so preoccupied."

Is that what I am? he wondered.

Preoccupied? With what? With retiring and getting away from this town I've worked in for over twenty-five years? Migrating down to Florida. The good life. Preoccupied? Or afraid?

Ellerton has been a quiet town, sleepy and easy to protect. The bad things he'd known in the city just never traveled up here. Many a day he'd ride through the sleepy streets of Ellerton and marvel at the whole range of horrors that just never made it to suburbia.

He looked at Edith. She had had a quiet life, and she expected to retire quietly, slipping into the peaceful routine of the "golden years."

Except that things were different now. Yes, now a little problem had fallen right in his lap. When people disappear in a small town, it's the police chief 's job.

His job.

And he wasn't sure he had the stomach for it.

The phone rang, jarring him out of his reverie.

"Should I get it?" his wife asked.

He shook his head and reached behind him for the pale blue wall phone.

"Hello," he said, his voice still flat and distant. "Yes, Bob," he said, recognizing the young cop's voice.

"Chief, we waited until we were sure you were up. Sergeant Russo went back onto the lake this morning. . . . He had that fellow from the first dive with him."

The writer, Rogers remembered. "And why the hell did you let them go?"

"He said it was okay, that you knew. They were going to search for the other two divers."

"Great. Now maybe we'll lose some more people." Rogers stood up. "When they come back out, don't let them leave. Arrest them if you have to. Just hold them there. I'll be over there in fifteen, twenty minutes. And, Bob, do me a favor. Don't let anyone else out there unless you see a written order from me."

He slapped down the receiver.

His wife was clearing away the untouched plates of food.

He walked over to her and put an arm around her. "I've got to go over to the dam, Edith. I've got a feeling it's going to be a long day."

"Call me," she said.

He pulled her close, hugging her hard. "Do I ever forget? Ever?" he said, looking right at her eyes.

Then he smiled and turned and walked out to his patrol car.

It's a cool morning, he thought, reaching the open air.

Almost nippy.

For days Emily Powers didn't let herself think about it.

No, every time she thought about that night she just told herself, "Stop." And literally forced her mind to think of something—anything—else. Except that morning it wasn't working.

Sure she prayed for Tommy Fluhr, really prayed. But she didn't let any creepy pictures into her head . . . pictures of Tommy swimming, getting a cramp, calling out for her—

"Emily! Emily!"

Calls that she didn't hear, plodding back to the car, ready to sulk and pout, making Tommy apologize for being so rude, so nasty.

But then he didn't come. And she had waited, listening to the deep hum of the cars and trucks as they barreled along the two-lane highway.

At first she just fumed, getting angrier and angrier at the obnoxious Tommy, who kept on swimming when their picnic was so obviously over. She thought of hitching a ride home (but that, of course, conjured up other images . . . images of even uglier things than fending off Tommy's horny advances).

So she just got out and stormed back through the opening in the fence, back to their spot, calling out his name even before she could see the water.

"Tommy, Tommy Fluhr?"

He wasn't there. At first she assumed he was hiding, a prankster playing tricks, ducking under the water, peering out from behind a tree. You know boys.

But she noticed the towels and the blanket, just as she had left them.

He hadn't come out of the water.

She looked out at the lake.

It was still, dark now, bluish-black with the coming of night.

"Tommy . . ." she had whispered.

And the nightmare began, the running through the woods, branches reaching out, scraping her skin, her face, while she whimpered. That was the only time she let the image of Tommy—gasping, grimly flailing at the water—enter her consciousness. It was also the only time she admitted, *accepted*, the terrible guilt.

If only I had stayed, he'd be alive. 1 could have saved him.

In a fog, she had flagged down a Ford four-by-four and took a ride with a beer-toting kid who, from his grinning face, couldn't believe his luck. But her choking story about her boyfriend straightened the driver right out. He quickly dropped her off at the Ellerton police station.

After that she prayed and forced herself to think of anything else.

Anything. Except the guilt. And the picture of Tommy under water.

But that morning it was all there for her. Not to be ignored. And somehow it wasn't all that horrid. There was an almost poignant sadness in Tommy's death. It was a tragedy—the young boy who died with his love un . . . un . . .

She searched for the word that Mr. Winan had used in his English class, talking of young Romeo.

Unrequited.

That's when she knew what she'd do that day. She wouldn't tell anyone. Not a soul. That would mar the beauty, the simplicity of her gesture. She'd bring flowers, not from the store but gathered from around the town's parks and gardens. Flowers from his home. She'd bring the flowers to their spot, right to the secluded place where she'd last seen Tommy. And she'd throw them in one by one, into the water.

A private memorial.

Just for her, and Tommy.

Slowly Billy Leeper found it easier to look at the lake.

At first it overwhelmed him with a tidal wave of memories. Biking with Jackie up to the Lakeview Hotel, where they would fish the small Kenicut Lake until someone from the hotel would come out and chase them away.

"And don't come back!" the caretaker would yell.

But they did, nearly every day of the summer, talking about the universe of things that boys value. What's a good knife? How quick would it take the U.S. to lick the Germans or the Japs? (Never knowing that Uncle Sam would have to take them on together.) Swapping comic books and debating whether this new crime fighter, Superman, would make it big.

Billy smiled a bit, thinking of those talks.

And rainy days, God, the hours they spent at the Glenwood, their Keds propped up on the seats in front of them, wolfing down popcorn and Junior Mints. (With more high-level discussions of just how was Buck Rogers going to get out of his latest impossible jam.)

A childhood gone forever, leaving only fragments, tiny traces of thought.

But his nostalgia faded—quickly, as if it were a false reaction—and Billy felt cold.

He rolled down his shirt sleeve over his powerful arms.

The house is down there. Sitting and rotting under the water. The bloodstained floorboards. The twisting hallway. The stairs leading to an ever darker basement.

(And what else, Billy? What else?)

He was here now. As much as he hoped and prayed that he'd never have to do this, he knew it was almost inevitable.

Fated.

Sixty-three years old.

A long enough life, he supposed. But he wasn't doing this for Dan or any of them—what do they call them?—yuppies who lived in Ellerton. That's not who he came back to this town to help.

(It's for you, Jackie, he thought. Unfinished business. Accounts to be balanced.)

He rubbed the grizzly beard sprouting on his cheek.

He watched Jack Russo crouched in the back of the small boat.

And if he hadn't been so lost in his thoughts, he might have noticed that someone was watching *him*.

For the first few minutes it was no different than any other morning dive. Cold water touched the small bits of his exposed skin. That first disconcerting moment when up and down seemed a tad indefinite. Then the soothing, almost primeval feeling of kicking, froglike, straight down.

And for a while he didn't see anything too strange. After all, his tungsten lamp only projected a beam fifteen, maybe twenty feet ahead. For all Dan knew, the story of a town down here was an enormous hoax, a local fable to drag suckers to the reservoir to look out at the water and imagine the buildings (and the stories) beneath such still waters.

But then the first shapes appeared, a hulking corner of a building that nearly clipped him on his left shoulder, and then a flat rooftop pockmarked with holes, and a yawning valley of what—unbelievably enough—had to be Main Street.

His equipment was performing fine. (He just wished he had a radio so he could talk to Russo—some chitchat and directions would be more than welcome.)

But he was alone.

He concentrated on following the directions to the church—straight north up Main Street, then right, onto Lakeview Road, toward the church. How thoughtful of them to put street signs down here!

And he thought of Tom and Ed. (He didn't want to find them. Not at all. Leave that for the guys with the body bags . . . the people who could fish someone out of the water and make jokes—jokes!—about the puffy, "dough-boy" look caused by all that gas building up in the corpse.)

He barely looked left or right, just enough to notice some of the signs, all encrusted with algae but still easily readable. The Gouldens Falls Post Office (no zip code here), F. W. Woolworth's, a red sign gone to a sickly greenish-brown, and the movie theater (he swam especially fast past that).

Until he reached Lakeview Road.

At first all the landmarks seemed to disappear. This was, according to the map, the end of the town. But even as he slowed and moved ahead more cautiously, he picked up some steps, leading to a massive veranda. It was the hotel.

Closed for renovation.

The church had to be close, just past the hotel, and up a slight hill.

He found himself lower to the ground (lower than he

wanted to be), and he reached the gentle grade of an incline. He kicked away violently.

I'm swimming uphill, he thought.

Over the murky deposit of years of dead leaves and trash.

The church appeared out of the water like a gray phantom.

He was glad to see it.

(Somehow it felt better here, even with the small building all boarded up and its steeple nibbled down to a blunt stub. There was no cross anywhere in sight. Still, it was a church.)

He circled the building, past the sign listing Reverend Duncan Passworthy as rector. He looked for some entrance. But the doors were crisscrossed with heavy two-by-fours, and the windows—the stained glass probably long gone—were covered with sheets of wood. *Damn. I could probably rip the door down,* he thought. *But how long would it take? Do I have enough air to struggle with the wooden cross beams and still do what I have to do?*

He checked his oxygen gauge. The pressure was down to nearly a half. Another thirty minutes or so left and he'd have to be on the surface. He wished Jack had gone closer to the church (but he had to give him the idea that he was looking for Tom and Ed, at least *somewhere* near where they were lost).

He went to the front door and pulled at one of the two-by-fours. After fifty years they should be a bit loose.

He tugged, pulling hard while his flippered feet pushed against the door. The wood struts didn't move a bit.

Nothing like old-fashioned craftsmanship.

He aimed his lamp upward to look for another possible way in (or maybe guidance from heaven). He saw the steeple. It was riddled with small holes. Perhaps he could widen one of them and work his way through. Or there was the top itself, open.

If it was big enough. *If* it was clear down to the church.

He kicked up. (*I'm breathing hard. Too damn hard, using up my air too quickly. Gotta calm down. Relax, don't worry—)*

Right. Sure.

No fuckin' problem.

He glided past the sealed windows, along the steeple, checking at the holes as he passed (all of them too small).

Catching glimpses of eyes—furtive, dotlike eyes watching his progress. The fish were about to have their hiding place disturbed.

He reached the top of the steeple.

It was open. Clear.

(Lucky me.)

He stuck the lamp in and aimed down.

It was unobstructed as far as the light carried.

Unfortunately all it showed was something that looked like a black hole.

He grabbed some of the wood girding the hole and snapped it back. A few chunks broke off, then a few more, until Dan thought it was wide enough.

(Like going into a mouse hole.)

He kicked around and stuck his hands in, the lamp held out in front, and slowly kicked forward.

Almost immediately his tanks got caught up in the hole. He twisted left and right. It had looked big enough, dammit. And he wasn't wearing fat tanks designed for an all-day excursion. He reached out to feel for something to pull himself through. But the walls, sharply arching away, were smooth.

He wriggled around, stuck in that hole, caught. He breathed even more heavily, his chest rising and falling. His hands continued to grope until he found a hole.

Great. Now if I can just pull myself through.

With only one hand free, it was difficult. But he strained, and with a sudden lurch he slid into the steeple.

He saw some fish scurry away. He moved straight down, trying to remember . . . what the hell is a church like?

(It *had* been a while.)

He couldn't see anything.

Then the faintest outline of—

A floor. Heavy stones. But no pews. (Gone to some other church, most likely.) No altar. (Ditto.)

No pulpit.

In fact, he thought grimly, there was absolutely nothing here to suggest that this was a house of God.

Absolutely nothing.

Her mom wasn't talking.

She was mad at her, mad enough to ignore all of Claire's attempts to talk.

The only thing her mom had said when they got in the car was "I'll take you with me, Claire, but I'm very angry. *Very.* And one way or the other, we're going to get to the bottom of these fears of yours."

Her mother was going to go to the office, and then, that afternoon, she would take Claire to the dam. Claire watched her abruptly snap the Volkswagen Rabbit into gear and back out of the driveway.

Her mother was *not* happy.

But she didn't care. It was better to have her mom mad at her, really mad. Much better than having her go to the dam . . . by herself.

Now, at least, I can warn her.

I can protect her.

But she never once thought that her coming along was maybe what was supposed to be happening all along.

The young cops were gone, into their car to slug at some coffee and eat some doughnuts.

Leaving Billy Leeper all alone on the tiny beach.

Jack Russo was out there, on the water, but he was carefully watching the blips that indicated where Dan was.

All alone. And Billy didn't like it.

Remember, he thought, ring-a-levio? Do kids still play that? He remembered hiding in the woods, waiting to be found. And sometimes no one came. It was creepy sitting there, expecting Jackie Weeks to come bounding around a tree, grabbing at his arm, yelling, "Cor, cor, ring-a-levio! One, two, three!"

They played down there . . . in the woods, near Old Man Boozer's hill, by the graveyard, in all the wide-open spaces of Gouldens Falls.

Not so wide now. Not so open.

The cops closed the door to their patrol car.

It was chilly that morning. Even getting chillier as it grew lighter. (No sunrise. Just chunky gray clouds. Dark October clouds in July.)

He rubbed his hands together.

And saw something.

Off to the right, away from the beach. A bit of movement that just barely registered in his peripheral vision.

He tried to look.

There was nothing there.

Then, again, the movement.

This time he turned quickly. But there was no need.

The person stood there, just a bit inside the overgrown woods past the beach, looking at Billy.

A guy in a blue suit. Damnedest thing.

Billy stared back at him.

Damnedest thing.

The man smiled. Billy smiled back. Just a detective, or some official, or—

No.

Billy's hand came up to the air, and involuntarily he pointed.

I know you. I know that face. The hair was different. But no mistake. Different. But the *same.*

He took a heavy step in the sand, away from the water, off toward the right, toward the man.

(Who stood there waiting.)

And every step convinced Billy that no, he wasn't crazy. It was him.

Thirty feet away. Twenty feet. He left the beach, pushing his way through the prickers and stunted maples that grew in the dappled shade under the tall, fully grown trees. Ten feet away. The man grinned. A big, welcoming smile.

"Billy . . ." he said quietly, almost soothingly.

(No fear? Why aren't I afraid? Why—)

"Billy . . . it's been a long, long time."

"Martin Parks," Billy said (or he thought he said). He wasn't sure he made any sound at all. His hands clenched. They were big, strong hands—he was proud of these hands—and the fingers pressed into his palms, cutting deep into the hard, calloused hands.

"You're back."

Parks laughed. "Yes. How observant of you. Unfortunately I know what you and your friend down there are trying to do." Parks put his hands together.

(Like some accountant delivering the bad-news bottom line.)

"I'm afraid the game is over, Billy."

He pulled his hands apart.

(Why aren't I afraid? Billy thought. *I ran all the way to Montauk to be away from here. Why . . . aren't . . . I . . .)*

Parks pulled his hands apart.

The pain bloomed in Billy's midsection, bright, flashing, doubling up the old man.

"No," he said with a moan.

"Yes, your time is up, Billy Boy."

Parks brought his fingertips together, such graceful fingers. The pain stopped. "All bets are off, Billy." Parks pulled his hands apart, and it was as if Billy's insides were being ripped apart.

This time he went to his knees.

Billy glanced back at the police car. The doors were shut.

(Please, he prayed now. Finish your coffee, your doughnuts, your bitching and complaining about low salaries and bills that just keep on coming. Please—)

"I'm sure you've got it all figured out, Billy. In fact"—the hands went together again—

(Oh, no, please.)

The pain stopped.

—"I'm sure you had it figured out fifty years ago when your friend Jackie Weeks ran into our little Club." He laughed, a sick, hollow sound. "After all, how could he know that they were all supposed to be dead?"

He moved his hands apart.

Now his body opened. A faint tear at first, like squatting down and—oops—splitting the backside of your pants apart.

A thin line ran from his midsection, then up, slowly, to his chest.

Parks laughed louder.

Billy fell backward, his hands going naturally to his skin, pressing it together, crying now—

A small boy who had hurt himself.

"Please, no," he begged, pushing the folds of skin together even as the tear widened, and he saw his insides, warm and steamy, exposed to the cool air.

The hands came together.

(Where is the pain? he wondered. It was as if it were all happening to someone else. Like the Scarecrow in *The Wizard of Oz,* when the witch's monkeys rip his stuffing out and scatter his straw all over the ground and he said, "That's me all over.")

So Billy looked down . . . amazed, horrified, oblivious

now to Martin Parks and those damn manicured fingers that went together, apart, together, apart—

"Gouldens Falls will live again," Parks said to the air, the lake, the trees. "I'm afraid you won't be here for the glorious revival. Not in the flesh, anyway." He smiled.

Billy looked up at him, knowing that pleading was useless.

Parks's fingers moved apart—slowly.

The pain was allowed to flow, along the tiny nerve endings, through the maze of neurons, along the spinal cord, to Billy's brain.

A tidal wave of pain. An eruption of pain that turned the world into a single burning point of white, lavalike fire, centered in this body.

The fingers touched. The pain stopped.

"Unfinished business, eh, Billy Boy? Our work was interrupted."

A sound from just behind them. A few feet away. In the water.

He turned to the side (away from his body—so oddly fascinating in its destruction).

Something slithering out, crawling out of the lake, onto the muddy edge. Grabbing at the vines and bushy plants.

A hand. Billy screamed. But there was no sound.

Except the gentle splash of something crawling out of the water.

NINETEEN

He dropped his knife.

It slid down, wobbling back and forth, somewhere into the darkness that surrounded him.

Damn. He retrieved the lamp from the small perch he had made for it out of some loose rubble, and searched the stone floor for the jagged blade.

It rested on the webbing of one of his flippers, looking incongruously shiny.

He snatched it up and tried to balance the lamp again, aiming it right at the chunk of stone he was working on.

(It had been no trouble finding the stone.) Just a matter of swimming over to the wall, counting the blocks, and now, just digging the sucker up.

The cement was soft, almost porous, and great chunks of it chipped away easily, swirling in front of him, blocking his view of the stone. He waved his hand with a swirling motion to clear the water. Then, back to jabbing at the rectangular outline of the cement.

How many minutes left now? he wondered.

He checked the gauge.

Twenty minutes. Should be plenty of time. Plenty. Four or five minutes to get the stone loose, get the diary—

(If there is such a thing.)

And if there's time, snap a few photos on the way out. His Nikon SU-50—a compact underwater camera—was strapped to his side. Not the most versatile piece of equipment, but small and reliable.

Chop, chop. Like an underwater archaeologist exploring a sunken city. He had cleared a two-inch-deep outline around the stone. Another few seconds and he'd try to lift it up.

He felt movement. The water had been still. Perfectly still, bottled up inside this old church. But just now he felt the water move against him, like an underwater current, or maybe—

Something moving. Inside the building.

He wanted to get the lantern and just take a look around.

(Just to check. Just to be sure.)

Keep cool. There's nothing here. Nothing.

He went back to work.

Chop, chop. He had finished clearing the stone. He put down his knife (feeling a tad defenseless). He grabbed the stone. The water moved against him, buffeting his body, and he looked around into the darkness. He waited.

Something was coming. Here. Just a feeling.

Like he could read it in the tiny eddies and swirls of the water.

He pulled on the stone. It didn't budge. Again. It moved—or did he imagine it?—a few millimeters. He placed his flippered feet firmly on either side of it. He grunted and pulled with all his might.

The stone flew up into the air. He knocked the lamp over. (The light beams fell onto the wall, outlining in a darker green some now departed religious icon.)

How much time now? Fifteen minutes? Ten?

He threw the stone to the side and grabbed the light. He

aimed up and around quickly. Ready to catch whatever might be inside the church with him.

(The knife . . . where's my damn knife!)

But he saw nothing, save the stray pumpkin seeds swimming by.

He aimed the light into the cavity he had just made in the floor.

At first he saw only the grit and sand. Then, brushing at it, he saw a small metal chest, no larger than a cigar box.

He picked it up.

(Screw the pictures, he thought. I'll get pictures later. Now I just want to get my knife and get the hell out of here.)

He started for the opening, kicking hard, checking the angle of the steeple as the walls curved to a point.

He reached the top and then moved toward the hole. It looked smaller than he remembered it.

He hurried—too fast—into the hole, holding the metal box in one outstretched hand and the lamp in the other. He got stuck.

And this time he wouldn't budge.

(Just like a human lobster trap.)

He kicked harder with his flippers, but it only seemed to wedge him tighter. Damn, he needed a free hand, some way to push himself out.

If he let the box go, it would tumble away, vanishing to who knows where. He'd never find it again.

If he let the lamp go, he'd be in the dark.

(Like when his car went off the bridge and he was in the dark, the water rushing in, pressing close.)

He felt the water move, swirl strongly now around his flippers.

He hastily searched for a place to hook the lamp, or to balance it at least. But there was nothing.

He let it fall. It tumbled silently, lazily spinning over and over, like an underwater cop's beacon.

(Pull over, sir, we're the fish police.)

He couldn't see anything except the milky-gray roof of the surface—a good fifty feet above him.

He brought up his free hand and pushed, while he squirmed left and right.

His tanks chipped at the wood, and once he thought his air hose was going to be ripped in two. Slowly he gained a few centimeters more space in which to move. Then a few more.

Until—as if it were all some kind of mistake—he was free, scuttling out of the hole.

(As he kicked away, his fins hit something just near the hole. Probably part of the steeple, he thought. Probably—)

He had to guess his depth, taking time to decompress. He couldn't rush to get to the surface quickly.

He didn't bother making his way to Jack and the boat. Straight up would do just fine.

He paused, then started up again.

The air tasted metallic . . . then—

Bingo.

My time's almost up.

The kicking of his legs became more urgent.

(No panic, no sir. Just a bit of precautionary extra speed. That's all. That's—)

Gone. No . . . more . . . air.

And how many more feet to the surface?

He spit out his now useless regulator and pressed his lips together tightly as he slowly exhaled.

Rogers held a megaphone in his right hand.

"Soon as he's up, you bring him over here."

Russo waved to signal that he understood.

Five cops stood around the police chief, their arms

folded, and he knew they wondered if they were all going to catch hell for letting those two jokers out in the water.

And maybe they would.

Maybe he'd pin their ears back like they've never been pinned before.

He broke the surface.

And gasped horribly at the air.

Filling his lungs once, twice, and then again.

He started coughing, his head almost bobbing below the water.

But then Jack was there, beside him, the steady *putt–putt* of the small inboard motor just a few feet from Dan's head.

"We're in some trouble, Dan," he said, gesturing at the beach.

Dan turned to look and saw the small phalanx of Ellerton's finest—all of them with their eyes trained on him.

"Trouble?" Dan said. "Here, take this." He handed Jack the metal box.

"What did you find? Any sign of Tom and Ed?"

Russo helped hoist Dan onto the boat.

"No. Nothing. Just what's in there."

Russo looked at the small box. "What the hell is it?"

"A diary," Dan said hoarsely, breathing still not the natural thing it had been. "About Gouldens Fails."

Russo shook his head.

Dan snatched a towel up from one of the seats. He pulled off his wet suit and started drying himself.

"Jeez, it's cold. What kind of weather do they get here?"

He looked back at the beach.

Where's Billy?

He'd expected to see him waiting there. Unless, maybe, it was all too much for him.

Russo turned the boat to face the shore. "Time to face the music."

Dan sat down, wondering, Where's Billy Leeper?

There were roses, mums, marigolds, and a scattering of black-eyed Susans. All neatly clipped from lawns and gardens around Ellerton.

Now she made her way toward the lake, retracing her steps of just four days earlier, down the small path to the secluded spot on the reservoir.

Their spot.

She wasn't scared, or upset, or anything bad. No, she felt exhilarated to be here, to remember Tommy. Already she had built their relationship into one of history's great love affairs.

Great *unrequited* love affairs.

The branches that had seemed to scratch and snap at her when she ran through there Monday night now seemed soft, gentle, almost welcoming.

It would be a secret shrine.

She reached the spot. It was clear now. No picnic blanket, no bag of food. Not even any footprints on the ground.

There was a small breeze, and she wished she had a sweater on.

She picked a rose from her bunch and tossed it into the water.

Herbert Blount did have a sweater on, A frayed, fire-engine-red acrylic with buttons.

It was cold. And he had it all buttoned up tight.

He started walking to the plaza after the workers vanished into the hole on top of the roadway.

Wonder what they're up to, he thought.

And having nothing better to do, he started to stroll,

vaguely, almost absentmindedly, toward the grassy plaza below the dam.

Reverend Winston was supposed to spend the morning at Tyler Memorial Hospital. Visiting the sick, the dying, all the poor souls who happened to put down "Protestant" under "religion" on their admitting card. Most of them would be startled to see him, a few pleasantly surprised. Others merely polite.

It was a job he didn't particularly like.

In fact, he thought of skipping it today. Call the hospital and plead a cold or some such story.

But there might be that one person for whom his visit would make the difference. Someone who'd feel better—all day!—because he had stopped and prayed with them.

So he eased out of his Dunhill slippers (a gift from the nice people downstairs) and put out his collar and his black suit. No casual minister clothes for him.

When you do the Lord's work, you look the part.

Shedding his pajamas, he felt cold. He took a look at the thermometer on the wall. It was sixty degrees, much too chilly for his taste. He wished he had a thermostat in his room instead of depending on the generosity (or the lack of it) of the family downstairs.

He grabbed his collar.

Funny.

Just then he thought of Dan Elliot.

Something about that boy—

That young man, he thought, correcting himself. Almost anyone seemed young to him these days. Yes, he worried him. The past, Winston knew only too well, was often better left undisturbed.

But even he admitted to a bit of curiosity about Dan's research.

What had he found out about the town and the dam?

Perhaps later he'd try to find him.

He picked up his Bible, its cover creased and criss-crossed with hundreds of tiny cracks. Opened the book and began the first of his many readings for the day.

Dan sat in a hardwood chair inside Paddy Rogers's small office.

"If you find Billy Leeper," Dan said, "he'll support my story. I'm not making this up."

"I'm sure you're not." Rogers nodded almost distractedly. "But the fact of the matter is, Dan, there is no Mr. Leeper. Sergeant Russo saw him, but he knew nothing about any diary—"

"I already explained that. I knew, if I told him, he might think the whole story is a bunch of nonsense. I wanted his help getting out there."

"Well, he had no idea what you were up to. Which is why you're here and he's not." Rogers shook a finger at Dan. "Though I gave him some hell too. I'll let his superiors deal with him."

"Chief, can't we at least look at the diary?"

Rogers sighed. "Sure, Dan. But I don't think it will help you." Rogers pressed his intercom button, and his secretary brought in the small metal box.

The lid was open.

"It's in there?" Dan asked.

"Sure is." Rogers took it from his secretary and handed it to Dan. "It's all yours."

It looked like a piece of hundred-year-old cheese that had been sitting in a tub of water. It was brown and green and dotted with puffy mold spots.

"There's some kind of worms living in the box, tiny things called tubifex." Rogers said.

Dan took the cover and peeled it back. It came apart like

a waterlogged wafer. He attempted another page, and a chunk of pages—all stuck together—peeled away easily.

"I'm afraid whatever secrets that diary had will remain just that, Dan. Secret."

Dan sat down, holding the tin in his lap.

Before the dive, he had been skeptical of Billy Leeper's tale. The Club, the occult mumbo jumbo. Now, seeing the diary, maybe something had happened fifty years ago.

But the diary's not what convinced him.

No, those last moments in the church before springing free—that was what had done it. He felt something surrounding him, coming closer. Like a wolf sniffing at its prey, circling closer, ready to pounce.

He felt it.

And now he believed Billy Leeper. Completely.

"We need what's in there."

Rogers laughed. "Glad you think so. But"—more laughter—"as you can see, Dan, it's all illegible."

Wrong.

Even as the pages slid away—all mushy and water-soaked—he could see that the writing was still visible.

"No, something can be done."

He stood up, placing the diary gently in the metal box. "There are people who work with things like this, documents from disasters, plane accidents." He looked right at Rogers. "There *are* things that can be done."

It was as if he were trying to convince himself.

Rogers arched his eyebrows—impressed, startled by Dan's vehemence.

"Easy, just sit down there a second."

He didn't sit.

"Chief, there are four people gone, down in that reservoir. Four people in four days. And you don't have a good goddamn clue what the hell it is. Do you?"

Rogers just stared.

"Do you?"

The police chief shook his head.

"This might have some answers, some clues. Maybe there's some weird current in there, some fatal design flaw in the dam . . ." He tried to keep things as acceptable to Rogers as possible. "This diary may have some of the answers."

Rogers looked at the soggy book, now in three pieces. "Sit down," he said quietly. "Please."

He sat. And watched Rogers look at the tin box . . . and the book.

Rogers started speaking, slowly. "There's a man in Hawthorn. He works with ephemera. Old magazines, books, all the stuff collectors like to restore. From time to time the local police in the towns around here use him to work on distressed material. Stuff that's been burned, damaged, or wet. Like this."

"Call him," Dan pleaded. "Tell him to drop everything and work on this."

Rogers looked at Dan. He picked up the telephone. "Okay. But I want you here."

Dan smiled. "Am I under arrest?"

Rogers didn't smile back. "You could be. You bulldozed your way past my men to a restricted area." He paused. "But let's just say you'll hang around here. Till I've got some of this diary back . . . if any of it does come back. Agreed?"

Dan nodded.

Rogers's secretary came onto the line.

"Sally, get me Wilson Smith."

TWENTY

James Morton stood to the side and admired the great Stu Schmidt at work. Schmidt kept up a constant barrage of orders aimed at his now very lively workers, telling them exactly how to move the heavy PVC tubing down into the dam wall. Stu himself carried two of everything to their one, even the great coils of plastic tubing over his shoulder, like they were so much fishing tackle.

But even Stu Schmidt was a bit subdued inside the cavernous dam.

"It's worse than you told me, Jimmy. The water's coming in fast. Too fast. I want to get this pumping started before we try to get a temporary cap on the leak."

He was right, of course. It was coming in a lot faster than the previous day. From a trickle to a spray to . . . now this—like a small fire hose left half open.

"Will you need any more help?"

Schmidt grinned. "Nah. We'll manage here all right. We'll just take a bit longer. You hear that, boys?" he shouted at the two workers, going off for more equipment. "We're talking overtime here. Just don't drag your fannies too much." His eyes twinkled as he looked back at Morton. "Good kids. Just like everyone else these days, though. Lazy."

He watched Schmidt arranging the coils of tubing. "We've got ten, maybe twelve hours of solid pumping here, Jimmy. Won't be able to use any concrete until it's been dry down here for a few hours. I told Eddie up there to hold the cement truck till tonight. We'll let them know when we're done." Schmidt looked down at the sizable pool at his feet.

How deep was it now? Morton wondered. Ten . . . twelve feet? That's a lot of water, and a lot of pressure for the outer wall.

He watched Schmidt crouch down close to the water, as if he were trying to look into it. "There's only one thing that bothers me, Jim." Schmidt turned and looked right at him, then gestured at the dam wall. "Just how strong are these walls? They're more than fifty years old. They weren't built for this kind of treatment."

Morton took a step off the landing, down the spiral staircase, closer to Schmidt. "Oh, I imagine they'll hold all right. There's a lot of stone and concrete down here."

"Let's hope you're right."

He heard Schmidt's workers coming back down the stairs.

Schmidt stood up, surveyed the tubing. "That should be enough to start pumping. If—"

Morton felt the vibration. Like electricity, he thought. Yeah, like when he was a kid and touched a socket—just to see.

So faint, it tickled the bottom of his feet.

"Hey, what's—" he heard Schmidt start to say.

Then the vibrations started to grow, seemingly rising up from his feet, up from the water, spreading until everything seemed to be slightly out of focus. Jittery.

"A quake," Morton said, too quietly to be heard. Then louder.

But by then it was all too obvious. He tumbled back, then down onto the metal floor of the landing. Schmidt's great bald head turned left and right, looking, looking . . .

The leak widened. One, two, then three inches. The water shot straight out now, rocketing across the pool. It hit Schmidt square in his bowling-ball face and knocked him against the far wall.

Morton tried to stand, but his right arm just wouldn't move.

Someone screamed above him. Then another voice. More screaming above the noise of the water.

Why can't I get up? he thought. *What's the—*

He looked at his arm.

Like tumbling into a mousetrap, he'd fallen back onto the landing, his arm dangling up into the staircase leading up.

Somehow the metal staircase had twisted, groaned, and corkscrewed, imprisoning his arm.

"Stu . . ." he yelled. "Stu!"

But Schmidt had tumbled into the water. Maybe he'd been knocked out by the jet that had gushed out and pushed him against the wall.

The two workers. Surely they could help. "Hey, guys! Get down here quick. Hurry!"

But the only answer he heard was some more pained groans, just barely audible over the sound of—

The staircase, loose, away from the heavy bolt that kept it attached to the twin walls of the dam. Loose, twisting, like it was alive.

I can't feel my arm.

He could see it. It was there, all right.

Just—hah, hah—no . . . can . . . feel.

"Stu," he said again, helplessly.

The water rose.

Fast now, lapping at the steps below, then climbing, visibly climbing as it started to fill the base of the dam.

It reached his feet, lying just a few inches below his metal pallet.

I'm trapped.

In that moment he thought of his wife, his kids, mowing the lawn, taking a nap on a Sunday afternoon. A cold beer.

He closed his eyes.

He felt the water at his back.

And a sound.

(Someone's coming! Yes, he heard a sound, above the moans of the workers. Yes, they must be trapped also.)

It was the door leading down to the dam! Yes, it was moving! Moving!

Shut. It slammed. A loud, final noise. The light bulb sputtered on and off, then off.

The water was at his shoulder, his ears, his cheek. Cold, clammy water.

He prayed.

She tossed the last flower in: a yellow mum. Then she watched them drift, floating, slowly moving away from the shore.

Out to where Tommy had died.

She felt naked now without the flowers. They had given her a purpose for being here. Now other feelings started to move through her. And questions . . .

How had Tommy died? He'd been a champion swimmer, one of Ellerton's stars. A cramp?

She looked down at the flowers, swirling, swirling. Faster, now, it seemed to her. Moving in a circle, picking up speed.

A rose sank beneath the water.

Plop.

Just like . . .

"I have to go, Tommy. I'll be—"

It happened as soon as she spoke.

The ground shook, and the flowers in the water seemed to blend together. She reached out to balance herself. She grabbed a small tree.

But then the ground lurched again and she fought to keep her balance. The angle of everything seemed wrong, as if she were on a hill.

She reached to the left, but there was nothing there to stop her from falling onto the mossy ground. Onto the odd little plants, black, mushroomy things that filled the ground. The rumbling stopped.

"Thank God," she said, knowing now it was just another earthquake like the one from a few days ago.

(An earthquake. She remembered that from her geology class. Made it somehow sound all safe, just to name it. An aftershock. They can go on for days.)

And it was over.

She started to get up.

She was stuck.

"What the—"

Emily looked down at her hands, at the small black things she had popped. Now she was tangled in something, something like a blackish vine. She pulled back with one hand, knowing that surely it would come snapping up.

It didn't move. Nor, when she tried, did the other hand.

Her legs, tan, bare, also were covered with the blackish stuff. "Oh, shit," she said, and she wriggled back and forth, pulling on the stuff.

"Great. Now I'm going to have to wait here until someone gets me out of this . . . this junk whatever it is."

She looked around. There were hundreds of them, *thousands,* stretching from the edge of the water all the way back into the woods.

It was like being in a spider web.

She grinned at the image.

"Well, might as well start hollering for help now." Sooner or later someone would hear her. No problem there. None at all.

She felt the tendrils tighten.

"What?" She licked her lips.

But nothing more happened. It was like taking a notch up in a belt.

She heard movement in the water.

A boat! Great! Now I'll get out of this—

But the sound came from out in the lake.

Out there.

The sound of someone swimming.

She turned her head and looked out at the water.

Stroke, stroke, stroke. It was someone swimming toward her with a nice, steady, smooth style. A sleek Australian crawl, a fast swimmer.

A swimmer like Tommy.

The swimmer reached the shore, stopped. And looked up at Emily.

Tommy.

(She was crying now. Saying his name through her gasps and tears.)

"Tom—mee—"

He stood up.

Still wearing the electric-blue Speedo bathing suit. And outside of a few very obvious nicks and gashes in his body—like three-day-old bait that's been chewed by some cagey crab—he looked pretty well intact.

Except for his face.

It was a gray, sunken thing. With eyes shrunk to tiny pricks of blackness. And the mouth—so rubbery, fishlike.

He stepped close to her.

She could smell him.

Her stomach heaved, spasming over and over as he came closer.

He opened his mouth.

(Like a spiderweb.)

"Tom—mee!" she screamed.

"Don't open the door," Samantha ordered. "You know what Momma says."

Joshua stood at the door.

"Don't. Until Mom comes back."

She watched him to see if he'd really do what she said.

"But where is Mommy, where is—"

"I don't know. Maybe she had to go to the store."

Joshua's lower lip began to quiver, a sure sign that he was about to cry. "But . . . but that was a long time ago . . . a *long* time."

And it was. Samantha still measured such things by TV shows, and she and Joshua had watched cartoons all morning until they gave way to the talk shows for stay-at-home mothers.

The cereal they had both wolfed down seemed like a long time ago.

"Still, Mom says never open the door when she's not here. Never."

"But where is she?" he wailed, crying now.

She went to him. Gave him a squeeze.

"C'mon, scuzzbucket, she'll be back soon. Sure she will."

Will she? Samantha wondered. Every car she heard roar past she hoped was her mom's. But none of them slowed.

"Let's go watch some more TV."

"You . . . you could call someone."

He was right. They had a list.

A special list. People to call, it said in big letters. In case anything happened. To Mommy. Or Daddy.

People to call. For help.

"Okay, I'll call. But I bet Mom will be mad that we just didn't wait, you know, like big kids would."

She imagined that she was Joshua's sitter. Yeah, and her mom would be so proud when she got home.

Such a big girl!

She walked, with Joshua trailing behind her, to the kitchen phone and the list.

"I'll call Elaine," Samantha said, pointing to the first number, her mom's best friend's.

She could reach the phone easily now—a relatively recent accomplishment. She picked up the receiver and held it next to her ear.

She started dialing the number.

She heard nothing.

You were supposed to hear a sound. A hum. Then those little beeps. Sure.

She hung up and tried again.

Nothing.

"What's wrong?" Joshua asked.

Samantha shrugged. "Dunno. It's not working."

Then an idea, a brainstorm. "That's where she pro'bly went . . . to tell someone to come and fix it. That's why she had to leave. Couldn't call, now could she, Joshie-washie?"

He raised his tiny fist to her, a warning against using his most hated nickname.

"And you know what she'd want us to do?"

"What?"

"Be good . . . keep the doors shut tight."

"Right."

There, she'd solved that. *Now all we have to do is watch TV and wait for Mom to come home.*

Which she hoped was real soon.

"Whaddaya say, sprout? Bored enough yet?"

Claire shook her head, then smiled at her.

She's so serious, Susan thought. Claire was curled up on a padded secretary's chair—somehow maintaining her balance. It was just a cubicle, her office, with a couple of cheapjack coatracks on the particle-board divider, a small two-tier filing cabinet, and the ever-present computer terminal.

All morning Susan had been checking the computerized morgue for other towns that had fallen under siege, hostage to either some maniac or some wandering sicko. She accumulated a hefty file. None of it, unfortunately, seemed to shed a bit of light on what was happening to dear old Ellerton.

Despite her annoyance, she didn't mind having Claire there—not really. It was soothing to see her curled up with a book, watching her mom at work. Sure, they'd have to deal with Claire's nightmares eventually. But for now, this was okay.

She sat down and opened a photocopied file just sent up from the press library. It contained the most recent reports on Tom Fluhr, crazy Fred Massetrino, the two divers (with an addendum on Dan Elliot, listing some of his published credits).

She felt guilty about how she had let him have it the night before.

Right between the ears.

It had just been the wrong time for him to lay any of that paternalistic macho bullshit on her. She was a reporter—no, a writer—and the last thing she needed was someone playing Indiana Jones to her damsel in distress.

She smiled. Perhaps she'd been a bit too hard. She liked him. He was different, fun, and he turned all the right switches—a rare occurrence these days.

She'd call him later, perhaps invite him over. After Claire had gone to bed. Her smile broadened.

"Mom, what are you laughing at?"

She tossed her head, shaking the imaginary wisp of hair off her forehead.

"Oh, nothing. Just something . . . funny." She turned

and looked at her daughter. "Let me finish checking this file and we'll 'do lunch,' okay, guy?"

Claire nodded. "And after lunch?"

"I have to go over to the dam."

Claire's face sagged.

Susan shook her head and went back to her clippings.

Wilson Smith, Conservator of Ephemera, had the book spread out on a large, plastic-covered table. The book was in three soggy, lumpish pieces. Smith wore plastic gloves, and a battery of draftsman's lamps bathed the table in brilliant white light.

Smith, a pear-shaped fellow with wire-frame bifocals and two small tufts of gray hair on either side of an otherwise bald head, was mildly discouraged by the item in front of him.

He normally worked with distressed ephemera. Damaged thousand-dollar stamps, torn covers to the first issue of Superman (worth $40,000 in mint condition), rare and valuable books with split bindings and loose pages. He could fill holes with a liquid substance that dried into the paper, easily match whatever yellowish shade of paper he was working on. He would carefully remove "magic" tape, touch up the color on the cover, and give the whole book a sharp, glossy look, increasing its value by a couple of hundred dollars.

But this . . . this looked hopeless. This wasn't distressed material.

It was destroyed.

"Oh, boy," he said aloud, breaking the quiet of his basement lab. He had dropped everything, at the police chief's request, to work on this. A squad car waited outside for anything he could salvage.

"Oh, boy." He sighed again. He reached down and

touched the larger part of the book. True, it was all stuck together, like a paper brick. But as his latex-coated fingers gently probed the perimeter of the book, he saw that the pages, by and large, still seemed fairly separate.

He brought his hands back to his chest.

Well, then, there's some hope. He could dry the book page by page, using the heat lamps, and pull the pages apart one by one. Of course, some would be lost, permanently stuck together. (And all those little worm holes running through it didn't make the job any easier.)

And a lot of it would be smeared. Totally illegible.

But—yes. He figured he would save about half the book.

He walked over to his storage shelves and brought over a pair of high-intensity heat lamps.

Dan sat, then stood, then sat, in the lime-green waiting room. Once in a while he wandered out to the front desk of the police station. But the bustling activity of the sergeant made him feel uncomfortable and in the way.

I can't spend all day here. If I have to push Rogers to the point of arresting me, then so be it.

But first he wanted to call Susan. She had been so angry at him the night before. (Just when things were going well. A typical Dan Elliot move.)

But he was sitting there with those notebooks, trying to figure out what the hell was going on. The idea of Susan near the lake was enough to give him the creeps.

And where had Billy wandered off to?

(He had wandered off, hadn't he? Hadn't he?)

You couldn't blame him. The old guy looked like his memories were washing over him, ready to knock him down. So he probably left.

But where did he go? The two cops remembered seeing him there, but they didn't see him walk away.

Where the hell are you, Billy? I could use you to back up my story. Your story.

He walked back to the small pay phone, just outside the cluster of jail cells at the back of the station.

(How many two-bit hoods made their one call from here?)

He popped a quarter in and asked information for the number of the *Ellerton Register.* If he was lucky, he could smooth things over with Susan. Having nothing to scribble down the number with, he repeated it aloud, then hung up and dialed quickly.

"Susan Sloan, please."

Then, after a long wait, the operator came back on the line. She was gone, out to lunch. Perhaps he could try later.

Someone tapped him on the shoulder.

He turned and saw Rogers.

"Thought you'd like to know, there was a small quake this morning. Little over an hour ago. Nothing much compared to Monday's shock. But my boys felt it over at the reservoir." Rogers looked him squarely in the eye. "Good thing you weren't down there when it happened."

Yes, he thought. Might have been nasty inside that steeple. He might have stayed trapped.

"Oh, and Mr. Smith called. Said things aren't quite as bad as we imagined. In fact, he should have half the diary ready in a couple of hours."

"Good."

"No word from your friend, Billy Leeper?"

Dan shook his head.

Rogers smiled. "Well, let's just sit tight until we get a look at the book, agreed?"

"Sure," Dan said, and made his way back the ugly green waiting room.

Max Wiley was finishing his chili dog, taking special care not to drip any of the dollops of red goo onto his seersucker suit.

He was parked just in front of the barricade closing the roadway to the dam. There was a big gray New York State truck next to him.

He took a long sip of his diet Pepsi.

No workers. There were some cops down by the beach, too damned engrossed in talking to one another to notice shit. But it sure as hell looked like the workers were done and gone.

He popped the last chunk of his hot dog into his mouth and stepped out of his car.

The banner was done, and it looked as smashing as he hoped it would. It was enormous, proclaiming, ELLERTON–GOULDENS FALLS FIFTY-YEAR CELEBRATION with the words KENICUT DAM even larger.

He walked up to the roadway. There was even a scattering of people down in the plaza, milling about, looking at the dam and the banner.

He kept walking, across the closed roadway. (Got to get it open by tonight, he thought. Everything's got to be all set for the celebration. No screwups allowed.)

He reached the door leading into the dam. He yanked on the heavy L-shaped handle, but it didn't budge. He pulled futilely at the door.

All locked up. Why, then, they must have finished the repair job. Yeah, finished up and gone off for some lunch.

Great! He felt exhilarated. Now things could get rolling again. He walked briskly back to his car. He'd call Rogers and tell him . . . tell him that everything was fine, the repair was finished, and please get the barriers down.

(And if he wanted to keep the cops on duty, that was fine. Just don't go scaring the townspeople.)

Then he'd head home, catch a few hours sleep before getting ready for the costume party at the Stonehill Country Club.

(Where he hoped he'd get a chance to thank Mr. Martin

Parks for his ever so generous contribution to his upcoming campaign.)

He pulled his jacket close.

He buttoned all the buttons, but the material was so thin, it didn't help.

Strange, but it sure was cold today.

TWENTY-ONE

The closer they got to the dam, the more weird Claire felt.

She thought of pretending she was sick, maybe start coughing, really hacking, or *something,* just to get her mom to go home.

But then her mother would just drop her there, maybe call horrible Mrs. Jones to come over and take care of her, and then head back to the dam. By herself.

And she didn't want that.

No, she was maybe the only one who understood the danger.

'Cause I've seen it. Night after night—

"Here we are," her mom said, pulling their Rabbit off the road.

"Darn! The roadway's still closed. I thought they'd have the thing repaired by now, opened and—" Her mother looked at her, running her hand through her hair. "You wait here, okay, honey? I just want to talk to the police, maybe jot down a few notes. Okay?"

"No."

Her mother gave her her best annoyed look. "What do you mean, no?"

"I want to come. I'll stay . . . out of the way."

Her mother shrugged. "C'mon, then. I don't know"—she opened the door—"how you expect me to become a rich and famous reporter with an overly imaginative eleven-year-old tagging along."

She trailed behind her mother, looking all around as they walked down to the beach and the two policemen.

She knew enough to stay back and let her mother talk. And again she looked at the lake. It was completely flat now, gray like the sky, flat like a piece of sheet metal.

Claire almost expected it to—what?—move, react to her coming?

'Cause I'm here. I'm here and I know about you. I know what you're trying to do.

She shivered. Then she looked up to the woods and hills on the other side of the lake. She could just make out the Bennys' house through tiny chinks in the trees. Bits of their wooden deck, small splotches of wood, the big, black gas barbecue.

So close . . . so close to the lake.

She was glad she didn't live there.

But then she thought of the two children.

And she was scared for them.

"Thank you. We'll just walk over and back. I appreciate it." Her mother had finished with the two policemen.

"We're going now?" Claire asked hopefully.

Her mother shook her head. "No, sweetheart, I'm walking over to the other side. From there I can see the beach, and some of the other spots more . . . er, clearly. Up that way, missy." She pressed an imaginary button on Claire's nose and pointed her head up to the closed roadway. "I can describe the place the way it really is. You can wait in the car if you'd like. I'll be right back."

"I'll come along," Claire said hurriedly, forcing a smile onto her face.

"Suit yourself."

She walked next to her mother, right next to her.

And the water seemed a bit different now.

It wasn't just flat anymore.

She could here it softly splashing against the wall. And out there, out where she didn't like to look, it seemed to make tiny little waves.

Claire turned and looked up at the trees.

There was no wind.

Her mother kept walking.

"God, it's cold here," she said.

They'd almost reached the other side, right near the other police barrier.

"Okay, sweetheart, this is fine. Right here."

Her mother was scribbling words down in her narrow reporter's notebook. Claire looked around.

(Stay away from the edge, she told herself. Just stay away.)

But then her mother took a step closer, as if to get a better look at something across the water.

"Mom!" she said, yelling without thinking about it.

"What, honey? What's wrong?"

"N-not so close," she said, stammering. "Not so close to the edge."

Susan shook her head, then begrudgingly humored her. She took two steps away. "There. Is that better?"

Claire nodded.

She looked around the lake, following the twisting shoreline, around and around and around, until—

She was looking at the Benny house.

They were near it now, it was just up a small hill. But her eyes followed a trail through the woods, down to the fence line. She saw something. On the ground.

A blackish lump. Lying half on one side, half on the other side, of the fence.

"Mom . . . Mom!"

"What now?" Susan snapped.

"Something's wrong at the Bennys'. Something with Joshua and Samantha—"

Susan looked over at the house and the fence. "Whatever are you talking about? How can you see?"

"There's something over there, down by the fence. Don't you see it?"

"See what?" she said, squinting. "There's no—"

But then her mother saw it.

(And that pause scared Claire more than anything she had ever dreamed or imagined.)

"You're right. There's something there. Okay, we'd better go back and—"

They both turned.

The police were gone.

Susan reached out and took her daughter's hand. "We'd better go—"

"No." Claire gave her mom's hand a hard tug. "Not that way, Mom. We have to get Joshua and Samantha out of there. Now, Mom. Now. Because, because—"

(They're coming. From the water. Soon. Oh so soon.)

"Okay," her mom said. "We'll call the police from there."

Claire was tugging her along, They ran, first off the roadway, then up the small trail made by the high-school kids who liked to sneak beers, and then up toward the Benny house.

He picked up the phone and misdialed the number, getting, instead of the switchboard at the *Ellerton Register,* some Latino hausfrau.

"Sorry," he mumbled, and he dialed again. This time he made the right connection.

Susan Sloan was still out of the office.

He hung up. Out of the office. And just where could she be? Where, oh, where—

He knew damn well where.

He walked over to Rogers's office to announce that he was leaving—unless the chief wanted to press charges. He knocked on his door.

A young cop came hurrying through the double glass doors, a thick brown envelope held tightly to his side.

The cop walked right up to Rogers's door, next to Dan.

Rogers opened it himself.

"Yes, what is it—"

He stared at the envelope, knowing what it must be. The diary.

"It's the first half of the material, sir, from Mr. Smith. He thought it should be brought straight over. He'll have the rest in a few hours."

Rogers took the envelope and looked right at Dan.

"Shall we look it over together?"

"I—"

(I was on my way out. Leaving. To look for Susan. But with the pages of the diary here . . . so close . . . maybe he could wait just a bit.)

"Sure."

"Mr. Smith said he did the best he could, but whole pages were useless."

Rogers nodded. "Come in, Dan. Let's look at what we've got here."

He closed the door behind Dan.

Claire ran ahead, and Susan had to struggle to keep her in sight.

My God, she thought, finally reaching the edge of the Benny property, this house is secluded. A long gravel road-cum-driveway led down to a narrow service road that ran around the reservoir and then up to Pennington State Park, just to the northeast.

The reservoir was surrounded by county-owned property. It was beautiful, the sleek wooden house, all angles and glass, with a neat lawn around it. There were tremendous pine trees, a few maples, and—standing near the center of the backyard—a full, plump willow.

"Claire!" she called, but her daughter ran ahead, hurrying, driven—terrified.

I'm scared too, she admitted. *Something wrong with my daughter, and I don't know what it is.*

Claire ran up to the back door, a sliding door.

"Claire!" Susan called futilely. She ran as fast as she could.

She found Claire kneeling on the floor (the TV on and blaring), right beside Joshua, who was crying. Claire looked up at her.

"Joshua says they've been alone all morning."

"Alone?"

Joshua nodded. "Our mommy wasn't here when we woke up." He looked up at Susan, his tears starting to ebb now. "We've been waiting for her to come back."

Claire suddenly grabbed Joshua's arm.

"Claire, easy with the poor boy, he—"

"Where's Samantha?" she asked sharply.

Joshua looked up, first to Susan, then over to Claire.

"The door was open this morning. I tried to shut it . . . it was cold. Samantha said maybe Mommy went out . . . maybe something happened. She went to look for her."

Claire stood up and went to the door.

"Claire, honey . . . wait."

Susan was lost, confused. Claire went out the door.

Susan turned to the small boy. "Joshua, wait here. We'll be right back."

He nodded glumly, and she ran out across the lawn.

Toward the woods. Toward the lake.

"Jeez, I don't know, Dan. I don't . . . really . . . know." Rogers stood up and walked over to his window. "This is all a bit much. I mean—"

Right. Too right, thought Dan. Even with the pages missing, terrible gaps in the story lost forever, what they had read so far was unbelievable.

Unbelievable. An absolutely incredible bit of insanity.

Which he nonetheless believed now—totally.

Reverend Passworthy, according to the diary, was careful who he had called to help him. Nobody who he expected of being close to the Club. . . . They met and prayed in secret. And once they accepted the inevitable, their path was clear.

The Club was in service to some other entity. A force. Dark. Ancient.

There was a phrase Passworthy used.

It sent chills up Dan's spine.

(Because he had felt it. My God, he had *felt* it. There. In the church.)

It was, Passworthy wrote, ". . . something as close as your own breath. As far away as the end of the universe."

Others of his small group called it names. The Demon. The Beast.

But Passworthy knew that it was, more simply, evil incarnate. The eater of souls. The destroyer of planets. The creator of chaos.

Aleister Crowley had named it Azathoth. And the Club had invited it to come.

Invited it!

Into their world. It helped them, served them, until it was time to claim its prize, its reward, its due.

Pain. Suffering. Death. The very marrow of chaos. It grew in power, ready to spread throughout the country, throughout the world.

Feeding. Growing.

In the end the Club members were no more than messenger boys—one of Passworthy's group had witnessed one of them being punished. Horribly. Slowly. A terrible torture that served to remind them all who was the real master.

As bodies vanished, it fed the demon, building the gate, opening the pathway, making it that much stronger.

Then Passworthy's group knew what they had to do.

There were rules, procedures, canonical actions for dealing with ancient myths.

They came to the end of the pages.

"It's all just too much, Dan. And besides, if they did something, what's all this that's happening now?"

The phone rang and Rogers answered it. "Yes. Fine. We'll be there." He hung up.

"Who was it?"

"Smith. Apparently the old boy is reading all this stuff. It's shaking him up. Says he'll have the rest done in forty-five minutes, an hour tops." Rogers turned toward him. "You'll wait?"

He was on his way out the door.

To look for Susan.

But if he waited, he'd have the rest of the story.

(Incredible! Unbelievable! And true.)

"I'll wait," he said, hearing the eagerness—an unattractive eagerness—in his voice.

She grabbed Claire.

"Don't go any closer."

Samantha knelt beside the blackish lump.

Pop, pop. With each step Susan heard the sound of these little . . . things opening up.

They were standing on them. *Surrounded* by them.

"Samantha. Samantha, sweetheart, I'm Claire's mom and—"

She wasn't listening. She crouched down.

(No, Susan thought. Stay up, away from the ground. Please, dear God.)

And Samantha brought her hand to the top of the blackish thing. To its head. She pushed at the blackened stuff.

"Samantha, honey, please."

She pushed hard. Grim. Determined. Until . . . Yes . . . there was a mouth. Then part of a nose.

Claire tried to step forward, but Susan held her tightly. Her hands like talons digging into her shoulder.

(Sweet God, get the girl out of here.)

"Step back, Claire . . . to that tree." She loosened her talons.

"Back, Claire!" she snapped.

Her daughter moved.

Samantha had the eyes uncovered.

They were open.

"Mommy . . . Mommy . . ." she cried.

(My God, is she alive? Is she *alive*?)

Pop, pop. More of the spore things opened and laid tiny tendrils around Samantha's feet.

"Mommy . . . Mommy . . ." She was blubbering now.

Susan tried to see the thing on the ground. She stepped closer.

Pop.

The open eyes.

Damn, was she alive? Open eyes!

But no. They were clear, cold, dead.

Waiting!

For who the hell knows what.

"No!" she screamed, and she ran over to Samantha, grabbing her around her midsection. She lifted her up.

But Samantha's feet held fast.

"No. Goddammit!"

Pop. Pop.

She pulled, spittle flying from her mouth. More, harder, more.

Sweet God, let me be strong enough.

She tugged, groaning, screaming to the woods.

(A tendril curled itself around her ankle.)

"Now!" And Samantha sprung free, her arms reaching out for her mom. Crying, screaming her mother's name over and over, a pathetic, hopeless litany.

"Run!" she ordered Claire. "Back to the house."

She felt the tendril on her ankle tightening. She snapped her leg forward, and the single vine shrugged off.

"Run!" she screamed, as much to herself as to Claire.

TWENTY-TWO

She reached the house, holding Claire with one hand and Samantha with the other.

Joshua was just inside the sliding door, his nose pressed against the double-paned glass.

Susan tugged on the door. It didn't move. Then she grunted and pulled, and the door slid sluggishly to the left.

"C'mon . . . c'mon, kids, inside." She looked over her shoulder.

(Half expecting to see a black figure trudging out of the woods toward them.)

She turned to Claire. "Where's their phone?"

"In the kitchen."

Claire began following her upstairs.

"Stay with them," she ordered. "Just stay downstairs."

But Claire stayed right beside her.

What will I tell them? she thought. *What will I tell the police? That these two kids lost their mommy to some black fungi? And you'd better get somebody out here 'cause the stuff is spreading?*

Sure, lady.

She picked up the phone and started to dial.

Joshua had followed them.

"It broke. My mommy went to get it fixed."

She went to him, pulled him close. "Right, honey. That's where she is."

Claire was staring at her, demanding, *What are we going to do now?*

"Claire, get Samantha up here. I want to get everyone out to our car . . . to . . ."

(Get out of here.)

Claire scuttled downstairs and led Samantha—now silent, her eyes glassy, blank—into the kitchen.

"Okay, group," Susan said, "we're going to walk back to my car and"—she looked right at Joshua, her voice bright—"see if we can find your mom."

"I know where she is," Samantha said dully. "She's—"

"Let's go," Susan said, interrupting.

She led them toward the front door, past the modern living room with its freestanding fireplace and beveled-glass table.

She opened the door. And looked outside.

"Oh, thank God."

She saw three people at the end of the long driveway. The two policemen—how'd they know she needed help?—and someone else. A man walking with them. Dressed in a blue suit.

"C'mon, kids, someone's here to help us. Hurry now." She turned to check that the children were behind her. She took a step out of the door.

A hand closed around her wrist. Tight, desperate, pinching into her skin.

"No."

She turned to Claire.

"Claire, honey, what's wrong? It's okay now . . . someone's here."

Claire walked beside her and stood rigid. She spoke quietly . . . just loud enough for her mother to hear.

"Mom . . . no . . . don't go out there. Don't bring us out there. We have to do something else."

The policemen were halfway up the driveway, with the other man just a few steps behind. Susan looked at them, and then at her daughter. "Claire, what on earth are you talking about?" Her voice started to snap, growing angry.

Claire looked right at her. "You have to get us away . . . from them." She paused. "Please."

Susan shook her head. "What? I don't see . . ." She looked down the driveway. The man in the suit had stopped, while the two young cops kept walking. Slow, plodding steps. She looked at them, smiled. She could almost see their faces . . . their eyes.

Her body went cold.

"Oh, God."

And in an instant she knew that they weren't there to help them. It was as if she saw them through her daughter's eyes. Their slow, measured steps. Their oddly vacant eyes.

Samantha and Joshua tried to push past her, eager to get out to the front porch, out to the policemen.

She slammed the door.

"Okay . . . over here." She backed away from the door, shaking.

What now? Surely not back toward the lake. Just where the hell were they? She tried to picture the Benny house, the lake, the dam.

The park.

To the northeast, surrounding the far end of the reservoir, there was Pennington Park. Named for the county executive who had ruled Westchester as his personal fiefdom for nearly a quarter of a century. It was almost a wilderness park. Just a few biking trails and a couple of hundred acres of woods.

The condo developers with their cheapjack duplexes itched to get at it, but so far the county had resisted the lure of easy money.

If they were to go into the park now, it would take them miles away from any help.

There was no other way to get out.

"Okay, gang," she said, pulling them close, "we have to go on a little adventure."

Joshua chewed his lower lip. It was all getting to be too much for him.

"We have to hike. Claire," she said, looking at her daughter, "will take the lead."

Claire seemed a bit steadier (now that they weren't going out the front door).

"And I'll be in the back. Okay?"

Samantha nodded listlessly.

"Hurry, Mom," Claire said.

She took Claire's head in her hands. "Go out the family-room door, Claire, and go left, straight into the woods. Don't go anywhere near the lake. Stay well away—"

She thought she heard sounds outside. The sound of feet shuffling along, kicking pebbles.

"Now run, honey."

Claire turned and led them out of the house.

"That's all of it. All he could save."

Dan pulled a chair close to the chief 's desk. He could see that there were many more gaps here, whole chunks of pages missing.

They sat together, pouring over the pages together.

There was enough, Dan saw, yes, more than enough to finish the story of Gouldens Falls.

Passworthy's plan had been simple. He and his group surrounded the Club one October night while a simmering Hudson Valley storm barreled down toward Manhattan.

A few men had run away—unable, at last, to face the Club. But Passworthy moved his circle tighter and tighter, and then knocked on the doctor's door.

Dr. Hustis appeared. Then the others.

Hustis laughed and threatened the men if they didn't leave.

(Pages were missing here. He and Rogers were left to their imagination to fill the gaps.)

Hustis took a step toward the invaders, then Thomas Raine and Jonathan Reynolds. That's when Passworthy acted.

The ceremony he was about to use dated from the late fourth century. It was a time when Christianity was still a disorganized assortment of rival sects. Real orthodoxy was two hundred years away, with the coming of the Holy Roman Empire and Constantine.

One of these sects had explored the border between the religious and the profane, the holy and the damned, where good and evil clash.

The ceremony had been banned for more than a millennium but never removed from the old historical texts of Christianity. It was nothing less than the mirror image of a black-magic rite. A White Mass designed to dispatch evil and to close the earthly gates to otherworldly dimensions of horror.

As the Club moved toward them, Passworthy began the ceremony. The members laughed, sipping their port, confident of their overwhelming strength, the pure power of evil.

But then they saw the daggers glinting in the moonlight, the swirling of the leaves, and a sudden warm breeze seemingly rising from the very ground. They knew. The power of King Solomon, the great magician, was invoked. Then a litany of holy names, culminating in the one, the powerful—

The Lord.

They screamed out obscenities, raised their hands, began to gesture, to summon their power.

But Passworthy had already drawn the intricate lattice of crosses and circles into the dirt. Finally the pentagram, filled with ancient Hebraic runes.

"By the power of the Lord, let the gate to him-that-never-sleeps be closed."

Above them the clouds swirled, and the air spun the leaves dizzyingly around the house. Passworthy's followers moved onto the steps, ready to act.

Their knives had been washed in holy water and blessed. They glistened in the just revealed moonlight.

Hustis called out a name.

"Azathoth!" But his power was too weakened.

He fell first, Passworthy himself plunging the knife into his heart.

(More pages were gone . . .)

There was nothing more about the Club, nothing about what had happened in those next few moments. Instead there was a description of that house on Scott Street . . . the sickening souvenirs that filled the walls. The unholy art, images of a horror that would haunt these men from that night until the day of their deaths.

The Club had been murdered.

All of them . . . except one.

Somehow Martin Parks had escaped, leaping from a back window, pushing past the young boy who'd dropped his knife onto the ground.

The one that got away.

Five points in a pentagram. Five members of the Club.

They gutted the house. Buried the members in the basement.

But Passworthy still feared the forces unleashed in the town. Somehow his group convinced the governor to approve the long-talked-about Kenicut Dam. To bury the town of Gouldens Falls forever. To seal the horror in . . . the bodies . . . the victims. Everything.

(More missing pages, and Dan was unable to discover

what Passworthy might have showed the governor to persuade him. Was it some kind of otherworldly artifact? Something left in Gouldens Falls? Or did Passworthy dare to threaten the governor himself, perhaps with a display of his newfound power?)

No matter.

The dam was built. The town inundated.

Rogers held the last legible page of the diary in his hand.

"It's only half here, Dan." He passed it over to him.

It was labeled "The Pentagram of Solomon," an enormous five-pointed star surrounded by words and runes . . . half of them gone.

He looked at Rogers. Was he buying any of this? *Am I?*

"Chief, what do you—"

Rogers stood up. "Dan, I'm not an especially religious man. Like most of us, I pray when there's nothing else left. I'd be lying if I said that this wasn't all . . . a bit hard to take. But, son, I'm afraid there's something that has to be done here." He looked down at the pentagram. "You have to find the rest of this somehow. It would seem like the job started fifty years ago . . . must be finished."

Easily said. But where would he find the rest of the pattern (if it's really true . . . if it's not some fable . . . a folk tale)?

And like a gift from heaven, he had an answer.

"Chief, I've got an idea. But I'm worried about Susan . . . she could be at the dam. I'd appreciate it if you'd get her away from there."

Rogers held up his hand. "No problem. I'll call my boys on duty there. I'll have them look for her. Go look for her myself if I have to."

Dan stood up. "Thanks."

He picked up the fragment of the last page. Fifty years ago it hadn't worked. There were five of them, like the five points of the star. Five.

But one had gotten away.

So it didn't work.

And now it was up to him, and maybe Rogers, to somehow settle the fate of Gouldens Falls.

He left the police station.

They were still coming! She sensed it, even though when she looked back, she saw nothing . . . just her own rough trail through the lush bushes and scrawny saplings.

"I'm tired," Joshua wailed.

"Me, too, Josh. Me too. Keep going, just a bit farther, and we'll take a break."

They were well into the park, making their own path through the thick mesh of plants and trees. Claire was keeping up a good pace, but the little ones were flagging.

But she knew that they couldn't stop.

What had happened to the two cops? And Mrs. Benny?

(She thought of the old Buffalo Springfield song; ". . . something's happening here . . . what it is ain't exactly clear.")

She had a plan. Not, certainly, to move toward the quiet roads to the west. Someone easily could have followed the road from the Benny house and be waiting for them there.

No, she was going to circle around the lake (staying clear of the water), around and over to Route 100C, a major highway. It would be easy there to get someone to stop and take them . . . somewhere safe.

(And just where is that?)

"Puh-lease," Joshua cried again, "I . . . can't . . . walk anymore." He was crying, a little boy on the edge of total collapse.

She went up to him, knelt down.

(Giving another check over her shoulder, and then a quick glance down to the water.)

"There, there, Joshua, you can keep on go—"

"No, I can't! I wanna go back home. I wanna—"

He fell into her, melted into her body, ready now for even a stranger to try to make him feel better.

There was only one thing to do.

Her arms circled around his small, well-packed little body. She lifted him up. His head collapsed immediately onto her shoulder, and his legs circled around her body, monkeylike.

Just standing there holding him was hard.

"Okay," she said breathlessly to Claire. "Keep going, honey, but start moving a bit more to the right."

She hoped that she had led them far enough into the park to pass the lake.

As they walked, she constantly checked the ground, searching for those funny black things.

And with each step she took, Joshua felt heavier and heavier.

Max Wiley woke from his nap feeling oddly disoriented.

Where am I? he wondered. *What day is it? Is it morning or night?*

But as he lay there he slowly remembered just what was going on. *I took a nap. Because tonight—oh, yeah—is the costume party.* The kickoff to the four days of celebration. And all the old families of Ellerton would be there.

(With all their nice old money!)

He sat up, got out of bed, and opened the blinds.

It was dreary and overcast outside.

Not a particularly nice summer's day.

He opened up his closet and took out his costume. It was all red, from the tip of his red tights to the thin, rubbery skullcap with two stubby horns.

The cape, trimmed with a golden brocade, was draped over a chair in the corner. Resting right next to it was a nice long pitchfork.

(Just the thing for loading the souls in the next meat truck to hell, heh heh.)

Some nice red makeup for his face (with heavy, dark eyebrows) and . . . *voilà*!

A perfect little devil.

He looked in the mirror.

Big party . . . big announcement . . . big doings in Ellerton.

It's gonna be a hot time in the old town tonight!

"I was about to go down to dinner. Mrs. Thomas gets so cross if I'm late." Reverend Winston smiled. "Besides, they like me to say grace."

Time seemed slow here. A small mantel clock on Winston's dresser leisurely clicked off the minutes.

And there just wasn't time enough to tell Winston everything.

Dan handed him the paper. "I wouldn't ask you to look at it if it weren't important."

"Well, if it doesn't take too long." Winston took the photocopy Dan handed him and started searching for his glasses. "I need my bifocals for this."

He put them on. "Oh, dear, wherever did you get this?"

Winston looked right at Dan, a startled expression on his round, gentle face.

"Billy Leeper led me to it."

Winston raised his eyebrows.

"It came from the First Lutheran Church of Gouldens Falls."

Winston shook his head. "Are you serious?"

"I found it there myself. Do you know what it is?"

"Why, certainly I do. Of course I do. It's the Pentagram of Solomon. Though I must admit I haven't seen a copy of it outside of a church text in years."

Winston studied it, following the crisscrossing lines, touching the symbols. "Nearly destroyed Christianity, it did. It was used by a splinter sect of the Albigensian Heresy. They had continued the traditions of the Cabala in the Old Testament. Do you know the Cabala?"

He shook his head.

"It was a very old form of black magic, from the earliest days of Judaism. Not exactly approved by the rabbis but often tolerated. It . . . infected some of the early Christian groups, who mixed the occult with the new, true faith." Winston fingered the truncated design. "They were very powerful . . . very. Until the group was purged."

Dan walked next to the old man, looked over his shoulder. "Do you think you could complete the design?"

"What? You mean, finish the pattern?"

"Yes."

Winston studied the paper some more. "You found this, you say, in the church?"

Dan let him study it some more.

Winston looked up at him. "I won't ask what you're doing, Dan. I just pray that you're not in over your head." The reverend walked over and removed a heavy, gilt-edged book from his library shelf.

Dan smelled the old worn leather, the tangy smell of paper.

Winston laid the book on his small bed.

"This book dates from, yes, 1923. *Documents and Articles Concerning Early Christianity. Volume 9. Heresies.*"

He flipped through the pages.

"Here we are. Let me have a pen."

Like an ancient scribe, Winston huddled over the massive book. The clouds—growing thicker and darker all day—now turned an ugly black as the invisible sun settled below the hills to the west.

It was getting late.

Winston's room felt cold and uncomfortable.

"There." Winston picked up the completed sketch and handed it to Dan.

Now came the tough part. (Stuff and nonsense, he thought . . . stuff and nonsense.)

Dan removed a small vial of water from his shirt pocket. Right from out of the tap.

"Would you bless this, Reverend?"

"Are you serious?" He looked over his glasses.

"Very."

Winston made the sign of the cross over the water. "God bless . . . whatever you're up to."

"Thank you," Dan said quietly. He turned to leave. "If all goes well, I'll come back . . . and tell you everything."

"Yes," Winston said. "Please do that."

But already Dan was moving down the stairs, taking the steps two at a time. Hurrying.

I'm late for dinner, Winston thought.

Nonetheless he knelt down on the cold, hard floor, placed his hands together, and prayed.

As he promised, Paddy Rogers put a call in to Susan's paper. He was told that she hadn't come back from the dam.

He knew she had a young daughter, so he called her home. The phone rang once, then twice, before an answering machine clicked on.

Perhaps she's still at the dam, he thought. Though it looked real nasty out then, with the heavy clouds bringing an early darkness to the summer evening. A thunderstorm was on its way. His office was so cold, he was tempted to turn on some heat.

He picked up the phone and had the switchboard patch him directly into the cops' radios at the dam.

Their radios had to be on—it was a regulation.

No one answered him.

He had told Dan he'd wait for him. Here.

(To do what? Help him track some phantom from fifty years ago? The more he thought about it, the more he thought it was a lot of silliness. Murder may have been committed years ago. But it was more likely over earthly matters.)

He then decided to take a run over and see what was going on at the dam. He told the night desk-sergeant that he'd be back in an hour.

He drove there himself.

The first thing he noticed was the people gathered around the plaza . . . dozens of them, some eating, some drinking beer. As if the fireworks and the celebration were tonight. It was still light enough to see the banner, but soon a battery of spotlights would be turned on.

He passed the plaza and curved up and around to the top of the dam.

The police car was there. The door was wide open. And another car . . . a Rabbit.

"What the—" he muttered, pulling alongside the Rabbit.

He got out of his patrol car. He looked right, then left, and saw no one.

He took a step closer to the water's edge . . . the better to see the shoreline as it twisted its way around the reservoir.

Up near the barricades there was a heavy truck. It looked like a State truck, but there didn't seem to be any workers around.

He was, he quickly realized, alone.

He took a step back to his patrol car.

Have to call this in. Get some more boys down here. Find out where the hell everyone went—

He took another step.

Someone grabbed his arm.

Herbert Blount was directly under the wall, looking—my God, yes—straight up. It was so grand the way it curved away from him, from the wide base to the narrow roadway.

It almost looked like he could climb it.

He took a bite of his ham sandwich.

Other people had brought their dinner here. To the dam. It was a regular picnic. A party. People just milling about, looking at the banner. Sipping coffee and chewing sandwiches.

Lots of people. Just hanging around.

All of them waiting . . .

For, well—a funny thing—Herbert didn't know *what* he was waiting for.

And that didn't bother him in the least.

TWENTY-THREE

He removed his knife from its sheath. The blade was over six inches long and one and a half inches wide, with a razor-sharp serrated edge. It could cut. It could tear. He once jabbed a nosy tiger shark in the snout with it (stupidly drawing a whole school of the medium-sized nasties, known to take a chunk out of a diver now and then). He also used it once to neatly fillet a water buffalo (and the meat had not been worth the effort or the stench—not by a long shot). He had used the knife to cut vines and small trees to make a lean-to in the Canadian Rockies right in the middle of a sudden blizzard.

But had he never killed a man with it.

He checked his watch. It was a little after six. He had called the police station, but Rogers had left. Another call to Susan's house and he just got the answering machine again.

(*Funny. No matter what goes on in our lives, no matter what crisis . . . what problem . . . the voice on the answering machine tape remains oh so calm and unflappable.*)

He knew where she had to be.

He knew it in the same way you know that, *God, you've*

done something really dumb, really stupid this time. Here we were, one by one, traipsing on down to the dam, hanging around—

Waiting.

Only now he knew what might be coming.

He fingered the sheathed knife. It sat on the seat beside him like a silent passenger.

The paper was in his shirt pocket.

Over his head. That's what Reverend Winston had said.

Could be, Danny, boy. Could very well be.

Her mom held Joshua tightly, but her breath was ragged. She was grunting, groaning—

How much longer could she carry him?

Her own legs felt like wobbly rubber sticks, ready to go all bendy and useless.

Once she saw them. Behind them. Searching for them.

They climbed a hill, and despite the too thick clusters of leaves, she could see down, to the small ravine they had just left.

The two policemen were there, the dark navy blue of their uniforms now looking so horribly black.

And someone else, trailing just behind them.

It was not the man in the suit. It looked more like . . . a woman.

Samantha started to cry.

"I can't . . . go . . . anymore," she wailed.

Claire took her hand. "Sure you can, Sammy. We're almost there."

Are we? Her mother thought she was taking them to the big highway, where there'd be lots of cars . . . lots of people.

But was she taking them the right way?

"I can't!" Samantha cried.

She gave Samantha's hand a gentle squeeze.

"Just a bit more. You can do it . . . sure you can."

Her mother's panting grew more hollow, more terrible in its pain.

How much longer can she go on? Claire wondered.

And what happens to us when she stops?

It looked like somebody was having a party. There was Susan's car. A patrol car. Another cop car with the word *chief* neatly lettered over the Ellerton insignia.

And there was nobody around.

Dan took the knife and looped his belt through the opening in the sheath.

He got out of his Rover.

The silence was total.

Where was everyone? In the woods . . . up on the roadway . . . or maybe in the goddamn lake itself?

The water moved.

Out there, near the center of the reservoir, he could see small whitecaps.

(Like it's alive.)

The movement of the water was erratic at first. It grew choppy, looking more like a small sea under a stormy sky.

But then it started moving in a slow, steady, circular pattern. Around and around . . . slow, steady . . . building.

A whirlpool.

Then, across the water, he saw some people climbing a hill. Two . . . no, three people. Clumsily climbing up a hill.

Perhaps Susan was there. Perhaps Rogers.

And, if he was especially lucky, perhaps Martin Parks himself.

Samantha lay down on the ground.

"C'mon!" Susan pleaded. "You can't stop now!"

The green of the trees had darkened, as if they were changing with the coming of night. She put down Joshua, ending the terrible pain in her shoulders that just grew and grew.

"I can't walk anymore." Samantha moaned.

Claire, her Claire, looked at her . . . looking for an answer.

Susan looked back where they had come from. No one was following.

No one she could see.

She looked at the jumbled mass of boulders, bedrock, and thick trees around them that were twisted into strange shapes.

She saw a small cave. Barely visible. A tiny crevice in the rock.

She looked at Claire . . . her Claire.

She went over to her and spoke quietly, stroking Claire's cheek as she tried to explain.

"Claire, honey, I can't carry the two of them. They're just too heavy. You see that, don't you?"

Her daughter nodded, but her eyes looked confused.

"The highway has to be just over that hill, right there. And up there"—Susan pointed to a large outcrop of rock above them—"I think I see a small cave."

Claire looked at it.

"I'm going to hide Joshua and Samantha there, and you and I are going to go get help. Okay?"

Claire kept staring at the cave, then looked back at her.

You're my baby, she wanted her eyes to say. *My baby. I have to think of you first.*

"Okay, honey? Understand?"

Claire shook her head. "No, Mom, we can't leave them alone. Not here."

"We have to, baby. We can't just sit here. We'll get help, we'll come back, and—"

"I'll stay." Claire got up and went over to where Joshua was sitting. The boy was shivering. "I'll stay . . . keep them quiet—"

Susan shook her head. "No, honey, no—"

"You should go now, Mom. The quicker you go"—she put an arm around Joshua—"the quicker we'll be out of here."

"I'm—" She turned and looked around. Still no one seemed to be following them.

She looked at Claire. Her brave, wonderful Claire.

(*I love you.*)

"C'mon, then. Let's get you up there. And keep quiet," she snapped. "Don't let anyone make a sound."

Claire took Joshua by the hand. "C'mon, Joshua. We're going to rest a bit."

She climbed up, half dragging the exhausted children up the leaf-covered slope.

Max Wiley's wife was dressed as the Good Witch of the West, as played by Billie Burke in *The Wizard of Oz.*

Thank God she didn't talk with that same high-pitched, obnoxious, singsong voice. It was bad enough how she looked, with her fluffy dress that threatened to cover the stick shift, and all that synthetic, curly blond hair. His car phone was already lost to her crinolines.

He tried, though, to be jaunty with her, cavalier. (Though he wished to hell he had Jamie with him, dressed as some leather-skirted kitten with a whip. Oh, yeah, a devil and a dominatrix, oh, yeah.)

But that would never do at the old Stonehill Country Club.

He entrusted his car to the platoon of teenage valets, all of them good-evening-ing him to death, desperately afraid of losing some of their tip.

His wife had some trouble navigating out of her seat. (And he saw some of the snot-nosed teenagers snickering at her—or were they snickering at him?)

His was a nifty costume, though, with his rubber horns

and devil's tail. But it felt a bit silly walking into the old club—usually such a reserved joint—in such a garish outfit.

So what? Once they entered the main hall, which looked like the giant lobby from the Loew's Orpheum, his old stomping ground in the Bronx, he was delighted to see a gaggle of cowboys, pirates, witches, and astronauts. An elderly clown at a nearby table turned and looked at him as he entered the room.

(Is there anything weirder than an eighty-year-old fart dressed in a clown costume? That guy can just about keep his oatmeal down, and he's stumbling around the dance floor, martini in hand, with a sloppy, oversize grin painted on his face.)

The cute hostess, not in costume but dressed in a very chic formal gown, led him and his wife to their table.

"Well, look who's here, Satan himself." It was Barney Cleat, president of the Mutual Bank Office of Ellerton. Drinks too much and laughs too much, but still a useful "friend."

Laughing at the joke, Wiley took his fork and jabbed at the air.

"And your lovely wife . . . who are you, Marion? Shirley Temple?" Barney cracked up at his own joke.

Fuck. You.

Wiley escorted his wife to her chair. "I'll get us some drinks, Marion."

Anything to get away from Barney.

And his wife, for that matter.

(*A discreet little divorce a few months after the election, that's the ticket. Then a new lady of the house more in keeping with my new role in life.*)

He navigated to one of the four bars.

"A dry sherry and a vodka on the rocks with a twist."

He looked around. At $150 a ticket, this bash represented the best Ellerton had to offer. Why, there were families here, moneyed families, that went back to the eighteenth century.

Some of their houses, in fact, once had rested in Gouldens Falls.

The bartender handed him his drinks.

Max made his way back, smiling at people who nodded, grinning at all those who said, "How are you, tonight, Mayor?" He slowly sipped his drink.

Until he saw Martin Parks.

Not in costume.

Parks was off to the side, near the Lamont Chester Orchestra, which was playing a big-band rendition of "I Wanna Hold Your Hand." He grabbed a free-floating busboy and gave him his wife's drink, and directions on where to find her.

Then he went over to Parks.

"Glad to see you could make it. No time to get a costume, eh?"

"Right." Parks laughed. "No time. And no interest."

Max winced at the apparent rudeness.

"I can introduce you around," he said eagerly, trying to impress Parks. "The best Ellerton people are here, the very best. They'll give you a good feel for the town."

Now Parks seemed to wince. His face darkened, as if a cloud had passed over the light. His hands fidgeted at his side.

"I have that already, Mr. Wiley. A very good feeling for the town, and the people."

God, it looked like his lip actually curled into a sneer. He was beginning to have second thoughts about inviting this snob here.

"Well, if you want to meet anyone, just let me know. Um, just—"

Everything stopped. The music. The clatter of plates and spoons. The chatter. All of it frozen.

Except for Max and Martin Parks.

Parks stepped right up to his face.

"I have to go now. But I hope you enjoy my little surprise."

Parks walked past him.

(Past the people who didn't move, the horns and violins that made no sound.)

Step. Step. On the tile floor, the only sound echoing inside the 1920s-style ballroom. Plaster cherubs grinned down lasciviously at Max. Strange, tan-colored fruit dangled from the corners.

A frumpy witch sat to his left, soup spoon poised at her open, gummy mouth.

I'm mad. I've lost my mind.

And then it started again. The noise, the sheer, blessed clatter.

The ice in his drink had melted.

He turned to walk back to the bar, shaking now. A refill was definitely in order.

Someone stepped on his tail.

"Ouch," he yelled. "Watch what the hell you—"

He looked down, at his tail. Just a piece of ropy material. Someone had just walked on it.

And he'd felt it.

(*I'm crazy. Bonkers. I'm losing it.*)

He put his empty drink down next to a Humpty Dumpty who gave him a slightly concerned look through his egg-shaped head.

Max gathered up his tail. He squeezed it.

(*Oh, dear God. Oh, no. I'm crazy, I'm—*)

He *felt* it.

The same sensation he would have felt if someone had squeezed his wrist, oh so gently.

He moaned.

"You okay?" Humpty asked.

Max nodded. But wait! He had a brainstorm. Another . . . test . . . of his sanity.

He brought his hand up to his horns.

(They don't know . . . they don't know, he kept thinking, looking out at the costumed scions of Ellerton.)

Slowly, gently, he grabbed the rubber horns and yanked. Lightly at first. Then good and hard.

He screamed. They hurt, as much as his nose would if he tried to twist it off.

The two horns throbbed with pain.

Humpty Dumpty stood up. At another table a gorilla moved his chair back.

Max was on his knees, wailing, screaming, babbling at the slowly growing crowd of onlookers.

He was trying to say something. It was totally unintelligible to them. It was too mixed up with moaning and screaming.

But what he yelled in that Art Deco ballroom with the puffy little cherubs gloating was: "You. Too. Youuu . . . toooo!"

The cave wasn't so very deep.

She had cleaned a few beer cans out of it, and some greenish chunks of glass. Now they all sat together, Claire between Joshua and Samantha, her arm around them (just barely reaching).

Joshua's shivering grew worse. His teeth chattered.

Samantha just sort of sat there, so quiet now. Too quiet.

But it was enough of a cave so that they wouldn't be seen from down on the trail. And if everyone stayed nice and quiet, they wouldn't be heard.

If that would save them.

If such things mattered.

Claire felt older. Like a mother. It made her fear go away somewhere. Not gone. Just . . . there, off to the side, waiting. She pulled them closer to her, sharing their warmth, trying hard not to count every second while she waited for her mom.

She was down the hill.

But there was no highway there. Nothing except more trees, a new trail for horses, and yet another hill.

"Oh, Jesus," Susan said. "Where am I?"

East had to be back there somewhere. So west had to be, yes, straight ahead. Over the next hill. And the highway, just past it. Sure . . .

But she wasn't sure. She just had to keep on going.

And I have to remember the way back.

(*God, can I find my way back here again?*)

She looked around, trying to memorize the various slopes, the varied clustering of the trees, half expecting to see something else.

Then she started running again.

There were lots of people here now, Herbert Blount noted. A veritable beehive of people. Such excitement! Everyone here at the dam.

He stepped back.

The floodlights were on and made the banner glow brilliantly. The low clouds picked up splotches of the light.

Everyone wanted to be here.

But he saw it first. A darkish spot, growing, like a stain on the wall. The yellowish stone turning a muddy brown. Then he saw it move. The stone sort of bulged out.

And now other people saw it, putting down their sandwiches, and the chattering stopped.

'Cause this must be what they'd been waiting for. This was it!

The bulge pressed farther and farther out, pushing, and he heard the stone grinding. He saw a tiny chunk of dried concrete clatter down the wall. It bounced once, twice, then three times before landing by his feet.

He bent down and picked it up.

A souvenir! Of the dam.

He looked up.

The stone shot out of the wall, exploded, flying across the plaza. It went over his head, back there, back where the late arrivals to the plaza were gathering.

Maybe it would land and crush a car.

Or pound someone into the grass. Flat as a pancake. Like some funny trick being played on the Roadrunner.

Beep. Beep.

Then the water. A solid stream, as thick as a tree trunk, most of it streaming over Herbert's head. But other water spilled, cascaded down the sides, so beautiful—like a waterfall.

More stones started to bulge.

Herbert (and all the other people, the ones not washed away by the first blast) stood and watched.

TWENTY-FOUR

They were out there now. Though no sound reached her, no snapping of a twig or shuffling of a foot disturbing dry leaves, she knew they were here.

She prayed that Joshua and Samantha would stay quiet. (Joshua slept now, shivering terribly even as his chest rose and fell with each breath. Samantha seemed frozen, with her spooky, wide-eyed stare.)

They were here!

Keep going, she prayed. Just keep moving, right along the trail, right toward the army she hoped her mother would bring back.

But no. She knew it was impossible.

Now she heard them, all right. Hands reaching out, grabbing small twigs, reaching for exposed roots, pulling themselves up, up to the cave. To Samantha and Joshua. But most especially, to her.

She saw it! Right there. Not more than fifty feet away. And already a few cars and trucks had passed.

Cars and trucks and people who could stop and help her.

She ran even harder, ignoring the prickers and the branches (almost invisible in the dark).

Happy. Almost crying.

Except suddenly she saw there was someone already there.

In the road.

"Oh," she said. "I didn't see you. Now, if you'll excuse me, I'll just—"

In the darkness he started coming toward her.

"No, no!" she screamed.

"Susan! It's me. Dan. Don't run away. It's okay. Really."

She ran to him, throwing her arms around him. She kissed him—not thinking, for a moment, that he could be like the others, the ones who had followed her through the woods.

"Hurry, Dan. I left them back there—my daughter and two other children. We've got to get them!"

"Show me." He grabbed the flashlight from his car, then ran to catch up to her.

Another stone block the size of a table shot out, then another, and the roar of the water drowned out the screams, the cries.

Herbert could still stand, even though the waterfall that ran down the side of the dam splashed in front of him like a stormy ocean wave.

It was beautiful. Wonderful. Exciting.

Then Herbert turned around and looked at all the people. They were all being swept away like ants, and he thought, as all of them were being washed away by the gigantic stream of water—for the first time—*why are they all here*?

He turned back to the wall. Other stones started to bulge. Not as quickly.

Why are we here?

Then an answer. He began to detect things flying through the air, inside the water. Dark, lumpy things. And long, twisted shapes. Strange things shooting out with the water.

Shooting over him.

But one of the shapes got caught up in the wall, caught up by a bit of ragged rock. It tumbled down the waterfall instead, and over and over, flopping around—

(All too blurry to be seen.)

Over and over until it plopped at Herbert's feet.

It stood up. It looked at him.

(*Do I know you?*)

It opened its mouth and came close to Herbert.

It grabbed his pudgy, out-of-shape body (he really had let himself go lately) and began munching on it.

(Like a piece of chicken at the county fair.)

Pretty hungry, fellow, Herbert thought, still—amazingly—feeling nothing. Not quite grasping just what the hell was going on.

He watched until everything somehow started to go black.

The water flooded the town. Seeped into homes, under doors, down to basements. All electricity was out, and all the phones too. People desperately tried to start cars, but the water formed rivers that flooded the streets and stranded the drivers.

But much worse than that, worse than the water and the panic, were the things that now came with it. Some dressed in clothes, almost like people, others with blackish, oily hides that resembled nothing anyone had ever seen before.

And the poor people—stranded in the town of Ellerton—struggled to keep the visitors from the reservoir out of their homes.

Just outside!

Claire wanted to cry out. *Go away!* Or *I'm here, you found me, now leave me alone . . . leave me!*

Joshua stirred.

(Did he smell that salty, sick stench now beginning to fill the cave?)

Samantha licked her lips.

Someone looked into the open cave.

"Momma."

It was Samantha's first word in over an hour.

She struggled quickly away from Claire's grasp, crawling out of the cave.

Toward her mother.

"No!" Claire yelled.

Joshua blinked awake. "Mommy?"

Claire grabbed at Samantha, a sturdy seven-year-old using all her muscles to crawl out.

"Momma . . ." she kept mumbling.

Her mother reached down for her.

(Bits of the black stuff still stuck to her hair, her eyebrows, her fingertips.)

Claire grabbed Samantha's legs. But Mrs. Benny—such a nice lady—yanked her daughter out of the hole, roughly pulling on her while Joshua ran behind.

Claire screamed.

The mother held Samantha while one of the policemen took Joshua and held him like a sack of potatoes.

There was another man there.

"Hello, Claire. I so looked forward to meeting you."

Joshua started kicking at the policeman. His hands flailed at the policeman's face.

(Oh, God. A chunk of the policeman's skin went flying down to the ground. Joshua kept struggling.)

The man stepped close to her.

"You are the only one I worried about, you know."

Another step closer.

"You were the only one out of the whole town. You're very special, Claire, and I"—he brought his hands together—"know how to take care of special people."

(She heard a terrible roar. Like lions in the zoo. And there! Just above it. She could make out the sound of people yelling, squealing, like the sounds coming from Playland's Dragon Coaster on a hot Saturday.)

The man's fingertips touched.

"I want you to meet someone."

Another sound. Now coming from the lake. She looked out there for a second. It was all funny and different.

There were things there, floating on top.

No. Not floating. There was a steeple—part of a steeple, anyway—sticking out of the water. And the very top of some buildings, their outlines just visible.

"So young," he said with a smile. "So powerful."

And in the center of the lake a terrible churning began, like water going down a bathtub drain, but so *loud*. She could see the white flashes of the water as it began to spin around.

Samantha yelled out something.

(It's a dream. Just another dream.)

Drops of spit—dark, purplish stuff—dribbled out of Mrs. Benny's mouth.

Then, from the bubbling lake, things began popping to the surface. Darkish shapes that floundered around for a moment before making their way to shore.

The man made his fingers part.

(*Don't.*)

She felt things moving at her feet. Things that popped out of the ground, opened up, and circled her bare legs.

She cried.

"Claire, please—" Samantha's voice sounded so hopeless.

Mrs. Benny lowered her mouth to Samantha.

Claire turned sharply. She looked at the monstrous woman.

(*Don't!*)

It was an order.

The mother howled. She blinked in confusion and looked at Claire, then at Parks, then back to Claire again.

"It's coming now," Parks said. "There's nothing you can do about it."

Claire's breath made a steam cloud in front of her.

The leaves took on the whitish sheen of frost, freezing into crinkly shapes. Her cheeks felt cold.

"It's coming," he said.

Something large, lumbering its way up.

Toward her.

The policeman let Joshua slip out of his grasp.

He ran over to his sister, trying to tug her down and away.

"Now . . ." Parks said.

(*It was winter here. Surely it would snow soon.*)

She looked past Parks.

There was someone there.

"Mom . . ." Claire said. The love, the relief—all almost overwhelming.

Parks turned.

"Too late, friends. You're just too . . . late." He sneered.

Dan ignored him. He carved a circle in the dirt.

One of the policemen lumbered over. Dan kicked the creature in the chest, and it staggered back like a rag doll.

Then the star.

(*So fuckin' cold.*)

Parks came toward her, his hands moving oddly. Susan grabbed a rock, a big heavy rock, and brought it down on the side of Parks's head.

(*Then the symbols. The names. The crosses.*)

She hit Parks hard, and he turned toward her, blood running down his cheek. His hand flew out quickly and knocked her to the ground.

Claire screamed. But Dan couldn't stop his work.

He stepped inside the star.

He flicked his light on and aimed it onto the paper. And read the words.

It got—by God—even colder.

The flashlight started to flicker yellow. *C'mon, c'mon, stay on . . . stay on!*

Parks came toward him again, his hands moving.

Dan knew if it was going to work, it was now.

Parks came closer.

Susan was up, and she barreled into Parks's back, sending him sprawling down to the edge of the circle.

He looked up, crazed now, right at Dan.

And then it was there. Still wet from the bottom of the lake. Looming over them. Massive. Alien . . .

(*"As close as your breath. As far away as the end of the universe."*)

The master of the Club. The real king of Gouldens Falls.

Parks tried to get up.

"By all that is holy," Dan said.

He brought the knife down.

Steady, careful, oh so steady. Driving it home.

It pierced Parks's shirt. (Parks brought his hand up to stop it.) Then through the shirt and on into his chest. And on. Deeper. Deeper.

To the heart of the Beast.

A warm breeze blew. Parks screamed. (Or did Dan simply imagine it?)

Parks twisted on the end of the knife, like a worm being cut for bait. Twisting, kicking, as his skin seemed to ripple and gather, till it seemed to start to pull away from his skull.

Parks's hands fell to his side, useless, skeletal.

Dan dared look up now.

It was gone.

They were alone.

Samantha collapsed onto her mother's dead body. The two policemen were curled up on the ground.

Susan held Joshua and Claire close to her, the three of them crying, arms encircled.

He let the knife fall onto the pile of twisted garbage at his feet.

(Like a week-old road kill.)

He walked over to Samantha and picked her up from the lifeless body. He crushed her to him.

"It's okay, sweetheart. It's okay."

He said it over and over.

As much for myself as for you. He whispered, eager again, to her heaving body, "It's all over."

EPILOGUE

Susan shielded her eyes from the glistening October sun.

It's all over.

Time was working its ancient magic of forgetting.

And just like the first warm breeze in April that announces that, yes, winter will end, flowers will bloom, and grass will grow, time brought its simple message. . . .

If you're still here, still in one piece when the clock ticks, your life goes on.

She looked at Claire, hammer in hand, standing next to Dan. They were building a fence for the pony he had promised her.

"A real pony!" Claire had said, her eyes alight.

(Both she and Dan hoped it would be one more thing to help her forget.)

It was Indian summer. The night before had been cold and they had built a fire in Dan's small but cozy house. And the crackling wood and the rich smell made her feel safe and secure, while winter seemed so near.

But that day it was summer again. The last dwindling

days of warmth and light before the land finally gave way to cold.

Claire laughed, so loud and clear, her voice carried easily on the wind. Dan was always telling her funny things, making her laugh. She loved him for that, and for what he now meant to her.

He was totally irresponsible. Bills were to be avoided, and he always had trouble with a deadline.

But he was a good man to know when all hell was breaking loose.

They both couldn't believe what had happened in those days following that Thursday night.

More than a hundred people were dead or had vanished. Nearly a thousand others had needed treatment for shock, exposure, and, unbelievably enough, frostbite. The newspapers were generally vague about what possibly could have happened.

When Joshua and Samantha's father came to pick them up, his eyes were red and blotchy from crying.

That was something else she'd remember forever.

The damage to the town of Ellerton was estimated to be over $100 million. The flooding eventually stopped when the reservoir reached the level of the hole. And while it looked like the dam itself might give way completely, somehow it held. A battalion from the Army Corps of Engineers worked around the clock to seal both sides of the wall, while an upstate crew temporarily diverted the flow of the water.

But before that was all gone, people got their first look at Gouldens Falls. The sunken town . . .

Dan waved at her. Winked. She smiled, the wind blowing her long hair behind her. Claire went on dutifully hammering.

Gouldens Falls. Only the top of it was ever seen, but that was enough. Like some quaint Atlantis, the roofs of the sunken village popped up, glistening with a grayish-green color. It was as if it had struggled to be born again, to crawl once more to the light.

And in that first morning people saw the bodies dotting the peaked roofs and tar-papered ceilings. Friends of hers at the paper said that positive IDs were made on Tommy Fluhr, Emily Powers, and the two cops from New York, Flaherty and Raskin.

Some of the others were beyond recognition.

Gradually the water was allowed back into the reservoir.

The official story spoke of the event as if it were some kind of natural disaster laced with mass hysteria.

But she—and hundreds of others—knew better.

And so did Dan.

He offered his home in Pennsylvania to her to get away.

("Small but mighty comfy, surrounded by acres and acres of land. Claire will love it.")

Land. That's what I needed.

She agreed, hoping he wouldn't read more in her agreement than she intended.

But he gave her space.

While she was officially on leave from the paper, she knew she'd never go back, despite the new, tall barbed-wire fence, complete with U.S. government warning signs.

Never.

She'd stay here. Write a book about it.

(Or maybe not. Maybe she'd write about something else. A children's story. Filled with hope and light.)

She'd stay with Dan. For now. Maybe forever.

Thanking him. Thanking God.

It was all over.

And they were alive.

Claire shielded her eyes from the sun's glare.

"C'mon, sprout, give that nail a good ol' whack!"

She smiled at Dan. We're almost a family. Doing things together, having fun, just like the families she always envied.

And her mom seemed happy now, not too busy to talk with her or play games.

She waited till her mom went back inside to ask Dan her question.

The one she'd been thinking about (over and over) since they'd arrived.

"Dan . . ."

He was trying to fit another split rail through the top notch of the post they were working on.

"Yes, Claire."

"Dan, do you think, I mean, is it possible that it could happen again?"

He gently lowered the rail into the notch. And slowly he crouched down beside her. He was close to her; his bright blue eyes and powerful arms made her feel safe.

"Claire, whatever happened back there is over. I can't pretend to understand it, but when that man was killed, it broke the spell." He mussed her hair. "Like in one of your fantasy books. The bad magic was licked, over. It's just another lake now . . . that's all."

She looked at him for some flicker of doubt.

He believed it. Completely.

She nodded.

"So you have nothing to worry about, okay, sprout? Nothing. Okay?"

"Okay." She smiled.

He stood up. "Now get back to work."

A lone cloud moved across the brilliant sun, cutting off the heat.

Nothing to worry about.

'Cause it's all over.

The bad magic is gone.

Whack. She hammered the nail.

Then why, she asked herself, *why do I still have dreams?*

Different dreams now . . . late at night.

Dreams of the town as it used to be, with old-fashioned cars and kids with ice-cream cones that melted too fast.

And then—whack.

Dreams of the town as it will be.

Whack.

She told no one. Not her mom. Not Dan.

But she knew this one fact as sure as she knew anything.

(The single puffy cloud moved on.)

She hit the nail home.

It's *not* over.